No Other Animals

Copyright © 2012, 2013 Jack Nease
All rights reserved.

ISBN 13:
9780615611013 (Pompano Press)

ISBN:
061561101X

Pompano Press
936 Intracoastal Drive 4F
Fort Lauderdale, FL 33304

For JACOB, my very talented son

No Other Animals

Jack Nease

Fort Lauderdale, Florida

The propensity to truck, barter, and exchange one thing for another . . . is common to all men, and to be found in no other race of animals.

Adam Smith, Scottish economist

If only we could pull out our brain and use only our eyes.

Pablo Picasso, Spanish artist

Chapter One

This was one crazy, bizarre, irredeemable stupid party. I knew I shouldn't have come. I hate all parties, and I'm usually successful in avoiding them. But I can't resist Mo. When she says she really wants me to do something, I usually go along. I owe her. More to the point, I love her.

So here I was with this other woman, Mo's friend Ginny, who was having a ball, flirting with every guy who got close to her, ignoring her son (except when she was telling him to do something or go somewhere), and paying me absolutely no attention. This last was all right with me, except that I'd thought we'd be gone by now and I'd be back with Mo.

"We can't leave until the fireworks start," Ginny told me.

"What fireworks?" I protested. "You didn't tell me anything about fireworks."

So she explained it to me, patiently like she would to a six-year-old. West Palm, the city across the lake from here, was having its annual arts festival and jazz concert, and this year it was putting on a fireworks display on both its opening and closing nights. This was Sunday, the last night, and she'd promised her son, Eric, he could watch

"We leave right after the show ends," I said as firmly as I could.

"Of course," the words barely out of her mouth before she turned her back to me and walked away. I'd already noticed that as the party wore on she seemed to swing her hips more and more. Damn her. But what had I expected? I'd told Mo this was a crazy, stupid, bizarre idea for a party.

Yes, I know I'm repeating myself. But I felt strongly about this. You decide: The purpose of the party was for former spouses to get together to wait return of their children by their exes, the ones who had weekend custody of the children. That way Sunday afternoons wouldn't be so lonely. OK, so far. But then the exes stayed and partied with all the other divorced men and women. They called it The Exchange.

It worked like this. A car would come down the long driveway, tall royal palms and tropical plants on either side, and pull into the covered entrance. A boy or a girl would pop out the passenger side door, an overnight bag and a doll or some other toy in hand (one a clown with its head sewed on backwards), and rush inside. The kid would find his or her mother or father, they'd talk a few minutes, then dart toward the lakefront to join other children playing by the water. Some of the children greeted their parents joyously, some just went through the motions, a few even reluctantly. Or was that fear on their faces? No matter which, the parents always wanted to talk more than the children.

Meanwhile the parent with weekend custody found a parking place, came inside, got a drink from the kitchen, and joined the other single parents by the pool. Once there, they plunged into the action with all the subtlety of a singles bar, a Meat Market no less. Dated music— Jimmy Buffet, the Beatles, the Beach Boys, Roy Orbison, even Sinatra and a sprinkling of BeeGees—flowed from speakers mounted on walls around the patio. A few couples danced on a small wood floor in one corner of the screened enclosure, while others stood around watching. It was early May, warm during the day, but cool enough at night for some of the women to be wearing light sweaters.

Have I said the party was being held in Palm Beach? Maybe the reason the reason I didn't was this was not a proper Palm Beach mansion. Those are two or three stories tall and hide behind tall ficus hedges so no one can see what goes on. This one was U-shaped with rooms built around a motel-sized pool and patio. The walls facing the pool were mostly sliding glass doors so I could see what was going on in almost every room and much of the driveway in front.

By now there must have been twenty or thirty children playing by the water, some on land and some playing on a dock that protruded into Lake Worth, the misleadingly named expanse of water that separates Palm Beach and West Palm. The kids—yes, I call them that—were too far away to see details of what they were doing, but the sounds they made were happy.

Colored floodlights bounced off tall royal palms, bushy philodendron plants, and showy bougainvillea vines on either side of the lawn. Big yachts and smaller pleasure boats paraded by on the Intracoastal Waterway, downtown West Palm silhouetted in the background, the scene proving once again that while money may not buy happiness, it can certainly buy access to beauty.

Since I didn't know anybody at this party and I was going to be stuck with these people for a while, I decided to play a little mind game I'd made up when I was a kid. I pretended this was a foreign movie without subtitles and devised nicknames for all the characters present, the silly, the wise, the bored, the ambitious, and the bewildered.

Take that tall young woman close to me, twenty-something, with frizzy blond hair and low-rider slacks that showed more of her stomach than fashion dictated. She was trying to pull an older, pudgy man toward the dance floor. "C'mon Wilbur, dance with me," she said. "Don't you know dancing for an hour's almost as good as fifteen minutes foreplay?" Wilbur broke away and darted inside the house. The crowd around them laughed with glee. Maybe they'd seen the act before. In my mind the two principals of the little play became Frizzy Blond and Shy Wilbur.

"Foreplay and sex," exclaimed a man wearing three gold chains and a skimpy shirt with sleeves cut out to display muscular shoulders and arms. "What's that, something people did before AIDS?" His tag was easy. Muscle Shirt.

"Condom, dumb ass," shrieked a thirty-something woman in a short pink-and-white outfit that made her look like a peppermint cane. "And get a blood test."

I tried to figure the odds of Candy Cane getting together later with Muscle Shirt. Not enough doubt to make a market on, as Mo would say.

Everyone within hearing distance joined in the joking and laugher except for one woman, mid-thirties and model thin, her nose upturned and her mouth in a pout. Perpetual Pout, as I dubbed her, stood alone silently taking it all in but making a point of not participating.

Now a tall woman in a black jump suit, her neck and arms, even her ankles, glittering with silver, walked up to Muscle Shirt and confronted him: "Your check bounced."

"Run it through again," he said, looking away but not moving.

Silver Bracelets poked her finger at his stomach, punching into flesh. "If it happens again, I'm taking your ass to court." Ah, yes. Another example of a friendly divorce, the kind Mo's friend told me she'd had. Just a matter of time, I figured, before this party blows up, especially with all the booze being consumed.

Across the pool I saw the back of a dead ringer for a bank president who'd never been married and almost everyone thought was gay. Can't be, I thought as he walked away. Gay Banker wouldn't have any reason to be at a party like this. Or maybe he sired a child before... I stopped the thought right there, deciding it was too complicated to follow to conclusion.

Wandering among all these characters were the two people I'd met at the door as we came in. Paul Brophy, gray-haired but not old, mid-forties probably, a well-fed plumpness about his face but no tan, a gold ring with a big diamond on his pinky finger, and a huge smile to show off almost perfect teeth, probably none of the ones God gave him the first two times around. Since he was the party's host, he became Host Brophy.

Then there was a big woman, Brophy's wife, drinking straight something over ice, vodka probably, pretty face but wearing a billowy, translucent smock over her bathing suit so I couldn't tell much else about her. Weather Balloon, I thought, colorful but still a big round glob like a balloon.

Down in the garden I saw Mo's friend–have I said her name was Ginny?—hugging a boy of about eight and figured him for her son. Eric. I'd brought her to the party (drove the car at least, although she was the one who got the invitation), so I figured I had the right to ask questions. "Which one of these is yours—your ex?" I asked, when I got closer.

She nodded, not so much with her head but with her whole body, toward a man of medium height, maybe five eight, at the far end of the patio. Curly black hair, white pants and boat shoes without socks. OK so far, but he also wore a white dress shirt and a maroon bow tie, an affectation rarely seen in South Florida. I figured him for an Aging Preppy.

"His full name's Clinton Drake, the third," Ginny said. "There's money in the family but he doesn't have any."

"What's he do?"

"His last job was at the *National Enquirer*. A half dozen other papers before that."

"He any good?"

"When he's not drinking."

As we watched, a big man with a white beard that accented his tanned face went up to Clinton Drake III and put an arm around his shoulders. The man was wearing a big gold Rolex and a red-and-white sport shirt, so I he became Santa-with-a-Rolex. The men talked a few minutes and walked away together.

That was when Ginny told me about the fireworks. Well, why didn't you…, my thoughts began, but I quickly decided it would be a waste of time to go there. She'd known about the fireworks from the very beginning and hadn't told either me or Mo about it. Nothing I could say would matter. But I knew that when somebody "forgets" to tell you something that would be important for you to know, it's usually no accident.

When the fireworks finally started, I resolved to pay more attention to the watchers than the show, but soon I was just as transfixed as everyone else. A single rocket soared skyward, higher and higher, and burst into three exploding clusters of red, white, and blue. Every face around me, child and adult, tilted upward. Each rocket soared higher and spread into wider circles of fire than the one that preceded it, the explosions growing louder and louder, the show building to a climax.

"Paul!" A high-pitched voice broke through the blasts. Our hostess, a ghostly gray balloon in the darkness, hurtled toward us, her voice shrill and piercing. "Paul, come quick!"

The urgency of her voice caused me to turn and run toward her, the Santa-with-a-Rolex a step or so ahead of me, Host Brophy a few steps behind. "In there!" Sally pointed. "In the pool." The Santa yanked open the door of the screened enclosure and ran in, Brophy and I so close behind we were inside before it closed.

Ginny's ex, Clinton Drake III, bow tie still squared, floated in the shallow end of the pool, his feet resting on concrete steps, most of his body just below the surface. A tiny thread of crimson ran through the water—deep red close to his chest, pinkish as it spread—but the flow of blood from Drake's body had stopped. Santa waded into the pool, lifted Drake's head from the water and pressed his fingers to Drake's throat.

The patio door banged open behind us. Adults and children crowded around the pool, oblivious now to the sight and sounds of the fireworks behind them. Santa shook his head and pulled Drake's body higher up the steps. He undid the bow tie, put a finger in Drake's mouth, and tried to breathe life into the body.

Then I saw the gun, short-barreled and blue-handled, glistening on the lighted pool floor. Host Brophy waded into the water, bent over and reached down, slipped his little finger through the trigger guard, and lifted the gun from the water. "Don't," Santa shouted.

Ginny pushed to my side and grabbed my arm. "Greg," she whispered. "That's my gun." The worse thing she could have said. For her. And as it turned out, for me.

Chapter Two

A phone call that morning got me into this. Mo and I were in bed, the smell of coffee and her perfume in the air, sections of newspaper scattered over the pink hibiscus flowers of the comforter, a coconut palm branch waving in sunlight outside. I'd fixed the coffee while she retrieved the paper from in front of the apartment door, a division of labor she insisted on from the beginning. Now, if this was like every other Sunday morning we'd spent together, it wouldn't be long before we'd make love.

Mo's cell vibrated on the stand beside the bed. "Don't answer it," I said.

She looked at the number on the caller ID. "Whoever this is phoned over and over again yesterday. I'll get rid of the pest." She picked up the phone, listened, then whispered, "Ginny. I haven't heard from her for years."

"Where are you?" Mo said into the phone. She listened, then, "Why didn't you phone sooner?"

I could tell by the excitement in Mo's voice that this wasn't going to be a short conversation so I pushed myself out of bed, vaguely aware that Mo's arm cut through the air behind me in an unsuccessful, half-hearted attempt to hold me there while she talked. "Slow down, Ginny, and explain again what this is about," she said.

In the kitchen, I filled two glasses from a carton of chilled orange juice, taking much longer than necessary because I wasn't interested in eavesdropping on Mo. We'd been living together almost two years, and one of the reasons our relationship works is we give each other plenty of space.

I walked to the window and looked out at the gardens that divided the twin towers of the apartment complex. Two children, ages about four and six, were playing in the swimming pool, mostly splashing in the shallow end but occasionally drifting into the deeper water. They were by themselves, not another adult or other child in sight. What would happen if they got in over their heads and couldn't swim to safety? It's child neglect, I thought. No other word for it. And the terrible thing is it goes on thousands of time a day all over South Florida.

"Where do you live?" I heard Mo asking when I got back to the bedroom, a glass of juice in either hand. Mo's tanned legs were folded under a short white nightgown, her reddish-brown hair barely brushed, no makeup except for the tiny bit of lipstick she'd put on earlier, a playful platinum angel hanging around her neck. She was gorgeous.

"The west side of Boca," Mo repeated as she wrote notes on the pad she keeps beside the bed. A few more questions and she clicked off, stared off into space a few seconds, and looked up at me. "We're invited to a party."

"I don't want to go," I said, my automatic response to all parties.

She ignored that and summarized the situation quickly: Ginny was going to a party where her former husband would be present. There'd be a lot of people there Ginny didn't know. She didn't have any idea what she was getting into. She wanted Mo to go along.

"Who's Ginny?" I asked when I finally got an opportunity to get a word in.

"Oh, I should have started with that." Mo wiped away any embarrassment she felt with a coy little smile. "My college roommate."

"Georgetown?"

"Yep. We were best friends for years. We'd talk for hours. The meaning of life—" Mo switched to a mildly self-depreciating tone, mocking her younger self. "—our lives in particular. Whether we were going into the right professions, whether we'd ever want to have children—"

"Then she went off to law school and I haven't seen or heard from her since. Until this morning." Had her tone and expression changed then, maybe betraying bitterness? I couldn't tell.

"Ginny has been married and divorced since college," Mo said. "She has a child. She's picking him up at the party."

"Why?" I asked. "Why did she agree to meet her ex there?"

"Ginny says her Sunday afternoons are terribly lonely. She hates sitting alone waiting for her former husband to bring her son home." Mo hesitated. "Sometimes he's been drinking." She looked at me for reaction, but I kept my face blank. What and how much other people drink is none of my business.

"Then Ginny heard about this group of divorced mothers and fathers who felt the same way," Mo continued. "They meet at a house in Palm Beach and wait for their children with each other. Dozens of them. They call it The Exchange."

"Exchange?"

"They exchange—return—the kids they've had for the weekend."

"Bizarre," I said. The word was mild compared to what I was thinking.

"With other mothers and fathers there, the likelihood of things getting nasty is reduced. Everybody's cool. In fact, Ginny says she's heard it's a pretty good party."

"Ex-wives and ex-husbands getting together for a party—?"

"When Ginny heard about it, she decided to try it out." Mo paused, and from the way she looked at me, I knew this was going to involve me. "There's just one thing." She moved closer. "Ginny wants company, but I can't go. My directors are meeting this afternoon. The meeting usually lasts late."

"On a Sunday? Again?"

"Sunday is the only time some of them can fly into town."

"Pay them something."

"Not this charity," Mo said. "Every penny goes to help homeless children."

Maureen is a dollar-a-year executive director of a billion-dollar charity, something she's very good at, not the least because she'd been a top-ranked stock market analyst on Wall Street for years before taking the job. Before that she'd been an investigative news reporter.

"Please, Greg." Mo put a hand on my knee. "I'd go with her if I could. Substitute for me. Just this one time." I hesitated, but there was no doubt in my mind what I was going to do in the end. There wasn't anything I wouldn't do for her.

"Look at this as a learning opportunity," she said. "All those children being returned to spouses. Are the kids happy or sad to be leaving one parent? How do the mothers and fathers react to each other? Do they show animosity, or have they put the past behind them? Do they try to pretend all is well for the children's sake? Do the children seem fooled?"

I knew—and Mo knew—that what she was saying would give me an opportunity to give in without seeming like a complete pushover. I'm a children's shrink, a description I don't like but people keep calling me, so sometimes I give up and use it too. It would be more accurate to call me a psychologist who specializes in helping children and adolescents, a job I like so much better than the professions I'd tried earlier—nursing in a hospital or being an administrator of one.

"OK, I'll do it," I said. "But we leave when Ginny's child is returned."

"Whatever you two work out." Mo's lips brushed mine, then she spun around and popped out of bed.

"What else do you know about her?" I asked. "What does she do now?"

"You can find out all about her on the drive to Palm Beach."

"Nothing good will come from this." I started to elaborate, to explain that she didn't owe Ginny anything, and I certainly didn't, and ask why Ginny hadn't phoned her before, and say the whole idea was stupid, but Mo was already out the door and probably didn't hear me. Or if she did, she wasn't going to let on. She never argued. She just didn't agree. And when she made up her mind, there was no changing it.

I'd loved Mo since we were kids. She lived next door and started coming over after school when I contracted polio through a terribly freak set of circumstances. She appointed herself my chief nurse and tutor, then taught me how to read, work basic math, and, best of all, to laugh when things went wrong. I'll be forever in her debt.

Nothing romantic developed back then, of course, or for decades. After all, she was four years older and when you're a teenager, four years is an eternity. But as we got to know each other, she took the initials of my name—Gregory Overman—and nicknamed me Go. Naturally I returned the favor, taking her name—Maureen O'Neal—and dubbed her Mo.

Later we went to different colleges and took different career paths, but we always kept in touch. I've had other women in my life, just as she's had other men, but Mo's always been the prettiest, smartest, kindest woman I knew. Until last year I never thought of her as anything but a big sister. Then some things happened that changed everything for both of us. My life is better than it's ever been.

It was time for me to get out of bed now and quit feeling sorry for myself over our interrupted morning, but before I could do anything more than think about it, Mo came back into the bedroom carrying a small plate in each hand. "Toast with marmalade," she said.

I said, "I thought you had to go to a meeting."

"We had time for either a long breakfast or whatever." She smiled in a way that left no doubt about her intentions. . "The toast is for after the whatever."

So I knew God was still in His, Her, or Its heaven, and all was well in the world.

Chapter Three

Ginny opened her front door seconds after I knocked, almost as if she'd been waiting on the other side. Short black hair, a loose pink blouse scalloped in front, white slacks, boat shoes—nothing wrong with her at all except her smile seemed a tad artificial.

Then I realized she'd been taking my inventory too. "I expected Mo would have good taste in men," she said.

Remarks like that always embarrass me because I'm no physical prize. I can bench-press two-hundred pounds, but the polio left me with from one leg twisted and shorter than the other, and. I walk with a limp. Some people say my short ponytail and small earring are ways I try to distract attention from the gait. I don't know about that, but I do know I won't get an operation to straighten the leg. Without my limp, I wouldn't be me.

"Mo has good taste in friends," I said, the best I could come up with.

"Just a minute while I set the alarm," Ginny said and closed the door in my face.

I'd had that happen to me before, everybody in South Florida being so security conscious, especially here in Boca Raton. Half the security systems have to be locked before the doors can be closed. But I wondered about the etiquette here: Don't I get invited in even if I don't want to take the time?

No matter. In the few seconds Ginny's door was open, I'd seen enough to realize the inside of the house was drop-dead impressive. The big oil painting hanging in the entrance hall—a lonely beach scene—must have cost thousands. The ornate glass chandelier overhead, well, who could tell? But they certainly don't sell carved oriental chests like that one at Kmart.

When Ginny came outside she carried a large brown purse, not at all something that matched her outfit. But we all have our idiosyncrasies and weaknesses. Mine was sitting at the curb, a Mazda Miata, my sole indulgence since moving to Florida. I pushed a button and the convertible top emerged from behind the seat.

"With this up, we can talk on the way," I said.

"I'm nervous," Ginny said.

"Me too."

That got a smile and a squeeze of my arm. "I'll protect you," she said.

"Then what will my job be?"

"We'll think of something."

The little flirt! Or was that just my imagination? Either way, I'd vowed to take her home the minute her son arrived at the Exchange, so what did it matter? Enough to set off a little alarm, I guess. And make it even more important to satisfy my curiosity about some unanswered questions. I turned onto Interstate 95, my driving and my mind on automatic pilot, questions flowing easily. I started with something I knew the answer to.

"Where did you and Maureen meet?"

"In college."

"Which one?"

"Georgetown. In Washington."

If I were working I'd ask fewer questions and listen more, but now I needed to verify everything that seemed the slightest bit odd.

"The law school is on the other side of town from the main campus."

"We were undergraduates together," Ginny said, enunciating each word distinctly. "After I went to law school, we lost touch and didn't see each other for years. When I moved down here, I saw her name in the paper and made a mental note to phone her when I could."

"And now?" I asked.

"I'm an assistant state attorney, one of a couple of dozen in Palm Beach county."

I thought back to Ginny's entrance hall, the huge oil painting, the sparkling chandelier, the carved chest. and asked myself, Do assistant state attorneys make that much money?

"You phoned Mo on her cell phone. How did you get her number?"

"Working in law enforcement has its perks."

I started to ask a follow-up question, but there were other topics I was more interested in. "You and your ex divorced long?"

"Less than a year." Ginny said.

"Joint custody?"

"Technically. The way we work it is Eric's with me weekdays, with his father on weekends."

"How old's your child?"

"Eric's eight."

"How's he taking it? The divorce."

"Wonderfully." She looked at me. "It was a friendly divorce."

"I've never known one of those," I said. "Usually after the lawyers get hold of them, one person comes out of court feeling like a winner, the other a loser."

"Well, *ours* was." She looked at me as if I didn't have any idea what I was talking about. "A friendly divorce." So I shut up, and we rode in silence until we got to West Palm Beach. When someone is as defensive about something as she was about her "friendly" divorce, you know darn well it's a gold-plated, thousand-percent, outright lie.

I turned off the interstate and we drove down Okeechobee Boulevard past the performing arts center and the larger-than-life statues of black elephants across from CityPlace Tower. "Tell me what I need to know before we get to this party."

"The host and hostess are the Brophys—Paul and Sally," Ginny said. "They have a big house on The Lake."

The Lake, I knew was Lake Worth, the wide body of water that separates the city, West Palm, from the island on which the little Town of Palm Beach sits. The Intracoastal Waterway cuts through the lake, running north and south, but the bigger dividing line between the two communities is defined by something more. Money. Big money. Millions. Billions. What comes after that?

"The Brophys have children returned to them too?" I asked.

"No children, as far as I know."

"Strange."

"I thought so too," Ginny said, but it was clear the subject didn't interest her so I let it drop

When we got downtown, she said to turn left on Olive. We passed the government center in front of the old courthouse where a Kennedy was tried on a rape charge.

"You take part in the trial?" I asked.

"No," Ginny said, not having to ask which one I meant. "I wasn't senior enough."

"Too bad. You might have—"

"I don't want to talk about work."

This was the second time that evening I'd blabbed without thinking. Wouldn't happen again. But I wished Ginny would remember I was doing her a favor by taking her to this party, not the other way around. I'd much rather be home waiting for Mo. Or almost anywhere else, really. Since I quit drinking almost all parties bore the heck out of me.

"Turn left on the other side of the bridge," Ginny said. "We're almost there."

As I made the turn, she put her hand on the inside of my thigh. "I didn't mean to be such a bitch back there. I'm still nervous." Then, more to herself than to me, she added: "This is a very big night for me."

I had no idea what she was talking about, but there was something about the way she said it that made me wonder even more if coming to this party wasn't a very stupid idea. I resolved to get in, get out, and get back to Mo as soon as possible.

Chapter Four

I've already reported most of the things that happened at the party before the murder, but a few things I left out stick in my mind. What Host Brophy said when we first arrived at the party, for instance.

When he greeted us at the door, he shook hands with me but his eyes never left Ginny. No surprise there. "Drink all you want, play around all you want," he said. "We've got only one rule here: No drugs. You don't look the type, but I make a point of saying that to everybody."

I hadn't thought of drugs until that minute, but what he said got me to wondering how Brophy made his money. Who but a dealer would wear a ring like that? I told myself to stop being ridiculous, nobody in Palm Beach is into drugs anymore. The days when every ritzy party had a Waterford bowl full of cocaine for guests to sample were long gone.

Standing next to Brophy was the woman in the big smock, the Weather Balloon. "Assholes," she said. "All men are assholes." Who was she talking to? I hadn't said a word to her. Then I realized she was looking at Ginny.

Brophy lowered his voice. "Sally says that about anybody in pants. Makes it interesting being married to her." So that was how I learned the Weather Balloon was Brophy's wife. I'm forever amazed at the couplings people decide upon.

The Weather Balloon learned Ginny's name, said she'd help Ginny find out if her son had arrived, and the two women walked away talking, presumably, about their not-so-recent discovery that men were assholes.

Brophy began walking away too. "Drinks are in the kitchen. The fireworks will start about eight." What fireworks? I wondered at the time, but there was no one I could ask before Ginny gave me the news.

Another thing I haven't mentioned was my phone call to Mo. Right after Ginny told me about the fireworks, I phoned her, my cell to hers, thinking she wasn't going to understand. I wouldn't either. It was one of those stories that's true but sounds fishy.

"I'm going to be late."

"I thought you wanted to leave as soon as possible," she said.

"There're going to be fireworks," I said, feeling foolish, and explained about SunFest. Maybe it would help if I gave her some evidence. "Listen." I held up the phone, trying to catch sounds of a jazz band across the lake. Drunken laughter, male and female, the women's shrieks seeming loudest, burst out close behind me. I covered the mouthpiece, but the damage was done.

"A lot of unattached women there," Mo said, more statement than question.

"Only thirty or forty." I was annoyed. "Ginny's your friend. I'm only here because you asked me to bring her." Then from somewhere deep in my brain I got a little message and guessed what might be going on. "Where are you?"

"At home," Mo said. "I left the meeting early to spend time with you."

"I didn't know—"

"Have fun." She clicked off.

Damn, damn, damn. I'm the one who should be miffed. This was a crazy event, not at all what I expected, all these former couples on the make for something, even Ginny working the crowd.

"Everybody down to the lake!" Paul Brophy's voice was so loud it could be heard above the music and the crowd. "Fireworks begin in five minutes."

Since I bought Ginny to this party, I thought I should watch the show with her, but when I found her she said she needed to find Eric and began walking back toward the house. I followed the others to the shoreline alone.

The sun had set low over the water, brushing the sky with wide strokes of orange and narrow bands of purple and yellow, Palm Beach sunsets just as spectacular as the more famous ones off Key West and Sanibel. Not as many people see them, though, because most of the Palm Beach oceanfront is walled off from rich and poor alike.

To one side of the yard, Clinton Drake III looked as if he was arguing with Muscle Shirt, but they were too far away to hear their words. When Drake saw me watching, he turned and stomped toward the house. On the other side, the Santa with a Rolex talked with Silver Bracelets until Host Brophy tried to join them. Then they stopped and walked off in opposite directions. Gay Banker (I was sure that's who it was by then) walked arm in arm with Frizzy Blond and Perpetual Pout on either side. Strange, but what's normal about this party?

Most of the children found places to sit on the dock while the adults stuck to the shore. The kids were happy, Latin, black, white, mingling and mixing with joy. Something about the scene seemed off, though. There were more black and Latin kids than parents to match. Or was that my imagination?

Brophy pulled an electrical switch throwing the yard into darkness. Then, surprise, Candy Cane moved over and stood next to me, pushing her body close, hip to hip, shoulder to shoulder. I moved a couple of inches away, trying to ignore her, but she was the sort of woman who could make a man's hormones jiggle and jump. Sally walked toward the house.

When the first rocket soared skyward, higher and higher, and burst into exploding clusters, reminding me of Mo's stories of what happens on Wall Street—giddy exhilaration on the flight up, burned- out despair on the ride down.

Then Sally's high-pitched voice broke through the blasts, yelling, "Paul, come quick!" and we found Clinton Drake's body floating in the pool and saw the gun and Ginny pushed to my side, grabbed my arm and whispered, "Greg, that's my gun."

Chapter Five

From then on, I saw and heard events as if watching an amateur video, images blurred and sound distorted. Santa told Brophy to give him the gun, but Brophy refused. Sally cried. Other men and women reached the pool, their initial exclamations soon awed into silence by the sudden demise of a man they'd partied with only moments before. I thought of Mo, the reality of death and the shortness of life bringing to mind an image of the most precious person in my life.

Brophy and Santa argued about whether to leave Clinton's body where it floated or move it. Santa won, only because Brophy left to make the 9-1-1 call. He took the gun with him. Why? Why not. I guess a host has as much right to custody of a murder weapon as anyone. Clinton's body stayed half in, half out of the pool, Santa guarding it. Again I thought of Mo, vowing to make every day with her count.

Now children came into the pool area, looking for their parents initially, then gawking silently at Clinton's body, the sight of real death not like what they'd seen on television. Parents found and hugged the kids they ignored only moments earlier, then tried to lead them away from sight of the body. Some kids began crying, others broke away from their parents, not wanting to leave.

I pulled Ginny aside. "What the heck is your gun doing in the pool?"

"I brought it to the party," she said.

"Why?"

"I always carry a gun. I've got a permit."

"Do you always kill off your ex-husbands?"

Ginny's arms fell to her side rigid, her fists clinched. "That's obscene!"

The third time that night I'd spoken without thinking. Ginny was right. I had no reason to believe she was in any way involved in her husband's death. I had overreacted, probably because of the shock of Clinton's death, of seeing his body laid out by the pool so soon after he'd been alive and walking around. Or, maybe it was because I'd just learned the woman I'd brought to the party was packing a gun. Packing? Where'd that word come from?

"I didn't mean—" I knew I was wrong. "I'm sorry. I apologize."

"I need your help," Ginny said without hesitation. "If not for me, for Maureen."

"I apologized."

"I need more than that." Ginny's fists relaxed. "Let's go inside."

She led me to a small room at the front of the house off the entrance hall. A big flat-screen television set sat in one corner, black leather chairs and sofas arranged around it. "Look." She pointed to a glass-topped cocktail table in the center of the room. Her large brown purse sat in the center surrounded by other purses, light windbreakers, and wraps, forgotten in the rush to see the fireworks.

"Somebody must have come in here and taken the gun from my purse," she said. "Then they shot Clinton."

"Why in the world did you bring a gun to this party?"

"I take it everywhere I go."

"Why?"

"I make a lot of enemies in my work," she said. "I send some very tough characters and their friends to prison." The yellow lights of a police car flickered in the window. Its siren cut off but others howled close by, the sounds growing louder and louder. "And don't forget," Ginny said. "I'm a single parent."

"That's not—" No, I told myself. You haven't much time before the police get here. Find out what you can before they interrupt. "Why did you bring the gun inside the house?"

Ginny shrugged. "We were in your car. Usually when I go to a social occasion, I leave it in the glove compartment of my car. But tonight—"

"Who do you think took it? Who killed Clinton?"

"I don't know." She bit her lip and waved an arm toward the pool. "It could have been anybody."

A uniformed cop walked into the room. "You two." He waved his arm. "Into the other room with the rest of them."

"Officer, I'm an assistant state attorney," Ginny said. "I'll show you some ID." She leaned over to pick up the purse.

"Don't touch anything!" the cop shouted.

Ginny straightened. "You'll find someone out there who recognizes me."

"When you get out there, lady. Now!"

Ginny took my arm, led me toward the door, and lowered her voice. "They'll let me go as soon as I find the right person. I can make a statement tomorrow."

"They'll keep the rest of us here," I said.

"If they do, how will I get home?"

"You could stay."

"Eric has school tomorrow."

What would Mo want? That was my conscious thought at the time. Only later did I realize I wasn't thinking clearly because I'd been feeling guilty about accusing Mo's friend of murder without any basis. Also wondering how I'd explain my remark to Mo when I reported this to her later. So I overreacted and like a bonehead told her, "If I have to stay and they let you leave early, you can take my car."

Ginny waited for the cop to look away to hold out her hand. I reached into my pocket and handed her the keys to my Miata. She covered them with her hand and dropped it to her side so the cop couldn't see.

Almost instantly I knew I'd made a mistake, but it was too late to back out. She squeezed my arm.

Chapter Six

There was chaos everywhere, inside the house and out. Parents tried to leave with their children. Police blocked them. The adults turned childlike, arguing, shouting, threatening. Nothing worked. A couple of parents tried to sneak away thorough side yards, but cops caught them. More shouting, more arguments. The police prevailed.

More police cars pulled into the Brophy's driveway, their drivers cutting the sirens but leaving yellow, white, red, and blue flashing lights spinning on top of their cars, the life-size kaleidoscopes waking the neighborhood to the fact that something important was going on. Neighbors emerged from their homes and gathered on the street in front of the Brophys' residence. Most stood in the street talking, but a few slipped around the side of the house and into the Brophy's backyard. Eventually police put up a yellow crime scene tape and pushed bystanders to the other side of the street.

Two medics pulled Clinton Drake's body from the pool. One tore the front of his shirt and attached adhesive pads to his chest. The other ran wires from the pads to a box-like device, a quick and simple EKG. By then the Palm Beach cops, none ranking higher than sergeant, had herded everyone, adults and children, to the patio where Clinton's body still lay.

"The children shouldn't see this," Silver Bracelets protested.

"Just stay there, ma'am," said a young cop, looking even younger in short pants.

"The children have school tomorrow," another woman protested, almost word for word what Ginny said.

"Stay put," said another cop.

One of the medics looked up and shook his head at the other, signaling no possibility of reviving Clinton, no life left in his body. The other put a blanket on the corpse. A couple of the cops talked softly into tiny radios on their shoulders, their voices too low to hear. Ginny kneeled on the other side of the pool, arms around her son staring at Clinton's body. She kept looking around the enclosed area, apparently waiting for someone she knew to show up.

More sirens screamed, more lights flashed outside. Sheriff's deputies in green pants and white shirts walked onto the patio. The blue uniforms nodded at them, acknowledging that the deputies and their boss would take over. Finally a guy in civilian clothes appeared, his deputy badge pinned to the pocket of a purple-and-yellow sport shirt hanging outside his pants, the bulge of a pistol showing under his shirt. From that point on, all the uniforms obeyed him. He looked back and forth between Clinton's blanketed body and the rest of us, his gaze stopping on the kids. "Jesus. Get everybody into the big room up front!"

Children stopped crying. They'd seen something like this on the tube, a strong guy coming in to take charge and solve the crime. Everything would be all right. The cops directed us to the living room, the floor there polished marble, the furniture covered in rich fabric, a large fireplace embedded in the rough stone that formed one wall.

Ginny walked up to the guy in the sport shirt and said something I couldn't hear. He put out his hands as if asking for identification. She shook her head and pointed to the room where she'd left her purse. The guy in the sport shirt looked toward the Santa-with-a-Rolex, who nodded almost imperceptibly. Thus assured, he motioned for a deputy to escort Ginny to her purse.

Other parents crowded around the man, each with a special case to plead. He put out a hand. "Wait. We'll get to everybody." Deputies pushed the parents away. Now he walked to the center of the room and waited. The noise level decreased slowly until there was an undercurrent of, "Shush, shush."

When there was complete silence, the guy took a cigar from a shirt pocket and rolled it between his thumb and fingers. He told us he was Chief Detective Louis Fourquet of the Palm Beach County Sheriff's Office and said the police chief of the Town of Palm Beach had asked the sheriff to lead the investigation because of limited manpower. "We're going to be in for a long night. If you all cooperate, you can make it shorter." Grumbling erupted throughout the room, but no one challenged him directly. "Now, who found the body?"

Sally Brophy raised her hand.

"Who else?"

Paul Brophy put his hand up too and pointedly looked toward the Santa and me. Reluctantly, we acknowledged we were also present when the body was found.

"You four, over there in that corner." Fourquet pointed. "I'll talk to you one at a time in the kitchen." He divided the rest into two groups and directed them to separate corners of the room. "We'll need identifications and brief statements. We may ask you to come in later, but tonight we'll try to make it as quick and easy as possible. Take your children with you."

With everyone's attention on Fouquet, I figured this was a perfect time to do something I'd wanted to do ever since we found Clinton's body. I turned my back on the cops, parents and children and pulled my cell phone from my shirt pocket and phoned Mo. She picked up on the first ring.

"I'm going to be even later than I thought," I told her.

"Why?" She didn't try to disguise the irritation in her voice.

As quickly as I could, I told her what had happened.

Her tone changed. "Are you all right?"

"Yeah, but I have no idea when I'm getting back."

"Need any help?"

"Later I'll need a ride." I told her about giving Ginny the key to my Miata.

"You loaned your car to somebody?" she said, incongruity in her voice.

"To Ginny. She's your friend."

"But your car? You don't even loan it to me."

Behind me, a cop said, "Turn it off."

"More later," I said and pocketed the phone. Brophy and Santa smiled approvingly at the cop.

Fourquet summoned Sally first, then the Santa, then Brophy. I was left to wait for more than an hour, pondering what had happened. Little of it was clear. The only thing that anybody could say with certainty was that somebody had used the fireworks explosions to mask sound of the gunshot that killed Clinton Drake III.

Some of my colleagues might think of this enforced confinement with others at the party as a great opportunity to learn more about this bunch, but I'm afraid I didn't discover much. I still didn't know most of the names. And I hadn't had any experience appraising a roomful of murder suspects. Did Candy Cane silently exchange information with Brophy, their eyes locking long enough to send an unspoken message? Did Silver Bracelets do the same thing with the Santa with the Rolex? Frizzy Blond fidgeted next to Gay Banker, looking most often toward Shy Wilbur, the guy she couldn't convince dancing was almost as good as foreplay. Muscle Shirt stood close to Candy Cane, who ignored him, then went to a corner and did push-ups. Those guys don't know when to stop.

Did any of this match anything I'd seen at the party? Candy Cane was still a puzzle. Hadn't ever been married, she said. Then what was she doing at the party? Why had she stood so close to me during the fireworks? I'd been wrong about her being interested in Muscle Shirt. He wasn't in her class. Maybe she was interested in one of the other men. Come play with me. That was the message her peppermint-striped outfit broadcast. Or was that just the message I was getting? Jesus. Time for me to get back to Mo before I get in trouble.

I looked around for Ginny. She was nowhere in sight. Maybe her prediction came true, the cops allowed her to leave with her son. Other mothers and fathers were just as anxious to get their kids to school on time, but she was given special treatment. Is an assistant state attorney free of suspicion? Privileged among law officials maybe, but trustworthy enough to be driving my Miata? I could see her, somewhere on

Ninety-five, mammoth semis passing on one side, hotshots from Miami weaving in and out of lanes on the other, her son in the passenger seat, her instinct to reach out an arm to protect him first, turn the wheel or hit the brakes second—

Stop it! When I bought the little jewel of a sports car I promised myself I wouldn't let it own me. Heck, it cost less than thirty thousand, strains to churn out only 166 horsepower, and won't beat any other sports car to sixty. But it is an orgasmic joy to drive. Only two seats, but when I sit in mine and press the little pedal down to the floor, I'm as close to heaven as I ever expect to get. A thousand percent better than booze. But it was just a thing. Just stuff. I had to remember that.

A deputy interrupted my thoughts. "You're next."

#

"Now you tell me," Fourquet said, "that you brought a friend of your girlfriend—a woman you'd never seen before, to this weird little party."

"That's right," I said.

"And you didn't have any idea she had a gun with her."

"That's right."

"You expect me to believe that?"

"Don't care what you believe. It's what happened."

Fourquet took a cigar from his shirt pocket, smelled it, then rolled it between his thumb and fingertips. The same cigar he did the same little exercise with a couple of hours ago. He probably never lit it.

"Get out of here," Fourquet said. "We can find you if we want you."

"Is Ginny Stonridge still here?"

"Long gone," he said.

"You've questioned her already?"

"Some. We'll question her at length tomorrow morning at the state attorney's office."

"Why the special treatment?"

He frowned and his face turned pink. "She's law enforcement."

"And therefore presumed innocent."

"Everybody's presumed innocent." His voice rose. "Now get out before we let you spend a night in jail."

Tired and close to anger myself, I was tempted to argue more but didn't. Sometimes my better judgment prevails. Sometimes.

#

I could tell by Mo's voice that the phone ring woke her up. I apologized.

"What happened?" she asked.

I gave her a short version.

"Your car. You gave her your car?"

"I could find a motel and spend the night in Palm Beach or nearby," I said.

"Not on your life. I want to hear all the details."

So Mo picked me up in her car, a sensible Toyota Camry, Sailfin Blue Pearl in color, and we talked on the ride back. She was interested in it all, but she kept repeating, "Your car, I can't believe you let her have your car" or variations of the same.

"Enough," I said. "I told you I might have made a mistake."

"Any idea who killed the man in the pool?"

"Your friend is the most likely suspect."

"Difficult to believe. The woman I knew—" Mo stopped. "Come to think of it, that was so many years ago that I have no idea what's she's like as an adult."

"If I'd have known that—" I stopped. I don't like people second-guessing me, so I wouldn't do it to Mo.

"But there's a possibility you're overlooking," Mo said. "She's an assistant district attorney. What if she were there on assignment? Some sort of undercover thing. What if the business of Fouquet asking for identification were a charade? .Surely he knew her. What if—"

"That's so improbable. They don't send prosecutors out as under-cover agents to investigate crimes."

"No more improbable than Ginny's ex-husband being murdered at the first Exchange she ever attended."

I was too tired to argue.

Mo was quiet for a while, the lips moving but no sound coming out. She did this every now and then when she was trying to figure something out. Mediating? Thinking? Finally she turned and said: "Tell me if I have this straight. When the cops let Ginny leave, they had no way of knowing that it was her gun that killed Clinton."

I hadn't thought of that.

"With your help she was able to leave before anyone else." she said.

"Right on both counts," I said.

"I wonder what will happen when the cops discover it was an assistant state attorney who owned the gun that killed Clinton Drake the Third and that she was married to the victim not long ago."

The answer so obvious I didn't say anything. Didn't want to think about it, in fact.

"Anyway," Mo said. "It's not our problem."

When we reached Fort Lauderdale, we crawled into bed and fell asleep almost immediately. In the middle of the night, I woke and found Mo's arms wrapped around me so tightly our body heat left us wet with sweat. I loved it when that happened. Loved Mo, loved us. We were one.

The digital clock read 4:16. Mo turned in her sleep, hair messed but just as beautiful as ever. Careful not to wake her, I lifted the sheet and tossed it to the foot of the bed. My life is better than it's ever been. Nothing can spoil it. Mo and I will be together forever. I put my arms around her, felt her nudge closer, and went back to sleep.

Chapter Seven

A piercing, terrible, end-of-the-world clanging was trying to stop my dream. No way, I wouldn't let it. I rolled over, searching for a way to block it out. Something ringing. Rang and rang again, louder and louder. The damn phone. I lifted my head barely off the pillow and forced one eye open. The digits on the clock read 6:36. Mo reached for her cell on her side of the bed. I rolled the other way and put my head under the pillow. Didn't work. I could hear Mo talking to somebody.

"This morning?" she said. "What? Where? Give me that address."

I felt the bed shift and knew Mo was sitting up, writing the address on her bedside notepad. She spoke a few more words into the phone, hung up, and shook me. "Wake up."

"What?"

"Ginny needs our help."

"She's your friend," I protested, my need for sleep momentarily overcoming all feelings of obligation.

"She says you can get your car back."

My Miata. Damn, damn, damn. I crawled from the bed.

#

We drove toward Boca in Mo's Camry, Mo behind wheel, an arrangement I hadn't challenged. Quick showers, coffee, and cereal on the run, and now there was time to talk. "What's the rush?"

"Ginny says they're suspending her. Topping's deputy phoned her a little after five this morning."

"Does that surprise you?"

"No," Mo said. "But apparently it came as a shock to her."

"What are we supposed to do?"

"Accompany her to the State Attorney's office and provide moral support."

Just like Mo. She was loyal. The expression "loyal to a fault" came to mind. Loyal even to this former college roommate who hadn't phoned her for years. The road signs flashed by. Lauderdale-by-the-Sea, Pompano Beach, Deerfield, Beach—all places people came to relax and get away from it all. Not us. We were speeding down an interstate, off on a mission to help somebody I hadn't heard of before Sunday morning and who may have murdered a former husband. We crossed the Palm Beach County line into Boca Raton. I asked, "You still think she did it?"

"I never have."

"But last night you said—"

"I remembered I didn't know her adult self. That's all."

She was right, so I dropped it. Mo reached over and touched my arm. I squeezed her hand.

#

My Miata sat outside Ginny's townhouse, its convertible top up, a thing of beauty even with tiny droplets of dew on its bright red paint. I checked for damage. None. Ginny saw us and came outside wearing her work clothes—a dark blue skirt, light blue blouse, dark hose and moderate heels. If she'd missed any sleep last night, she didn't show it. She nodded to me and turned to Mo, who gave her a light hug and asked how she was holding up.

"It's a suspension with pay, but still a suspension," Ginny said. "It hurts."

"You'll be reinstated soon," Mo said.

"Not a chance until after the election."

Then I understood. State Attorney Seymour Topping was running for Congress. He hadn't been in a courtroom for more than five years, according to the papers, but he was extraordinarily popular on the business lunch and chicken dinner circuit. His pitch: Crack down on crime with mandatory federal death sentences for a short list of crimes and mandatory life for many others. The slick little demagogue won't put Ginny back on the payroll before the election unless they find someone else to hang Clinton Drake's murder on. Maybe not even then.

"How's Eric?" Mo asked.

"Not good," Ginny said. "Frightened. Confused. Seeing his father like that—

"Where is he now?"

At a day care center." Ginny said. Then quickly, "It's better than it sounds. Really a pre-school, run by a friend."

Then Mo and Ginny discussed which car to take to the State Attorney's office in West Palm. My Miata was ruled out because it had only two seats. Ginny wanted to take her car, a black Acura, since she'd be bringing some things home. They gave me a choice: I could ride with them in the Acura or follow in my car. I opted to travel with them, riding in the back seat and picking up my car later. No telling what I might learn.

#

Ginny's office was in the short building next to the new high-rise courthouse on Dixie Highway. We passed two women talking in the lobby. "You mean everybody there hated everybody else?"' asked one, astonishment and glee in her voice.

"They must have," said her friend. "The paper said they were all divorced from each other."

"Can you imagine?"

Ginny ignored them. We rode the elevator in silence. In the hallway, a maintenance man stood on a short ladder, stretching to remove plastic white letters from the green felt of a directory. He was taking down Ginny's name, G S T O N R I D G E, the first name of everyone, male and female, shortened to an initial. I wondered: Had Ginny ever used Drake for a last name when she was married? Probably not.

A copy of the *Palm Beach Post* lay on a reception desk. "Murder at Mad Swingers Party," the headline read, the Sunday copy desk staff having a bit of fun, the reporter not having time to get it right before her deadline. The story ran on the top of the front page, but only eight to ten inches long. I could imagine what would happen when reporters for *Post, Miami Herald*, and *South Florida Sun-Sentinel* along with crews from half a dozen television stations had all day to chew on the story. They'll do things that would make even Clinton Drake's *Enquirer* blush.

The receptionist told Ginny that Topping wanted to see her. Ginny nodded but didn't say anything. We followed her to her office, the desk and chairs a Spartan tan metal, nothing but calendars on the walls. Not much on top of the desk either, except for a photo of Eric and two empty cardboard boxes about the size of a file drawer.

Ginny motioned us to sit, went to the closet and took out a hanger holding a dark suit jacket, one that matched her skirt. "Be back soon," she said, walking toward the door as she put it on. Almost there, she turned and looked at Maureen. "Could you get the personal stuff from my desk and put it in the boxes they've left?"

"Sure."

Mo transferred items to the cardboard containers. A pair of flat-heeled shoes. An address book. Emery boards. A box of tampons. Cards from a personal Rolodex. Nail polish. Not much else. "Someone's already removed all official papers," Mo said.

I pointed to a credenza behind the desk, dust covering all but a rectangular area. "There was a personal computer there. It's been taken out, too."

"Along with any disks," Mo said.

"I wonder—" I began.

Mo put a finger in front of her mouth and pointed to the air conditioning ducts, then the phone. Someone could be listening. So Mo and I spent the next thirty minutes saying very little to each other, both understanding that anything we said might be heard or recorded. I walked to the window and looked out. Good Sam, stood to the north, Palm Beach and Singer Island to the east, clear air and bright sunshine giving the outside a feeling of purity and tranquility. Not like in this office.

I should explain. Good Sam is the affectionate nickname for what used to be Good Samaritan Hospital, now officially the Good Samaritan Medical Center. In many ways it is what ties Palm Beach and West Palm Beach together. By itself, Palm Beach doesn't have the population to support a hospital, So Good Sam, sitting on the shore of Lake Worth facing Palm Beach just a few blocks north of downtown West Palm, is daily reminder to all the millionaires and billionaires of Palm Beach that they may be next—next to make the ride over North Bridge late at night, chests tight, hearts beating a zillion times a minute, pain getting worse by the second, sirens screaming on top of medical vans announcing that the end of the world was near (or at least the occupant's residency in it), these rich old men and women who could buy almost anything—anything but life—in terror knowing any second could be their last.

Then they'd see Good Sam sitting at the end of the bridge. glowing in light. Halleluiah, they'd been saved! They would live. Tell me what to do to show I much appreciate this Lord, they're thinking. Anything. I'll do anything. And they do. When the next fund raising ball for Good Sam comes around, they give and they give big. Just say how many zeros to put on the check. As a result, for decades Good Sam was able to purchase the most expensive and advanced medical equipment money could buy. Or so one of Mo's Wall Street friend had told us.

Voices in the hallway brought me back into Ginny's office. More time passed. I opened the office door and paced in the hallway. "Calm down," Mo said, but I couldn't. Another ten minutes went by. Then Chief Detective Louis Fourquet unlit cigar in hand, emerged from an office at the other end of the hall. He looked disgusted or perplexed, saw me, stopped, started to say something, thought better of it, walked through the lobby and out the door. I went back to Ginny's office and told Mo about Fourquet. She nodded.

Five minutes later Ginny burst into the office and threw a yellow pad on the desktop. "These bastards actually think I might have done it. They read me my rights. They asked if I wanted an attorney." She sat down behind the desk. "My God, I almost asked for one."

I looked toward Mo, telling her this was her game, but Mo sat silently, watching her old friend.

Ginny stretched both arms outward, palms up. "I thought they'd say something—something to let me know they were just going through the motions."

Of course not, I thought. Ginny wouldn't either if she were in their place.

She began pulling empty desk drawers open. "After ten years—"

"What did you do?" Mo asked.

"I stood by my Fifth Amendment rights." Ginny slammed a drawer shut. "What'd you think I'd do?"

#

We were almost out of the courthouse lobby when a woman came from behind us and touched Ginny's shoulder. Ginny turned and they hugged, both close to tears. Ginny introduced her as Lucy, a secretary she shared with another assistant.

"I couldn't say anything to you upstairs," she said. "But, Ginny, if there's anything I can do for you when you're not here—"

Ginny put her arms about the woman, then stepped back. "Actually, there are some things."

"What?"

"Keep your ears open and call me from time to time," Ginny said. "I'll need to know what's going on here."

A big risk for the secretary.

"Will you do that?" Ginny asked.

"Sure. You know I will."

And a risk for Ginny, too. Who can you trust in a deal like this?

#

At the parking lot, Ginny stopped and said, "I can't go back to Boca now. It's too early to pick Eric up, and I'm too keyed up to sit in an empty house."

I looked at my watch and saw I had a couple of hours before my first appointment.

Maureen said, "Is there a Starbucks nearby?"

"I want to go somewhere where no one will see us," Ginny said. "Nobody who would recognize us."

I knew just the place. "There's restaurant over on Singer Island. It's a bar really, but they serve food."

Maureen gave me a look. "Should you?"

"As long as other people are present, there's no problem."

Ginny had no idea what we were talking about but didn't seem to care. "We'll take my car but you drive," she said, and handed the keys to Mo. We loaded the boxes from her office into the trunk, Ginny sat in the front seat beside Mo, and I crawled into the back. Ginny gave Mo directions, then turned the radio on and tuned it to WWPB, the news and music station.

When the music stopped a female voice, excited and breathless, blasted from six speakers: *"State Attorney Seymour Topping this morning announced that Assistant State Attorney Ginny Stonridge has been placed on indefinite leave of absence following the slaying of her former husband Sunday night."*

The bastard worked fast. Must have had someone phone reporters minutes after we left Ginny's office.

"Topping said the action in no way reflected upon the competence or integrity of Ms. Stonridge, who worked in the office for ten years. However other courthouse sources said they did not expect her to ever return to the office in an official capacity."

Who are they kidding? Topping's the only possible source.

"Meanwhile, sources said police continued to pursue leads in a murder that climaxed a bizarre Sunday night party of ex-spouses. They said Ms. Stonridge is a suspect in the slaying."

They got that from Topping, too.

"The state attorneys' office is known to be concerned about Ms. Stonridge's possession of two firearms. The guns had not been authorized by Topping or anyone in his office. Sources say no charges will be filed until the case is presented to the Grand Jury later this month."

"He's gone too far," Ginny screamed. "Too fucking far,"

I felt rage building within me, too, Topping violating all sense of fair play, turning his back on a loyal employee who served him well.

"Son of a bitch," Mo said, a phrase she used about once every ten years. Her faced flushed with anger, also a rare sight.

I didn't realize it at the time, but I know now that at that moment we quit being bystanders and got involved. We were in this up to our eyeballs, as a matter of fact, and I started losing my objectivity.

#

Following Ginny's instructions, Mo drove north on Dixie, cut over to Broadway at Northwood, continued north on Broadway and finally turned east on Blue Heron. Soon we were climbing the Blue Heron Bridge between Riviera Beach and Singer Island, a fixed span rising so high above the Intracoastal that even the tallest sail boats could pass beneath without the span being raised, a rarity in Palm Beach County.

"Careful," Ginny said, "It's steep."

"Never fear," Mo said, pushing the accelerator down harder. "I passed my high school driving test with honors." The car leapt ahead. If Ginny understood the putdown, she didn't show it.

From the top of the bridge, the scene was something out of a Chamber of Commerce brochure. People in pleasure boats and in the water on the skis behind them looked for all the world as if they had no problems. Even the island they circled—Peanut Island—seemed frivolous. Sun, water, and sand, just like the ads said, they seemed to live in a world of endless play.

In the distance we could see tall condo towers lined up along the Atlantic, unattractive white structures that grew like toadstools along the beach, symbols of a past era when white developers were able to bribe black city officials on the mainland to build whatever they wanted. I knew that and many other things about South Florida second-hand from a friend of Mo's who handled bonds for the county once. I wondered how much, if any, things had changed. Does development always lead to public corruption?

"Which way now?" Mo asked, and I pointed into Fathoms' parking lot. Get a grip, I told myself. Pay attention to what's happening right now. Are we riding with a murderer? Or not.

#

We stepped from bright sunlight into a barely lit room. It took a while for my eyes to adjust, but eventually we made our way to a wood table near a window shaped like a porthole. Fish netting hung from the ceiling, a circular bar sat on the opposite side of the room.

At the next table, a man and woman ordered peach schnapps with beer chasers. I looked at my watch. Barely eleven o'clock in the morning. We ordered coffee and sandwiches.

When the waitress left, Mo turned to Ginny. "The radio said guns. Two guns."

"That's what they don't understand," Ginny said. "To me it's simple."

Mo didn't say anything, and of course I didn't either. I'd learned to use silence while working as a therapist. She used the same technique in interviewing, both as news reporter and stock analyst. It worked the same for both of us. Say nothing, and eventually the other person will fill the void with words. Follow them up and sometimes you get to something significant.

Ginny shrugged her shoulders. "When I took this job, I figured I'd make enemies. And I'm single parent living alone."

"I understand," Mo said.

Did she? I wondered. Or is she just saying that to encourage Ginny to talk? If every single parent living alone in South Florida bought a gun for protection there'd be shootouts in most neighborhoods every other night.

"I got a concealed weapons permit from the county seven years ago. That was when I bought the little gun they found on the bottom of the pool. A .22-caliber Derringer made by the North American Arms Corporation, if it makes any difference."

Mo nodded.

"Then a policeman, a friend I met at the courthouse, told me I should get a big gun to keep at home," Ginny said. "So I did. A thirty-eight."

"Weren't you afraid Eric would find it and—"

"I keep it in a locked box up on a shelf in my bedroom closet."

"And the other one you carry with you?"

"I usually keep it in my car," Ginny said. "But last night—"

Mo looked toward me. I gave her a half shrug. I know little about guns or where to keep them. The admonition to leave them at home unless you plan to use 'em had always made sense.

"Topping didn't understand either," Ginny said. She mimicked his voice: *"Leaving your gun in your car! Don't you know it takes only twenty seconds to break into any car made?"*

Our sandwiches and coffee arrived. The scene outside a little round window behind Mo caught my attention. A group of surfers lifted boards from the top of their cars and walked toward the beach. A green and white sheriff's car pulled into the lot, a uniformed deputy behind the wheel.

"Ginny," Mo said. "While everything's fresh in your mind, tell me everything you saw last night that might have a bearing on Clinton's murder."

Ginny followed my gaze out the window, then turned to Mo. "Nobody really liked Clinton, but as far as I know nobody wanted to kill him."

"Not what I mean," Mo said. "I want everything you remember about the party, from the top. Go and I might be able to help you."

What was she doing? I guess I frowned or something, because Mo gave me a look that said, *Shut up*

"OK," Ginny said. "When we first got there…." Her recollections were Fremarkably similar to mine, but more detailed. She knew the names of some of the people there and how they made a living. When she finished, she said, "Mo, level with me. Do you think I did it?"

Maureen took two beats before she answered. Then, "No, Ginny. I don't."

"And, Go? Do you?"

"Any of the people at that crazy party could have done it." Excessive honesty was not required at this point.

"Why?" Ginny asked, turning the question back at me "Why does anybody kill anyone?"

"Revenge. Greed. Fear. Response to blackmail," I said. "Any of the hundred things."

"But until they learn something new," Mo injected, "You're the chief suspect, Ginny."

God bless her, I thought. Outside, the deputy sat in his car, windows up, engine running to power air conditioning. Early May and already it's too hot to sit in comfort without it. An unmarked car, a dusty white

Ford Crown Victoria with a little aerial mounted on the roof, pulled up beside the deputy.

Inside at the table, Mo said, "So you can't just sit and do nothing, Ginny. What would you do if you wanted to discover who killed Clinton?"

Ginny cocked her head to one side, thinking only briefly. "I'd talk to Sally first," she said. "She knows more about those people than anybody. Then, one by one, I'd talk with every adult at the party."

"That'd take weeks, maybe months," I protested, my attention back inside the restaurant now because I knew what Mo was thinking. "Ginny's used to working with testimony and evidence brought to her. She doesn't know what it takes to conduct a one-person investigation."

Mo knew it, too, I knew. Whether she was doing investigative work for a news story or researching a company for a stock report, she interviewed everybody imaginable. Then, after she'd talked to all the obvious players, the real work began. We'd talked about the process many times when we first got together. Something she learned would lead to something else, and so on, until—often when she least expected it—she hit pay dirt. I'd try to talk to her about the roll of the subconscious and synchronicity in the process, but she wasn't interested. For her it was simple. Look long enough and you find the answer.

"We can't just sit and do nothing," Mo said.

Outside, the man in the unmarked car got out and walked to the deputy's car. I recognized him, right off. The Santa-with-the-Rolex from the Exchange. Can't be, I first thought, but there was no mistaking him, even wearing a blue sports shirt now, not the red and white one that caused me to give him the nickname. What's he doing here?

The deputy put his window down. Santa talked to him briefly, then got back in his car and drove off. I didn't understand what they were up to, but I was convinced it wasn't good. Not for us, anyway. "Let's get out of here."

If Mo was startled by my abruptness, she didn't show it. "Your turn to get the check," she said, a joke between us that Ginny didn't, indeed couldn't, understand. I've never let Mo pick up a check, not once in more than two decades, a tiny attempt to pay her back for all I owed her. "I'll get the next one."

I shook my head. "You buy the ice cream tonight," I said, knowing our freezer was full of the stuff.

#

Outside Mo gave me the keys and said, "Your turn to drive."

"I'll get in back," Ginny said, but Mo wouldn't let her. Ginny sat next to me.

In the rearview mirror, I saw Mo buckling a seat belt. Next to me Ginny left hers unfastened, but I figured it wasn't my place to tell her to buckle it. As we pulled out of Fathom's parking lot, the uniformed deputy watched us but his car didn't move.

I turned onto Blue Heron and started up the bridge. Almost to the top of the span, a black truck with a big front grill suddenly filled the rearview mirror. Before I could react, it rammed our back bumper, knocking the Acura forward. My body slammed backward, into the rear of the seat. Ginny yelled, "Damn."

"That crazy—" Mo said.

The truck hit us again. I pushed the accelerator to the floor. We reached the top of the bridge. The truck fell back. A Ford F-series pickup, I knew when I saw it better. As we began our downward descent, the truck came at us again, this time hitting the Acura at an angle, jamming our car into the curb, the right wheel climbing onto the sidewalk.

I jerked the steering wheel to the left. We dropped back into the roadway. The truck bumped us again, hard. The blow slammed the Acura into a slow, circular orbit. This can't be happening, my mind kept telling me, but I knew it was. I yanked the wheel again, but the car wouldn't respond. We kept sliding. My body strained against the seat belt, the car's spin pushing me toward Ginny. Her body pressed against the opposite door, blood on her forehead.

The rear of the Acura, leading the forward motion now, hit the concrete median and bounced back. I tried to twist around to see Mo, but centrifugal force held me back. Outside, the grill of a big Lexus rushed toward us in the left lane. It would hit us head on. Can't do a damned thing about it. Inevitable, my mind shouted. This is the way life ends.

Mo screamed. No sound from Ginny. A muffled C-U-R-U-N C-H outside, then a loud, jolting T-H-U-N-N-K! Metal tore into metal, the windshield burst into tiny diamonds, an airbag exploded in front of me and slammed into my face. I couldn't see anything. Something crashed into us again.

The Acura began rolling, careening down the bridge, climbed the curb again, this time with greater force, and hit the bridge railing. Inside, we were knocked backward, then to the side. The car rocked slowly, then finally came to a rest. I fought off the airbag and reached to unlock the seatbelt. The damn thing was stuck. Ginny lay on top of me, panting, blood on her head and neck, splattered on her blouse.

She began to speak, her voice tiny and indistinct. "Don't," she said. "Don't let them get away with—" She gasped. "—with this." Then she was silent.

Images and sounds melded into each other, the sequence of events churning in time, nothing clear but everything registering somewhere in the depths of my consciousness. Ginny's body, not moving, dead weight. No, God don't let it be true, I turned to see Maureen, her body motionless, slumped to one side, gravity pulling it toward the left rear door, the seat belt holding it back. I tried to push Ginny off to reach back to Mo, but Ginny's body resisted with fierce stubbornness. Again I thought: Dead weight.

Tires screamed outside. Somebody climbed on top of the car and pulled at the door but it wouldn't open. A gruff voice said, "Don't move the bodies," a pair of arms stuck through a window on the other side, then retreated, then a face, a bearded face, a red beard not white like the suspicious Santa Claus in the parking lot, looked down. "Just hold on, help's coming," he said, but I didn't hear any sirens and I kept thinking, I've got to get to help Mo, got to get Ginny off me, then I heard Mo say, "He's right, stay there."

Eventually there were sirens and medics and cops, all very professional, "Gentle there," one said as they pulled first Ginny, then Maureen, from the car, then looked down at me. I said, "I'm OK, I'm OK," and tried to climb from the wreck on my own, but they lifted me up and outside, then insisted I lay on a cot while someone checked my pulse and blood pressure. I realized they were going to take us to a hospital and from somewhere deep in my mind I heard two words and said, "Good Sam, take us to Good Sam," my near death experience producing not a review of my life but some almost forgotten advice from the bond dealer Mo knew.

Chapter Eight

They took each of us —Ginny, Maureen, and me—to the hospital in separate vans, those lime-yellow truck-like vehicles that substitute for ambulances these days. Inside they had enough emergency equipment—oxygen tanks, heart monitors, and such—to staff a small hospital. But nobody had any information.

"How's Mo?" I asked one of the medics.

"Who?"

"Maureen O'Neal. The woman in the back seat."

"She'll come along in the other van," he said. "You two, you and the woman in the front seat, you're the worst hurt."

"I'm not hurt." I tried to push myself up.

The medic pushed back. "You've got an awful lot of blood on your for an unharmed man."

"Not mine," I said.

He nodded but didn't say anything.

"The blood's not mine."

He turned away to adjust something.

"I'm sure Maureen O'Neal is hurt more than me."

He began cutting my shirt off, so I gave up. I'd find Mo when we got to the hospital. Now I began wondering how badly Ginny had been hurt, and then I got to thinking what she meant by her last words. Or whether we could believe anything she said. But the black truck had clearly intended to hit us. To hit Ginny's car. So Ginny had been their target.

"I can't see that you've been hurt," the medic said. "No cuts. Not even any bruises. This must be somebody else's blood."

"I tried to tell you." Once again I tried to sit up.

He pushed me back, "But you've still got to be checked out for internal injuries."

It is a sign of my late arriving maturity that I didn't argue. But when we drove up to the hospital, I saw a sign out the side window of the van. "This isn't good Sam," I said. "The sign says St. Mary's Medical Center."

"I said take us to Good Sam,". I told the medic,

"No way. St. Mary's is the area's official trauma center. Besides it's closer to where the accident happened."

"But—" I didn't know how to finish the sentence. I had wanted the best for Mo, but I knew that wouldn't matter to this guy.

"And for what it's worth, St. Mary's is where the Kennedys kept Rose alive for so many years," the guy said. "If it was good enough for them, it should be good enough for you and your friends."

"Can we go faster?"

"You in a big hurry now, huh? Like on the bridge?"

I started to tell this guy that we hadn't been speeding when the truck hit us, but what was the use? I was in a hurry to get to Mo now, to find out if she was OK, and for us to get on with our lives. I had a half dozen appointments with children and adolescents that afternoon and evening. I'd have to cancel them. I reached for the cell phone holster at my side. The medic saw me.

"No phone calls from here," he said. "Policy."

Of course. Why had I expected anything to go right today?

#

Across the emergency room I saw a couple of orderlies rolling Ginny though a doorway but Mo was nowhere in sight. A nurse leaned over my cot and said, "Where does it hurt?"

"It doesn't," I said. "I'm not hurt."

"A doctor will determine that," she said and turned away.

Left alone, I realized I was shivering. Why do they always keep hospitals so cold? Something about germs, I knew, but I was freezing. No shirt, no sheet over me even. Hours passed, or so it seemed. All my protestations of bodily soundness backfired. The more I said I wasn't hurt, the more they ignored me, all the while saying, "Stay right there."

Finally, a woman came from another room and handed me a clip board with papers attached. "Here Fill these out."Hospital and insurance forms. Simple enough.

She looked around the room, not seeing who she was looking for and handed me a second board. "These are for your friend, Gemini."

"Never heard of her," I said.

"They say she came in the van ahead of you."

"You mean Ginny?"

"Don't care what you call her. Her ID says Gemini Stonridge."

"I don't know enough about her to—"

"Do what you can." She thrust a third set of papers toward me. "How about Maureen O'Neal?"

"Where is she?"

"Upstairs in a room." I took Maureen's paperwork.

"I need to get up there ."

"When they get through with you," she said, nodding toward the nurses, and walked away.

I could fill out most of the information on Mo. Address? An apartment on the Isle of Venice in Fort Lauderdale, which I still thought was a stupid name for a street. Employer? Providence Trust, the non-profit charity she runs. Next of kin? None, her parents dead, no brother, no sister. In case of emergency notify? I put down my name, with our phone number and address. But I refused to sign liability releases for her. Mo could sign them herself.

When I got to Ginny's—Gemini's—forms I realized how little I knew about the woman. Address? I remembered the street, not the number. Occupation? Assistant State Attorney, I wrote, not acknowledging the suspension. Next of kin? I put Eric's name in the slot. The rest I left blank.

I found a woman behind a desk who would take the forms but wouldn't or couldn't give me any information about Maureen or the woman I now knew as Gemini. "You should put a shirt on," she said. I took that as a license to open a door that said, STAFF, found a sink, and washed off. A guy came in wearing a white lab coat soiled with blood or something, not nearly as badly messed up as my shirt had been. He took it off and reached for another from a stack.

"Twenty bucks to borrow that shirt for the next hour," I said, holding out the bill.

"Hell." He pocketed the money and pointed. "Take a clean one from the stack."

I did and became Orderly for a Day.

#

The visitors desk in the lobby didn't have a record of Maureen, Ginny or Gemini being admitted, so I began riding elevators and walking corridors. Luckily there was no dress code for the pants worn underneath light green medical coats, so I and my khakis fit right in.

"They bring a Maureen O'Neal up here?" I asked at each nursing station. Finally a guy gave me a room number.

"You look silly," Mo said first thing. She was sitting up, two pillows at her back, still beautiful in hospital garb, still, as far as I could tell, healthy and unharmed.

I bent over, brushed a lock of mussed hair away, and kissed her on the forehead. "Not as silly as that gown looks on you," I said.

She reached for my hand. I took hers and sat on the side of the bed. "How's Ginny?".

"Haven't found her yet."

"Try Intensive Care."

"Later. Tell me how you are."

"I'm not hurt," she said.

"I keep denying it, too."

"We get no respect," she said, laughing, and I knew she was all right. "I tried to get us into Good Sam. They wouldn't listen to me."

Mo tilted her head to one side as if trying to figure what I was talking about, the blank look registering that she had no clue.

"You know," I said. "The bond guy we had lunch with last year."

"Oh." Her face brightened with understanding. "His information is way behind the times. Good Sam and St. Mary's are owned by the same company now."

Now I didn't understand. "A company owns them?"

"Sure. Hospital chains were all the rage on Wall Street for a while. a growth industry. Big national companies were able to buy out hospitals all over the country. Then somebody realized that hospitals are at the mercy of forces over which they have no control. Governments and insurance companies dictate how much they get paid."

"But your Wall Street friend said—"

"He was a bond guy. They don't know much about equities or specific companies. To them it's all interest rates, safety ratings, and guessing what the Fed will do next."

I didn't need to ask about the Fed, knowing she meant the Federal Reserve Board from her previous, mostly unsuccessful efforts to educate me about markets. So I said: "Get some rest. Busy executive like you needs—"

Mo cut me off. "I've been thinking."

"I knew it, I knew it," I said, holding the palm of my right hand against my forehead.

The ends of her mouth curled into a smile, before she said, "Seriously."

I shifted my weight on the bed. "Tell me."

Mo said, "Somebody's setting Ginny up."

"I doubt it."

"Think about it, Go. Someone takes her gun and kills her ex. Then somebody tries to kill her."

"Us too," I said.

"Nobody knew we were going to be in her car," Mo said. "Besides, who'd want to kill us?"

"About a hundred people I know." I dropped her hand, made a mock notebook of my left and began scribbling with an imaginary pen in my right, pretending to start a list. "Let's see. All those people I worked with at the hospital in Maryland—"

"Go, be serious!"

"The truck bumping us could have been a coincidence," I said. "Whoever was at the wheel could have been so beered up he would have bumped any car in front of him."

"Go, you don't believe that," Mo took my hand in hers again.

I changed the subject. "When will they let you out of here?"

"Tomorrow morning. They're making me stay overnight for observation."

"Where are you hurt?"

"A little cut, here." She pushed her hair back, disclosing a bandaged area high on the side of her forehead. "No damage, I keep saying, but they said head wounds are sometimes more serious than they appear."

"Jesus," I said.

"It's nothing."

So much like Mo. Here she was, injured badly enough for doctors to insist she stay overnight, and all she had thought about was Ginny. Which reminded me of something. "Did you know your friend's real name is Gemini?"

"Sure."

"I thought Ginny stood for Virginia."

"Except when it stands for Gemini," Mo said.

"Explain."

"It's a long story."

"Give me the short version."

"Her parents met in a bar in Washington D.C.," Mo began. "It was in the late sixties or early seventies, so you can guess how the conversation started."

Easy. I'd been in single bars, too. "What's your sign?"

"Exactly. And the Zodiac talk continued all through their very short courtship."

"One consummated amid the aroma of pot, I assume."

"Natch," Mo said. "So, when barely nine months later, Ginny arrived in early June, they named her Gemini."

"That the one with the two fish?"

"No. Two faces."

"So she's two faced?"

"She says she can be of two minds about anything," Maureen said. "A valuable trait in an attorney."

I looked down and saw that Mo's hand and mine were still tightly clinched. "If she doesn't like the name, why doesn't she change it?"

"She says it would be too much trouble now," Mo said. "Lean toward me." I obeyed. She gave me a quick kiss on the mouth and released my hand. "Now get out of here and go find her."

"Who?"

"Who, who? Ginny, darn it."

#

I figured everyone who worked at the hospital surely knew where the Intensive Care Unit was, and since I was supposed to be one of them I couldn't ask. Instead I rode an elevator down to the lobby and looked at the directory. A vaguely familiar woman interrupted. "Aren't you Ginny's friend?"

I recognized her then. Lucy, Ginny's secretary. "Yes," nodded, figuring this was not the time to make a distinction between friendship and bare acquaintance. "How is she?"

"They don't think she's going to make it." Lucy's eyes were moist.

"I'm on my way up. What room?"

Lucy began crying, but blurted out a room number between tears. "They won't let you see her."

We'll see about that. Armed with my trusty orderly's coat, I'm invisible.

#

I needn't have worried about a room number, only the floor. Only one door in the hall had a policeman standing on one side, a sheriff's deputy on the other. Were they guarding Ginny against harm or making sure she doesn't leave? A stainless steel cart stood near the elevator, so I stepped behind it and pushed it toward Ginny's room. The cop and the deputy looked me over but made no move to block my entrance.

Ginny lay on her back, eyes closed. A clear plastic hose ran from a face mask to a cylinder that fed her oxygen. A smaller tube protruded from her left arm to a plastic bag that hung upside down beside the bed, bat-like. A wire connected her chest to a device that charted her heart rhythm. Red digital numbers flicked from a black box. I walked to the end of the bed, looking for a chart that would tell me how Ginny was doing. Not there. Maybe they keep them somewhere else in this hospital. I saw a small closet near the entrance door.

"You!" A gruff voice penetrated the room, followed by its originator, State Attorney Seymour Topping. "What are you doing here?"

I recognized him from newspaper photos but didn't see how he could know me. I put out a hand. "I don't think we've met."

"You know damn well who I am. I saw you at my office with Ginny."

So Topping watched us while we were in the State Attorney's office. I'd seen a mirror on one wall of the reception room, but hadn't thought much about it. Now I understood why they had a one-way mirror there: To look at witnesses before they're deposed. And size up visitors, like Mo and me.

"Who are you?" Topping demanded.

"A friend of a friend of Ginny's."

"I doubt it," he said. "But whoever you are, get out of here."

I smiled. It wasn't the first time in my life I've been told that. Probably won't be the last. I didn't move.

Topping turned toward the sheriff's deputy. "From now on, nobody gets in here except people from our office, the sheriff's department or cops." He twisted back toward me, "And you. Get out of that orderly's outfit."

"You want to see my chest?"

"Just get out."

I looked back at Ginny to see her reaction to all this, but her eyes remained closed, her face blank as if stating toward the ceiling. Maybe she could hear. "Ginny has a very good friend named Maureen O'Neal," I said loudly. "If she feels she's in any danger, she should call Maureen. And any friend of Mo's—Maureen O'Neal's—is a friend of mine."

"Get out," Topping said.

"Maureen and I would do anything for her," I said, still not moving.

"Officer," Topping yelled.

I'd done all I could so I turned and walked out the door.

"Seymour Topping wants to talk to you," I told the deputy outside the door as I passed him. "Now!"

Chapter Nine

I reported what had happened to Mo, giving it to her almost verbatim. "So you see, nobody likes me. Everybody tells me to leave."

"We probably have good reasons," Mo said, smiling enough to let me know she didn't mean it. "Be quiet a minute and let me think."

"First, I should tell you some things you don't know." I told her about the sheriff's deputy sitting in the air conditioned car outside the restaurant, about the Santa pulling up beside him, the two of them talking, then Santa leaving—things she couldn't see because of where she was sitting with her back to the porthole window at Fathoms.

"The guy with the big gold Rolex," Mo said. "That the one you mean?"

I nodded, reveling at Mo's power of recall. She hadn't been at The Exchange, but she'd absorbed everything I told her on the night of the murder, even details like the Rolex.

"Just as I thought," Mo said. "Someone's out to get Ginny. Someone in law enforcement."

"Ginny is in law enforcement."

"But—" Mo pulled her hand from mine, arranged her legs in a yoga position, closed her eyes, moistened her lips with her tongue, and started what she calls thinking—the practice others might call meditation or reflection. I knew she wouldn't talk or listen to me until she was finished. Mo was always doing this. Even when we were kids and next-door neighbors, she did it. We think differently. I try to find out all the facts of a situation and then reach a conclusion. She intuits an answer, then finds facts to support it. Left brain, right brain? Anima, animus? Or maybe a basic difference between men and women.

With considerable reluctance, I joined in the exercise. I don't have much respect for solo thinking. At least mine. Usually, what I and many others call thinking merely recycles old ideas, giving them new names. My breakthroughs come only two ways—from talking with others or from my subconscious. And my subconscious won't work for me unless I keep feeding it; otherwise it figures I'm no longer interested.

I put these reservations aside and tried to think about Mo's theory. There is rivalry between law enforcement agencies, no doubt about that. But why? Why would either someone in the police department or someone in the sheriff's department be after Ginny? Some cop or deputy angry at Ginny because of a trial they think she botched? Improbable. But why was the deputy at the beach? And Santa? Maybe he was in law enforcement, too. Had one of them followed us and radioed the other? If so, why?

Mo took a deep breath, then returned to her trance, alternately wetting her lips and pursing them.

For myself I couldn't shake the idea that someone was after Mo and me, not Ginny. The deputy saw us when we left Fathoms, The Santa with a Rolex, too. Both Mo and I have made enemies. Mo makes decisions about the distribution of millions of dollars every year. She may have offended some would-be beneficiary who felt strongly enough about his or her cause to kill because he didn't get what he wanted. She'd also told me she was on the hit list of every charlatan investment adviser she'd exposed earlier in her career. And I wasn't kidding about me making enemies. People bring their kids to me expecting me to get them to "behave." Often I discovered that the children are more emotionally mature than their parents—that their acting out is a cry for self-preservation. Then the fun begins.

Mo opened her eyes, sipped from a glass of water on the bedside table and announced, "The purpose of The Exchange wasn't for ex-spouses to exchange their children. The host, the hostess, banker, the Santa Claus, the flirt with the low-rider slacks, the woman who stood real close to you to watch the fireworks—none of them have children."

"Right."

"So whoever killed Clinton Drake is the same person who's trying to kill Ginny," she said.

"That's a stretch."

"They're setting Ginny up."

"You said that before," I said.

"I'm doubly sure now." Mo took another sip from the glass. "First they put out word they suspect she murdered her ex. Now they're cutting off communication with the outside world."

"They could want to protect her," I objected.

"By isolating her? Not likely."

"But they couldn't have had anything to do with her accident."

"How do we know that?" Mo said.

"You're saying the state attorney's office would kill or maim one of its own? Far-fetched."

Mo shrugged. "Stranger things have happened."

"Simple explanations are usually better than strange ones," I said.

"No matter how you figure this, we've got to help Ginny."

I took her hand again. "How?"

"By finding out who killed Clinton."

"How?"

"I haven't determined that yet."

"Well, here's a novel idea," I said. "We'll leave it up to the police and the sheriff's deputies and the state attorney's office."

"The same bunch of people who tossed her out of her office," Mo said. "Out of her job."

"Suspended her."

"Same thing."

I stopped. As so often happens when Maureen and I argue, either one of us could take either side. At this point. I'd been thinking many of the same things as Mo, but I didn't want her to get involved in this. So I said, "Topping will probably re-instate her."

"If she's still alive," Mo said. "We have to find out who killed Clinton Drake and wants to kill Ginny" Mo sai.

"It's not our business."

"It's my business," Mo said. "She's my friend."

Not that close a friend, Mo had said, but now she had the determined look of a woman who'd made up her mind.

"You don't have to get involved.," she said.

But I knew I did. I couldn't let Mo run down this road alone. "I'll help," I said.

"First thing tomorrow—," she began.

"You stay here for as long as they tell you to." I bent over and kissed her lightly on the mouth. "Now get some rest. I'll get things started."

"Wait for me," she said, but I was almost out the door.

"When God made testosterone, She was sure having a bad day," Mo yelled. But I'd heard that one before.

#

Outside the hospital I realized how quixotically I was acting and resolved to slow down. The wind had come up, and I shivered under the light orderly's shirt. I needed clothes and I needed a car. Both my Miata and Mo's Camry were in Boca, sitting in front of Ginny's house. I could take an expensive cab ride to Boca and spend the night in Lauderdale, but that didn't feel right. I wanted to stay as close to Mo as possible.

Briefly my mind went to the Breakers, the five star resort on the ocean, but I told myself not to waste money. The beds there don't sleep any better than any other hotel, and sleep was all I wanted. And clothes. I remembered seeing a Macy's sign at City Place when we drove into town and a Hilton somewhere near the interstate. Could I walk to the Hilton from City Place? I could try.

The cab took forever getting to St. Mary's but it was a relatively short ride to Macy's. I bought a sport shirt, some underwear, a couple pair of socks, and a light sweater. "Nice outfit," the woman at the cash register said of my orderly's shirt. I left it in the dressing room. The tension of the day had set into my body now, weakening flesh and resolve, so I called for another cab to take me to the Hilton. I hadn't taken two cab rides on the same day in years. I thought of our two cars outside Ginny's. Mo and I had given each other keys to them for just occasions such as this. Would she be so trusting now that I'd so cavalierly given Ginny keys to my car? At least it's safe, sitting in front of Ginny's. I don't know what I'd do if— That was a silly thought. I'd get it repaired if it was fixable. Otherwise no big deal. I've resolved not to get attached to it or any material object.

In the room at the Hilton the bed beckoned, but I wanted to see Mo one more time before I slept. She'd be eating now; so I'd wait and go to the hospital after she finished. I phoned Enterprise Rent-A-Car and asked them to send a car to the hotel; they said they would. Then I flipped on television and watched the local news shows. Most had live feeds from somewhere in Palm Beach but broadcast only still photos of the front of the Brophy's house. I could see it, the Palm Beach cops chasing television crews away from Lake Drive, not for a second considering their pleas to block one of the road's two narrow lanes to accommodate their rigs.

An assortment of young men and women, every hair in place, stared from the tube, trying to appear knowledgeable and trustworthy, their intent foiled as soon as they began speaking. They reported what they knew about Drake's murder, which was very little. To make up for what they didn't know, they used words like exotic, strange, extraordinary, way-out, phenomenal, unparalleled, singular, unique, odd, queer, off-the-wall, peculiar, fantastic, grotesque, ridiculous, remarkable, surprising, astonishing, over-the-top, mysterious, inexplicable, unimaginable, incredible, improbable, unnatural, shocking, scandalous, mind-boggling or mind-blowing and my continuing favorite, bizarre, to describe the party at which the murder occurred. Stripped of such puffery, it was soon clear most of them had learned nothing more about Clinton Drake's murder than I knew the night before. In fact, they hadn't even learned that the participants called it The Exchange.

I wasn't being objective, of course. My disdain for what passes as news on television and the pretties who deliver it began years ago when Mo was working as an investigative reporter at an old fashioned newsprint and ink enterprise called a newspaper. Too often to count, soon after her newspaper hit the stands I would hear her words delivered over the air by one of the airheads without a syllable of credit.

Finally one of the television news people, a woman who used less makeup than most, came up with something new. She said Deputy Louis Fourquet of the sheriff's department had announced that he'd soon release a list of all people known to be at The Exchange at the time of the shooting. Fourquet's purpose, the reporter said, was to solicit information from members of the public who might know why any of them would want to kill Clinton Drake III.

Form a line. I thought. If half of what Ginny said about her ex was true, a quite a few people at the Exchange wished him harm or knew someone who did. Creditors, former girlfriends, husbands, subjects of his news stories, sources of his stories. The list went on and on.

Maybe I could make a list of my own sometime. Not now, though. Now that I had transportation and a place to sleep, I needed to get back to Mo.

#

Mo sat on the bed watching television and pretending not to notice me as I came into her room. I kissed her on the back of the neck and when she turned I handed her a bouquet of mixed flowers I'd made from the two bundles I bought at a grocery store, all regular florists being closed for the day.

"I'm getting out of here in the morning," she said,

"The doctor say that, or you?"

"Both," she said, sticking the flowers in a water pitcher.

"Good. I'll drive you back to Lauderdale."

"No. I've got work to do."

"What?"

I've got to find out who killed Clinton Drake and who's been trying to kill Ginny."

"How?"

"Ginny told us ," Mo said. "Talk to Sally first. She knows more about the people at The Exchange than anybody. Then, one by one, talk to every other adult at the party."

"But that would take weeks—"

"Maybe months—ta da, ta da, ta, da. Go, I heard that speech at Fathoms and I wasn't impressed then."

There are times when I really don't like it that Mo's remembers so much. Too much. I wouldn't want her to be a bimbo, but sometimes— Stop, I told myself. That's not the issue. The real problem is she knows and I know that I'll ride shotgun for her for as many weeks or months as it takes. I could lecture her about co-dependency, about doing so much for her friends than they'd ever do for her, about putting her interests second to theirs so often. I could give chapter and verse of examples from her life. But it wouldn't do any good. So I face facts. If she wants to investigate this, I'll be along. Where she goes, I'll go.

"Are you with me?" Mo said.

"Of course."

She looked at the water pitcher. "Oh, by the way. Thanks for the flowers."

I must have smiled in some way that conveyed a message.

"Did you think I wasn't going to thank you?"

"Not for a second."

She looked around the room, then back at me. "You know what I've been thinking about ever since you and Ginny told me everything you remembered about what happened at The Exchange?"

I was almost afraid to ask. "That you missed a good party?"

"Nope."

"That you're glad you weren't there."

She shook her head. "Nope, again."

"What then?"

"You'll never guess."

"I've stopped trying."

"Children."

That stopped me. Maureen was forty-one and never had any children. Once when we'd discussed the subject, she said she never would. —It's too late." I'd looked at her as blankly as possibly, waiting for her to explain, and she did. —Before you and I got together, I'd never been with a man who'd make a good father. Now that I'm with one who would be, it's too late. Much too late." I knew to keep quiet. My experience is that when people start repeating themselves, they are not sure that what they're saying is true. —I have no regrets, — she'd said. — I've had a full life working in some fascinating jobs. You know how it is, a woman dedicated to a profession shouldn't have children. You can't be really good, best of breed, at two things at once. Either you're an excellent mother or a five-star stock market pro. You can't be both."

"Do you really believe that?" I'd said.

Mo never answered, not then or since, and until this moment she'd never brought the subject up again. So now I said, "What about children?"

"When first you and then Ginny told me about what happened at The Exchange, neither of you said much about the children. It was all about the adults. Who was hitting on whom. Who was acting in mysterious ways. Who didn't seem to have reasons to be there."

I realized then that I'd misinterpreted what she was talking about. "Not true," I said. "I told you about the boy carrying a clown with its head on backward."

"That was about the clown—not the boy," Mo said. "You barely noticed the children themselves. You of all people."

She was right. I was so absorbed in watching the adults I didn't pay attention to any of the kids except Ginny's son. Me of all people. A children's therapist. Someone trained to pay attention to kids.

"It was as if the children were invisible," she said.

"So, what's your point? Why were you thinking about children?"

"Nothing," She looked away. "I was just thinking."

Nothing, huh. Nothing. I knew Mo well enough to know I'd hit an emotional iceberg. But this wasn't the time or place to plumb this one. Or so I told myself.

#

On the way back to the hotel, I drove past a bar and restaurant named E. R. Bradley's Saloon and recognized it as the successor to the old Speakeasy Mo's bond buddy told us about. Old Jimmy Buffet tunes, lyrics about latitudes, longitudes, women going crazy on Caroline Street, floated through the royal palms along Flagler Drive. "The food's not bad," Mo's friend had told us, "but watch the drinks. Ask for a martini on the rocks and they fill an ice tea glass with ice cubes, then pour straight gin or vodka up to the brim Two of those could numb an elephant."

I used to hang out in places like that. I'd feel so emotionally drained at the end of the day, dealing with other people's problems and unable to offer any quick or easy solution to any of them, numbing out seemed to be a good idea. At first it was one drink, then two, then—as they say—the stuff turned and bit me. That was how I ended up in the rehab in Lauderdale. When I was ready to get out and find a job, I phoned Mo for help. But that's another story.

Now I thought: I could have a burger and a Coke at Bradley's Saloon and ignore the booze. Just listen to the music and chill out. Yeah, no harm in that. The idea sounded so good I'd started to turn the steering wheel to pull into the parking lot, when I had second thoughts. I'm hungry, feeling alone, tired, and a bit melancholy at the prospect of dropping everything but essentials and embarking on a wild search for Clinton Drake's murderer. A terrible time for me to be around alcohol.

So I swerved back to Flagler, found a 7-Eleven on Southern Boulevard, and rushed inside to the freezer. There it was, the old dependable. A whole shelf of Ben & Jerry's, the cartons lined up like soldiers, ready to do battle against gloom and weariness, a pint for less than the price of a martini, and exactly in the middle of a middle shelf (trumpets sounded in my mind) Chunky Monkey! I bought a pint and, standing in the parking lot, downed the whole thing with a plastic spoon. Not healthy, some people say. Oh yeah? They think burgers are made of yogurt and granola?

Chapter Ten

I slept fitfully that night and woke early. Mo had warned me that even when a patient is ready to check out, the hospital wouldn't allow visitors before eight in the morning, so I had time to kill. I picked up Mo's car at the county parking garage, found an old diner on South Dixie Highway named Howley's, and settled in. Diners usually serve a decent meal at an honest price, but I like them for a different reason. They don't care how long you sit at a table or booth, even when you sit by yourself at a table big enough for four, which was what I did that morning.

The *Miami Herald,* the *Palm Beach Post* and Fort Lauderdale's *South Florida Sun-Sentinel* all had news racks outside so I bought one of each, spread them out of the table, and went to work. The murder at the Exchange was the lead story in each, a banner in the Post, smaller above-the-fold headlines in the others. How could it have been otherwise? Take a murder. Put it in a posh house on the Lake in Palm Beach. Add some people with political and financial connections. Make the story break too late for the papers to do much with it Sunday night. Let it lay there for newsrooms to sink their teeth into on a traditionally slow Monday. Sure, they'd play the story big.

I'd learned quite a bit about how newspapers operate from Mo, who taught me, for example, that if you ever want to loot City Hall, you do it late on a Friday afternoon. At the most the papers devote a little brief to you and your crime Saturday morning and by Monday morning everybody would have forgotten about it. But do something on a Monday morning when reporters and editors were rested from the weekend, and you'd get banner treatment.

But I digress. Two of the papers featured color photographs of the Brophy's house on their front pages, but the *Herald* used a picture of Frizzy Blond in a skimpy bikini sitting on the bow of what it identified as Raymond Siegel's racing boat. The photograph had little to do with the story but gave The Exchange an appropriately salacious hue. In addition, each of the papers carried mug shots of anywhere from three to seven of the people who attended The Exchange—whoever they had available in their files. These were scattered among lengthy stories and one or two sidebars each paper devoted to the party and Clinton Drake's murder. *The Herald's* stories were the best written, the *Post's* the most detailed and the *Sun-Sentinel's* the most matter of fact and dull.

Reading them all, I had a pretty good idea of how the police viewed the murder. Nobody had an alibi. There was so much movement between the dock area and the house that anybody could have gone from lakeside to the pool, found Drake alone and shot him. Nobody had much of a motive either. Ginny was a suspect because it was her gun and her ex-husband, but no one had a reasonable theory of why she wanted Clinton dead. In fact, Clinton's death was going to cost her money. Her child support payments would stop, and the *Post* had learned Clinton wasn't covered by life insurance. Whether this was relevant or not it didn't say, but some reporter had discovered the factoid somewhere and by God if the *Post* knew something it was going to use it.

Many others at The Exchange weren't fond of Clinton, the *Herald* said, and some might have wished him dead. But none seemed to have any concrete reason to do the deed. As a result, everyone at the party at the time of Clinton's death was a suspect.

I pushed the breakfast dishes aside, put my little pocket notebook on the table and listed the suspects, summarizing facts from the papers first, then adding my recollections. By the time the fireworks started, there were only thirteen adults at the Brophy's house:

HELENA KATZ, 41, a.k.a. Helena Katz Schneider, Wellington real estate agent. Active member of the county Democratic Executive Committee. Formerly married to Alan Schneider. Sometimes still used his last name. Not married at the time of the party. Silver Bracelets, I'd tagged her, although she wore as many necklaces as bracelets with her black jump suit. Also memorable as the woman who raised hell with her ex about a bounced check.

ALAN SCHNEIDER, 37, a builder, mostly of single-family residences, both freestanding and attached townhouses. Drove a top-of-the-line Porsche but rumored to be in financial trouble. Credit exhausted at every bank in the county, the *Post* said, and looking for new money in Miami. Muscle Shirt, the guy with the three gold chains around his neck. Writer of the bounced check. Bantered with women about sex and AIDS.

PAUL BROPHY, 45, host for The Exchange and managing partner of a large accounting and business consulting firm. Possessed a rare combination of computer know-how and social skills. Rotary Club member, active in Palm Beach County Chamber of Commerce. Sally was his second wife. Pale, big smile, little pot belly, Big Diamond Ring. Why had I thought drug money when I first saw him?

SALLY TRAIN BROPHY, 35, Paul's wife and owner of a chain of high-fashion clothing stores called Salli's. Used maiden name, Sally Train, in business. Considered smart, personable, talented. Paul was her first husband. The Weather Balloon, the drunken woman who called me an asshole and later found Clinton Drake's body. I'd read about the clothing stores. Why hadn't I recognized her at the party? Never mind. On with the list.

CINDY CATHCART, 27, employed as a "special assistant" to Paul Brophy. Married briefly twice but neither husband identified. The *Herald* called her The Exchange's "Cosmo girl," apparently not realizing that times have changed so much that Cosmo Girl was the name of a magazine aimed at teens. Drove a MINI Cooper convertible. At the party with Raymond Siegel. Frizzy Blond, the looker who said dancing for an hour's as good as fifteen minutes foreplay.

RAYMOND SIEGEL, 48, banker. Identified as a bank president, but in fact the Palm Beach County manager of a Florida bank controlled by a big out-of-state bank. Proud owner of a fast and powerful racing boat, a Cigarette named Courtesan. Sometimes took bank customers on quick trips to Bimini and other nearby islands. Member opera, ballet and symphony orchestra boards. Never married. Relationship with Cindy not explained. Gay Banker, I remembered, elegantly dressed, his brown mustache speckled with gray. Why was Cindy with him?

DUANE SAUNDERS, 38, variously described as a contractor, real estate developer, and rancher. Thought to pilot a private plane based at Palm Beach International Airport, but much about him unclear. The man I remembered as the Santa with a Rolex. The man who so professionally checked Clinton Drake's body for signs of life and who pulled him onto the pool steps. The man sitting in the car outside Fathoms on Singer Island. Why?

STEPHANIE ROYCE GANTZ, formerly Stephanie Royce, 34, president of the Greater Palm Beach Day Care Association and owner of a day school in Green Acres City. Formerly married to Wilbur Gantz. Two children. May have dated Clinton Drake, one newspaper said. The Model. Dark red blush on her checks, a model's slim figure and arrogant walk, the one I pegged as wearing a Perpetual Pout.

WILBUR GANTZ, 42, another accountant, but not in Paul Brophy's league. His was a one-man operation. Handled some small jobs referred to him by Brophy. No marriage since divorce from Stephanie. Shy Wilbur. Cindy's foil about dancing as foreplay. Limp handshake. Face crossed with the small red lines of a heavy drinker.

MARILYN BARR, 36, manager of the Palm Beach office of a national stock brokerage firm. Frequent speaker to women's professional organizations. Marital status not stated. Close friend of Sally Brophy's. The Candy Cane in the pink and white playsuit. No children. Seemed to come on to me. Reasons unknown. Maybe did the same with all men. Made my hormones giggle. I re-read the last sentences, pulled the page out and tore it into little pieces. Then I rewrote the summary, leaving out the part about her hitting on me and my hormonal reaction. Maureen was going to see this.

CLINTON DRAKE III, 37, the victim. A freelance writer or unemployed newspaper reporter, depending on the account. Worked for the *Herald* and the *Post* before the *Enquirer*. The papers used the words playboy and wealthy although the *Sun-Sentinel* pointedly said a computer search revealed he owned no real estate and leased his BMW 540i. The victim. Probably the only man in South Florida wearing a bow tie that night.

GEMINI STONRIDGE DRAKE, 35, known to her friends as Ginny and to her detractors as Stony because of her cool demeanor in court and out. She hadn't gone through the formality of changing her last name on county pay records. Georgetown law, moved to Palm Beach County to be with unspecified relatives. Interned at the state attorney's office, became an assistant immediately after passing Florida bar exam. Married to Clinton less than a year before the divorce. Gemini. The obvious suspect, but the sheriff's office was discouraging speculation that she did it. Why?

I was the thirteenth adult at the party when the murder occurred, but I exonerated myself, asked for more coffee and re-read the news accounts. Theoretically, the murderer could have been someone other those attending The Exchange, but investigators thought this possibility very unlikely. It didn't seem credible that a stranger walked into the house, discovered Ginny's .22 in her purse, found Clinton by the pool, and then shot him.

There was more to be learned and much to speculate about. The *Post*, for example, called Sally Brophy "an energetic party-giver and reveler." Did that mean she was widely known as a drunk? The papers carried the most about Raymond Siegel, the banker, and the least about Duane Saunders. Was that because they knew the most about Siegel and the least about the Santa with a Rolex? Neither the *Post* nor the *Herald* played up the fact that Clinton Drake was a former employee of theirs, but both emphasized the *Enquirer* connection. The *South Florida Sun-Sentinel* lumped the other two newspapers with the *Enquirer*—somebody, editor or writer, having a bit of fun with the competition.

All three papers included news of Ginny's suspension, but none made a big deal of it. I detected some skepticism on their part about whether any action Topping took could be viewed as anything but political. Ginny might be a suspect, but as far the news accounts were concerned, any ex-spouse could have done it. What else could come of such a gathering? The question was implied, not stated, but on this point the papers were only slightly more restrained than the television reports. To their credit, though, they used fewer adjectives.

I knew the situation wasn't as simple as the stories implied. Most of the ex-spouses, those with the youngest children, had left The Exchange before the fireworks and the murder, so when it occurred the only formerly married couples still present were the Stephanie Royce and Wilbur Gantz, Helena Katz and Alan Schneider, and—of course—Ginny and Clinton. The others hadn't been married to someone else at the party, nor did they have children. This unusual circumstance was certainly enough to make the cops suspicious (Wasn't the return of children the purpose of The Exchange?) but the papers didn't raise the question.

If Maureen and I were going to solve this mystery, we'd have to learn a lot more about this group, which is exactly what Mo had in mind. She didn't know what she's getting into. We could be involved in this for years. Darn that woman. It sure would be nice to be in love with someone less protective of her friends. Or would it?

#

I took more flowers to Mo, these from a real florist, but I needn't have bothered. She was up, dressed and ready to go, sitting in a chair beside a stack of newspapers.

"Let me show you something," she said and handed me three sheets of paper. On them, in Mo's neat handwriting, was a list of a dozen names, the people the papers identified as being at The Exchange, and notations next to each. "Putting together what the morning papers reported with what you told me, these are the people we're dealing with," she said.

I looked through her comments and saw they were eerily similar to mine. I handed her my pocket notebook, glad I'd deleted the reference to Marilyn Barr's coming onto me. "Look at mine."

"Not now," she said with a wicked little smile. "I've seen it."

"My list," I said, glad to know her libido hadn't been injured in the crash. "My list."

Mo took her time with it, reading slowly, occasionally looking back at the notes she made. When she finished she said, "You didn't tell me Marilyn Barr looked like a candy cane."

"An afterthought," I said.

"I wish I'd been at that party."

"Me, too," I said, really wishing I'd done a better job bowdlerizing my notes.

"You can wheel me out of here soon," Mo said.

"Where do you want to go?"

"To Sally Brophy's," she said.

"Tomorrow or the next day." I said. "You need to rest."

"Today. This morning."

"You don't even know where she'll be."

"At her company's headquarters,." Mo said. "I've already phoned and made an appointment."

Chapter Eleven

We found Salli's Inc. on the second floor of a three-story building on Palm Beach Lakes Boulevard, just west of the Interstate. One of its retail stores occupied the first floor, and the corporate offices were on the second. When we got off the elevator a very young and chicly dressed receptionist waved us straight through to Sally's office and to a surprise.

Sally was a completely different woman, a transformation so great that if we hadn't been in her office, I wouldn't have recognized her as the drunken hostess of Sunday night's Exchange. She wore a dark blue business suit and a peach blouse, but more than the clothing was different. As she rose to greet us, she was smiling and radiant, gracious and charming with an aura of understated authority, a little heavy set but not really overweight. Why had I seen her as a weather balloon?

She shook hands with Mo, but spoke to me. "I believe I owe you an apology."

"Not necessary."

"The next morning Paul told me how I'd acted and what I called you," she said. "You may be an asshole, but I don't even know you."

"He can be, believe me," Mo said, and the two women laughed. "All men are at times."

I smiled politely, but underneath I was thinking: Why can't women find a new song? They must know this they're-are-all-assholes stuff isn't any more true about men than women and indeed wasn't even accurate back in the days of Betty Friedan and Gloria Steinem. But I noticed the sexism had a beneficial effect. Maureen and Sally had never met each other a minute ago. Now they were buddies. Or to use a cliché from the nineties, they'd bonded.

Sally motioned us to sit in the Queen Anne chairs in front of her desk, then took her seat behind it. The room was clearly Sally's stage, every detail selected to enhance her appearance. The desk and other furniture were made of light woods, ash and teak accented by small bits of walnut inlay. The upholstery, walls and drapes blended together in shades of pink and green with touches of white and brown. Framed paintings of sunny beach scenes, quiet harbors, and racing sailboats hung from every wall. The scent of cologne lilted through the air.

"That—drinking a little too much—happens every now and then," Sally said. "When I'm in that mode, it seems to sneak up on me."

"Us too," Mo said, and while—except for one slip—this had not been true of me for many years, I didn't challenge her. This was Mo's show, and I'd resolved to be an observer.

Sally tilted her head to one side. "Maybe that's the reason I went into business on my own. This way I only have to answer to myself."

Mo's head slanted to mirror Sally's. "Whatever the reason, going into business for yourself was a very successful idea."

Anyone who read the local business pages could attest to that. Salli's Inc. began with one small store in North Palm Beach, then expanded until it spread to every prosperous community in Palm Beach and Broward counties. It sold only sportswear at first, but soon added more formal clothing. A framed map of Palm Beach County near Sally's desk told the story. Magenta stars marked the location of each Salli's location, two in Boca Raton and one each in Manalapan, Palm Beach, Delray Beach, Boynton Beach, West Palm Beach, North Palm Beach and Jupiter, none in the western parts of the county, the area populated mostly by frugal retirees. It was a war map, I realized, business and the military organizations becoming more alike every year that passes.

"Anyway, I do apologize," Sally said. Then the smile vanished and her tone became serious. "I was horrified to read what happened to Ginny. How is she?"

"They aren't saying much about her," Mo said.

"I'll send flowers." Sally wrote on a notepad.

"You can do more." Mo leaned forward. "She was going to ask you for help."

Sally looked back and forth between us, a blank expression on her face.

"Before—before the accident," Mo said. "Ginny told us she wanted to find out who killed her ex-husband."

"Why on earth—" Sally said.

"To clear her name of suspicion," Mo said.

Sally nodded but looked dubious.

Mo said, "Can you think of any reason someone at The Exchange would want to see Clinton dead?"

Sally smiled broadly. "Probably half the people at the party wanted harm to come to that little prick. He was a snoop and a pest."

"Can you be more specific?"

"That's the problem," Sally said. "It's obvious many people didn't like him, but the reasons aren't always clear." She looked toward me. "For example, did you see him arguing with Alan?"

I made the association: Muscle Shirt, the builder. "From a distance."

"There's bad blood between them, but no one knows what it's about," Sally said. "Something to do with money, I guess."

Mo kept pressing. "Who else?"

"I know Clinton dated Stephanie after he left Ginny," Sally said. "A few of the other women there, too."

So, Clinton left Ginny. That was news, but I put it aside to picture Clinton and Stephanie together—the statuesque woman with the perpetual pout and the aging preppie with the bow tie. Not a good match. Had they been talking at The Exchange? I couldn't remember. The only clear image I could recall of Clinton alive was of his discussing something with the Santa with a Rolex, then walking away when Paul Brophy approached.

"In fact, Stephanie was one of the women who brought Clinton to The Exchange before Ginny asked him to bring their son there," Sally said. "He played the field."

That was news, too. Up until now, I'd thought Sunday night was the first time at The Exchange for both Ginny and Clinton. Had Ginny been there before, too?

The superior smile on Sally's face telegraphed what was coming next. "I guess several women would have liked to see Clinton castrated," she said and laughed. "But dead? I don't know."

Mo laughed, too. I didn't. Why do women find the subject so funny?

"And Helena." Sally turned to me. "You remember Helena? The one who had the little fight with Alan about a bounced check?"

I nodded.

"She's never had anything good to say about Clinton."

"Was she there with the man with the white beard?" I asked.

"That's right," Sally said. "I wonder about him."

Something about the way she said that, or maybe her frown, made it clear she wanted to say more about Duane Saunders, the man I still thought of as the Santa-with-a-Rolex. Mo must have seen it, too. Neither of us spoke.

"All of a sudden, maybe six weeks ago, Duane started showing up every Sunday night with Helena," Sally said. "He laughs a lot and doesn't say much, but there have been times I've seen him eavesdropping on conversations."

"Listening to anyone in particular?" Mo asked.

"No.'

"What's he do for a living?"

"Good question," Sally said. "Nobody seems to know." She turned slightly, looked up at the map with the magenta stars, a general surveying her troops, then turned quickly back to Mo. "Does Ginny know anything about him?"

"I've never heard her mention him," Mo said, staring back.

Sally looked at me. "Me neither," I said.

The phone on Sally's desk buzzed. She picked up the receiver and twirled her chair away from us. "Tomorrow again? Isn't that cutting it close?"

We couldn't hear the response.

"Okay," Sally said into the phone. "Take care."

She turned back to us and replaced the receiver. "Good help is hard to find."

Something's wrong with that conversation, I thought. What kind of help does the boss acquiesce to, then tell to take care, then denigrate? But Mo went to another subject.

"Why was Clinton invited to The Exchange if nobody liked him?"

"It's a convention of the evening," Sally said. "We don't make value judgments about the exes. We just want them to return the children."

"And the dates they bring?" Mo said.

"Same thing," Sally said. "That's why nobody objects to Helena bringing Duane Saunders."

Mo said, "Your children. What do they think about The Exchange?"

I knew damn well I'd told Mo the Brophys were childless. What was she up to?

Sally reached for the pink pencil cup on the right side of her desk and moved it toward the middle. "Paul and I don't have children."

"Oh," Mo said, the look on her face almost one of genuine surprise. "I guess I thought— Strange that a childless couple would host a party to return children of divorcees."

"The sheriff—what's his name—Fourquet—he thought so, too," Sally said. "I told him over and over that I can't remember who asked us to hold the first one. But somebody did, somebody who lived in an apartment or something and didn't have room. That's honestly all I can remember."

Bingo, Mo, Bingo. When somebody tells you something *honestly*, nine times out of ten they're lying through their teeth.

Sally pushed the pencil holder back to its place. Her voice rose. "I don't see what's so difficult to understand. We have a big house, and we know a lot of people. Some of them are divorced and some of them asked us if they could use our house. So I said, 'Sure. I love parties.' "

"Do you think Ginny killed Clinton?" Mo said, and I wanted to applaud. Ask the tough questions when they're on the defensive.

Sally took her time with it. When she finally opened her mouth, the answer came out softly. "No."

"The police say one of us did it." I said. "You agree?"

"What they say makes sense." Sally said, pacing each word. "But I don't see any of us as a murderer."

We waited.

Sally swirled her chair toward to the map and the magenta stars that meant so much to her. "These people are my friends. I don't want to get anybody in trouble."

I barely breathed, and I knew Mo was just as still. This was it. I don't want to get anybody in trouble. That's what they all say, just before they rat on their friends. That's the way it is in business and government, the way it must be in violent crime, too.

Sally turned and faced Mo. "But if I were looking for someone to substitute for your friend Ginny as a suspect, I'd look at Helena. Or her friend, Duane Saunders."

Mo didn't move a muscle, didn't acknowledge a word.

"Helena's not what she seems." Sally's raised voice. "And she's up to something with that fellow Duane."

Silver Bracelets, the real estate agent, and the mysterious Santa with a Rolex. An odd couple, but so are they all.

Before we could ask any questions, the phone on Sally's desk buzzed, and she quickly reached to pick it up. I'd have bet big bucks she pushed a button or something under her desk, signaling the reception-ist to phone her. "That's all I know," she said. "Can you find your way out?"

"Sure." Mo stood. I followed her lead, waving at Sally as we left. We both know we'd gotten all she was going to give us.

#

Outside the building, I slid behind the wheel of the rental car and asked Mo how she was holding up.

"Good as new," she said, but I could see she needed rest.

"We'll go straight home from here, and you get in bed."

"Bed. That's all you men think about."

"To rest."

"A likely story," she said, but she was smiling broadly and it sur-prised me when she changed the subject. "Fancy digs, huh?"

"What? Sally's office?"

"And the reception area, and all of the building we could see."

"I suppose."

"When I was plying my trade as a stock analyst, we had a rule of thumb, about new companies" she said. "The more elaborate the furnishings of its offices, the lousier its balance sheet."

"You still think about stuff like that?"

"The memory got me wondering just how much money someone could make from a chain of dress shops," Mo looked at me. "It's a notoriously fickle and cyclical business, and every season's clothes are bought on credit. Sally probably does her own buying. A few bad seasons and she could often skid pretty close to bankruptcy."

"What's that got to do with why we went there? I thought you were trying to solve a murder that took place at The Exchange."

"Just this," she said. "It makes me wonder whether the owner of a little chain of dress stores could afford a home on Lake Worth. Or whether her husband with the drug-lord ring, supposedly an accountant. And then I'm back to wondering why a childless couple hosted The Exchange. Sally was certainly defensive about it,"

"And what do you think about Sally offering us Duane Saunders and the woman with the silver bracelets as murder suspects?"

"Could mean she thinks it's anyone but them," Mo said.

"Agreed. They don't seem like two people who'd enjoy spending time with each other."

"Opposites attract," she said.

"Then they attack," I said.

"Really?"

"Check it out."

She thought about it for a couple of beats. "And us?"

"And us what?"

"Are we alike?"

"Not last time I looked."

"I mean— You know what I mean. You're a shrink."

"I'm not a shrink," I said. "I'm a counselor, a counselor of children."

"What do counselors say?"

"More or less they'd tell you that common interests and common values are more important than anything else in predicting whether a relationship will work." I'd assumed the tone of a college lecturer, I realized, and switched tone and message. "That, and not being able to keep your hands off each other for thirty years."

"But we didn't do anything for thirty years," she said, playing her role.

I leaned over to kiss her, thinking of a demure little kiss of the sort you'd give your gal on an interstate ramp with three cars waiting behind you. But that wasn't what Mo had in mind. She pulled me to her with one hand, squeezed the inside of my thigh with the other, kissed me quick and hard on the mouth, then pushed me away. "Now, let's get back to work. Turn right at the Okeechobee exit. We'll let Helena speak for herself."

Chapter Twelve

Wellington was only twenty miles west of Palm Beach, but it seemed like eighty. Traffic was terrible, and the roads worse. So when Maureen told me she'd already made an appointment to meet Helena at the restaurant in Wellington's Polo Club, I shuddered.

The pretense of the place. Wellington wasn't any different than the rest of South Florida—a barely drained swamp—but it tried so hard to be different. A polo field, for Christ's sake. An indulgence of one of the original developers, a rich old man who amused himself riding about the field while talent imported from South America made the plays. Prince Charles played on the field, and Zsa Zsa Gabor came every season for years. I don't know if you have to pay a promotional fee to a prince, but I'm sure Zsa Zsa didn't come cheap. Even with the draw of these celebrities and others, the polo field lost money. Few people in South Florida know a chucker from a charley horse, so the games were mostly Sunday afternoon social events. There was even a tailgate crowd.

All this was on my mind as Mo and I rode west on Okeechobee following the second half of Ginny's planned actions. Talk to Sally first. She knows more about the people at The Exchange than anybody. Then, one by one, talk to every other adult at the party.

Helena Katz Schneider, the real estate agent with all the silver jewelry, had told Mo she'd meet us for lunch at a clubhouse near the field. I didn't like the idea, but Mo said we can't be picky about where we interview suspects. Suspects! Ha! This was a job for Fourquet and his gang of investigators, not us. But I had to play along with it, hoping Mo would tire of the adventure soon.

"Isn't this just the most marvelous place?" Helena said as we sat down at a table.

I started to shake my head, but Mo, always more tactful than I, said. "It's certainly different."

Helena wore a burgundy suit and a dark green blouse. Her hair was dyed a tangerine red, her long nails painted bright red. Gold earrings shaped like seashells and a gold watch were Helena's only jewelry that day, but even without all of the silver bracelets she looked gaudy. She'd probably given much thought to her image, thinking the outfit made her look both professional and feminine. Missed the cut on both counts. My opinion, anyway.

"It's just so beautiful?" Helena looked at me. "Where else could you find a place like this?"

"Not many places," I said.

"Absolutely gorgeous," Helena said.

Her gushing stopped only when a waiter brought menus. Helena suggested the lobster salad, which Mo decided to try, but I stuck with chicken. Then, finally, we got to business.

"I called the hospital from the car," Mo began. "They said Ginny is still in critical condition."

"How terrible for Ginny!" Helena said, her eyes still on the vacant polo field.

"We're trying to help her," Mo said.

"I'm sure you are."

Briefly, Mo explained that her friendship with Ginny went back to their college days and that she feared Ginny was being set up as Clinton's murderer. "You can help her by giving us information that might lead to the real killer."

"Of course." Helena looked at me. "But I don't know anything—"

"We know nothing," I said. "So you're way ahead of us."

Helena studied us, looking from Mo to me and back.

"Anything you can tell us about the individuals at the party might help," Mo said. "For example, what's Alan like?"

"There's nothing to tell about him."

"You were married to him.'" Mo said.

"A horrible experience." Helena sighed. "The worst experience of my life."

I tried to imagine their life together. If the newspapers were right about their ages, Helena was six years older than Alan, he muscular and athletic, she a professional martyr. How do people who are so different get together? Opposites attract, then they attack, I heard my mind saying. Always? I wondered.

Mo asked, "Did Alan have anything against Clinton?"

"How would I know?"

"You and Alan keep in touch."

"I need to or he wouldn't make the monthly payments."

"Child support?"

"We call it that." Helena sighed again. "It's not nearly enough."

"I gather some of the checks bounce."

"It's humiliating. This last time. It was the most humiliating experience of my life."

Mo glanced toward me, so I tried a question. "Why were Alan and Clinton arguing Sunday night?"

``How should I know?" Helena drummed her fingers on the table.

I looked around the room, then out at the polo field. Maureen did the same. Helena opened her purse, pulled out a pack of Virginia Slims and lit one. "All right, I'll tell you something," she said.

I turned toward her, trying not to show any expression.

"Alan owed Clinton money." She blew smoke across the table. "Of course, Alan owes almost everybody in the county."

"How did a loser like him get money to loan?" I asked.

"He inherited it."

"How much?"

"I don't know exactly. Alan told me hundred and fifty one day, two hundred thousand the next."

"Why did Clinton loan it to him?"

"They were to become partners."

"Partners? Why would Alan—?"

"You don't see it, do you?" Helena's words came out quickly now. "Alan drives a Porsche and wears a lot of gold, but he isn't worth a dime."

She looked from me to Mo and back again. Mo nodded and after a second's pause I did the same.

"He calls himself a builder, but he's really nothing more than a glorified foreman," Helena said, her voice growing louder. "He borrows development money to buy land, and he borrows construction money to build on it. When the houses sell, he repays the loans and borrows money again."

"Isn't that's the way they all work?" Mo said.

"But Alan's never been able to hold on to any of it," Helena said. "He spends more than he makes, and when a recession comes along he has to sell properties at a loss."

"Bad timing," Mo said.

"In more ways than one," Helena said.

Across the table I saw Maureen suppress a smile, but I kept following the money. "I'm surprised banks keep backing him."

"Allen gets people to co-sign notes."

"Who?"

"Raymond Siegel. Maybe Wilbur."

Improbable. A banker wouldn't co-sign a note at another bank, and CPAs are notorious skinflints. Maybe Alan did go to them and they refused, forcing him to go to someone like Clinton Drake for money. But I was out of my field. I'd ask Mo's opinion later.

"You don't like any of them, do you?" Almost before the words were out of my mouth, I saw Mo frown.

Helena pulled her shoulders back and stuffed out the cigarette. "You said you wanted my help."

"We do," Mo said, but the damage was done.

Helena looked around the room, then out the window. "Don't you think this place is absolutely gorgeous?"

"There was one man at The Exchange who's a mystery to us," Mo said. "A bearded man by the name of Duane Saunders."

"You two ought to buy out here," Helena said.

Mo tried again. "Can you tell us anything about him? About Saunders."

"It's a wonderful place to live and an even better investment," Helena said. "I know a marvelous townhouse I could show you."

"You were with Duane Saunders Sunday night," I said. "You must know something about him."

Helena drew a deep breath, then looked at me more directly than at any time since we sat down. "Absolutely nothing. Absolutely nothing."

I looked to Mo for help, but her head was down, her lips tight.

Helena looked at her watch "Oh, the time. I'm late for an appointment. You two enjoy the rest of your lunch, and let me know when I can show you that townhouse."

We watched her walk away, looking around the restaurant for someone she might know. Mo shook her head back and forth, and I knew we were in for a chilly lunch. Alan wasn't the only one with bad timing

Chapter Thirteen

When we were kids and next-door neighbors and I had polio, Mo she would come over every day after school and fill me in on events of the day. She'd climb the stairs and burst into my room, and yell, "Hi Go, guess what happened today?" Then she'd tell me the highlights of her day at school. Sometimes she'd tell me what a teacher said or did, but more often her reports were about what some outrageous things another boy or girl was up to. I especially relished her accounts of the stories kids brought from home, spilling secrets their parents thought nobody would ever learn. I guess those were the roots of my interest in family counseling.

But she reported other school activities, too. One day, for example, she reported a group of older students had performed a play titled Cyrano de Bergerac. She described each scene, the sword fighting, the romance, the pathos. She said she thought I'd like it. I probably would, I said. Could she get me a copy of the play to read? Already have, she said, and pulled a library book from her backpack. I read the play over and over again, memorizing the passages I liked most. Even today, three decades later, it remains my favorite play.

I have some bitter memories about those days, too. One day when I was strong enough to get out in a wheelchair, Mo took me to a swimming pool. Her idea was that swimming would be good for me. We were casing the place and didn't plan to participate. Some other kids about my age, maybe a little younger, were playing a game called Marco Polo. One kid, who was "it," would have to tag the others, who swam under water. When one emerged, he or she would yell out, "Marco," and dive under the water again. Another would pop out of the water and yell "Polo." The idea was to confuse the "it." Stuck in a chair that day, I wanted in the worst way to join in but couldn't. A few months later, I was swimming, but I never did play the game. The kids had moved on to other things. Variations of Hide and Seek, Fruit Basket Turnover, and Red Rover, Red Rover.

I don't know why the Marco Polo story sticks with me and seems important to this day. Probably something to do with lost opportunities. Mo knows this and sometimes refers to dear old Marco Polo completely out of context. I think she's trying to relegate the story to insignificance by repetition.

Mo taught me an even bigger lesson in those days, too, and this is probably why these stories come to mind now. More than once back then I'd say or do something that offended her or made her angry for some other reason. Then she'd get very quiet, not saying a word for ten, fifteen, even twenty minutes.

"Why don't you say what's bothering you?" I'd ask.

"Because I want to make sure it's really you I'm angry at and not at some part of me," she'd say. That from a girl not yet ten years old!

And now, decades later in this restaurant overlooking a polo field, I knew Mo was into that same process while she waited until we finished eating before speaking. She had cleared herself, and it was my turn.

"You know better than that, I know you do," she said.

"What?"

"Accusing somebody of something when you're trying to get information from them."

"It works sometimes," I said.

"As a last resort," Mo said. "That's what you've told me."

"She irritated me."

Mo motioned for a refill of her iced tea, giving me time to think about what I said. When the waitress left, she said, "Is she the first person in the world who ever irritated you?"

"Of course not."

"Are most of the people who irritate you women?"

"No."

"But you have higher standards for women than you do men."

I started to deny it, but couldn't. Mo was telling me something, maybe giving me a lesson.

"You glorify women," she said. "You think they're all perfect and when one isn't, you get pissed off."

Bingo! What she said was so brilliantly true I couldn't deny it. In fact, like so many other buried truths about myself I'd realized this many times before, but the reality had slipped from my consciousness. "Your fault," I said. "I think all women should be like you."

"More to it than that," Mo said. "Ever since you were a kid you've thought women were made of sugar and spice and everything nice. We aren't. None of us."

"They sure don't taste like it." I said. There, maybe that would stop this amateur psychoanalysis.

Mo didn't even smile. She stood and patted my head. "Get the check," she said. "It's your turn to pay the bill."

#

The drive back to downtown West Palm in mid-day traffic took almost an hour. Mo used my cell phone to call the hospital, and I heard her ask how Ginny was doing. She listened, then, "I'm a close friend. At least you can tell me her condition."

Again Mo listened. Then she said, "No, I don't understand it, but thank you." She pushed a button on the phone and turned toward me. "The state attorney told them not to give out any information."

"You told Helena that Ginny's condition was critical," I said. "You said you made a phone call while we were driving to Wellington. You didn't."

"A surmise," Mo said. "I thought that's what they would have told me if I'd called them."

"Based on what I told you?"

"Yes."

"A lie, then," I said

"I wouldn't call it that."

"You'd call it a white lie."

"Go, you get so hung up on labels," Maureen said. "I needed to convince Helena to help us."

"Did she?"

Mo smiled. "I've been thinking about that. Your opinion?"

"She gave us her ex as a suspect," I said. "She said Alan owed Clinton money."

"And that's worth?'

"Darn little."

"But a little."

"I suppose," I said. Interstate 95 was just ahead. "Now what do we do?"

"We stop by Ginny's and pick up our cars. Then I drive mine to Lauderdale. I've got a staff meeting this afternoon that I can't skip."

"And I can get back to work." I said. "Maybe I can reschedule some appointments.

"No. You drive back to West Palm."

"Why?"

"You have an appointment to talk with the Candy Cane."

"I do?"

"I made it this morning."

"When? When am I supposed to see her?"

"Four thirty. Right after the markets close."

"Why?"

"You should be able to get more out of her alone than if we were both there," Mo said. "A chemistry thing, you know."

I waited, because I knew Mo wasn't finished with me. A mile passed. Two. Three. Finally she said, "I wish I looked like a candy cane."

"You're better. A box of chocolates."

"God, no."

"A bottle of champagne?"

"Too hippy," she said.

"The Eiffel Tower?"

"You're making it worse."

"Sugar and spice and everything nice."

"I told you about that."

We passed through Boynton Beach.

"Isn't this just beautiful?" she said, mimicking Helena's voice.

"Simply marvelous," I said, knowing that only the passage of time would allow me some measure of redemption. Whoever said fate was cruel didn't know the half of it. Fate is nothing compared to the power of an angry woman.

Chapter Fourteen

The brokerage office of Marilyn Brooks, a.k.a. Candy Cane, was on a top floor of a stark angular structure, all black except for a few horizontal red lines, one the developer called Northbridge but which the public had more aptly nicknamed the Darth Vader building. When Maureen first saw it she said that if its owners were smart, they'd make the change official. Don't fight the Fed, don't fight the tape, don't fight the crowd, she said. Mo was always saying stuff like that, and I didn't know enough about markets to argue. Didn't want to, actually.

I told the first person I saw that I wanted to see Marilyn, hoping she wouldn't ask me for a last name. She pointed toward the back. I walked down the hall, passing through a brokerage office that I knew from Mo's descriptions was like almost every other retail shop in the country—young reps sitting at desks in a bullpen in the center, older men and women in glass paneled offices surrounding them, occasionally the glare of a television set tuned to a financial station coming from a corner, every one of them talking into phones, selling, smoozing, pushing, advising—anything to get a commission.

Marilyn's office was the best in the suite, the corner of course, her desk strategically placed so visitors could see yachts parade by in the window behind her, the Town of Palm Beach glistening in the distance.

She stood to shake hands, but didn't bother with hellos and such. Instead, she ran the back of her hand over her forehead, as if wiping sweat from her brow. "I sure hope it's true about the first million being the hardest, because the first one was a bitch."

She delivered the line with the mock sigh, and I figured she used it often. "Brag, brag, brag," I said.

She laughed. "Okay. On the way to the first million."

Like Sally, this woman was completely different in her office than at The Exchange, more confident, very businesslike. She even seemed taller. Wearing a gray skirt and dark green blouse, small gold earrings and a pearl necklace today, her blond hair tied in a bun behind her head, its waves controlled and hidden now. Steady practiced eye contact, the Candy Cane replaced by a take-charge professional woman.

Marilyn motioned me to a chair and sat behind her desk. "About Sunday," she said. "All men are assholes. That's not negotiable." A sexy little smile. "But everything else is."

Jesus! Does she flirt with all men like this? Her costume's different, but the come-on just as strong as at The Exchange.

"Everything always is," I said.

The office revealed little about her. No personal photographs. None of men, women, or children. No degrees on the wall. No vacation photos or mementos, the only items on the credenza behind her desk three computer monitors. One displayed twenty or so stock symbols and prices. Every few seconds, when a stock traded, the line blinked and the numbers changed.

"Hypnotic, isn't it?" she said. "Let me show you what this one can do." She stood, walked to the monitor farthest from her desk and pushed buttons on the keyboard. A green bar graph popped up on the screen, then a red line traced a smoother path across the bars.

I tried to look interested, but Mo had given me this lecture before.

"Those are moving averages. And this is a cumulative volume line. When the cumulative volume line drops below...."

Her skirt stretched across her hips as she bent over the keyboard. Her breasts moved under the blouse. Wearing more clothing than on Sunday, but somehow much sexier now.

"But you know all this, don't you, Mr. Overman?" Marilyn said, looking straight at me.

"You know my name."

"And I've heard of your friend, Maureen."

"How? Why?" My surprise was genuine.

"You were the only new man at the Exchange that night who didn't hit on me. I decided to find out more about you, and that lead to Maureen. I'd heard about her, of course. Used to be the most famous stock analyst on Wall Street."

I wondered how she found out about Maureen so fast, but just nodded. She'd taken charge of the conversation, so give her all the rope she wants.

"I don't have any respect for most analysts. They sit in offices and regurgitate what management tells them." She was on a roll, her voice growing louder and faster. "And even then, they cover their asses so much you can't tell what they really think. In what other business does 'hold' mean 'sell?' "

I didn't say anything.

"But I hear your Maureen did it right. Went out and interviewed people. Talked to employees and customers—especially the disgruntled ones, people who'd tell her what was going wrong."

I wondered why she was going into all this.

"So I'm not surprised that she's got a boyfriend who's doing the same thing."

Oh. "Not usually. I usually stay in an office. But Maureen and I are trying to help her friend Ginny and we're talking to people who can help us understand The Exchange."

"For what purpose?"

I hesitated, then let it out. "To find out who killed Clinton Drake."

Like that, bare-assed without context, it sounded silly.

"So?"

I decided to go at her straight-on. "Why does a woman without children go to a cocktail party whose sole purpose is to return children to former exes?"

Marilyn stared at me dead faced. "I heard you two were asking around."

From who? I wanted to ask but knew better. Keep to the subject. Marilyn finished her stare, swung her chair around so she faced the window, her back to me. I let her think in silence. When she turned around, she was smiling again.

"I'm going to save us both a lot of time. You could ask a dozen questions and you wouldn't worm out of me what I'm going to tell you." She stood, walked around the desk, pushed a chair closer to me, sat down and looked me in the eyes.

"First, I didn't tell you the truth when I said I wasn't married," she said. "I'm still married to a man I haven't seen for seven years. He lives in another state."

I nodded.

"We find it mutually convenient not to get a divorce."

"Any children?"

"None."

"So what were you doing at The Exchange?"

She arched her neck, her breasts moving forward. "That was the second thing I was going to tell you. I go to The Exchange because I'm like a friend of the family. Particularly Paul's."

I had an inkling.

"He comes by my apartment two or three times a week. We don't always keep our clothes on," she said. "Rarely do, in fact."

I did what I've learned to do, let nothing show on my face, my lips closed, forehead relaxed, not giving the slightest reaction, certainly not the hint of a value judgment, but part of my brain was trying to picture the host of The Exchange and Marilyn together.

She seemed determined to maintain eye contact. "I'm not fooling myself. I know it isn't going to lead to anything. Maybe that's the real reason I stay married."

Maybe, but probably something deeper.

"I don't see him because I think he could help me in business," she said. "I don't need that."

I turned away, then back. I hate staring contests with women.

"What I'm saying is I don't do it for money. I do it for sex." She looked away quickly, then back at me. "I know all women aren't like that, but I am. And I like a man like Paul. The power." She leaned forward. Her knees touched mine.

"Does Sally know?" I asked.

"Probably. But Paul and I've never talked about it."

She looked at the office wall as if it would help her decide if she wanted to say more, shook her head slightly, stood and walked to the seat behind her desk. "My now you've probably guessed that my relationship with Paul is why I stood so close to you during the fireworks."

What?

"I come on to the new man at every Exchange. As a decoy. To throw people off the track. So they won't possibly guess that my real interest is Paul."

I suppose she expected this information to deflate me, but it didn't. Her role at the Exchange or toward me never made sense. I said, "I still have some questions."

"Shoot."

Methodically, I ran through the list. I asking what she knew about each of the people at The Exchange, any information that might explain the murder. The answers are about the same as Mo and I got from Sally and Helena. Some of the people at The Exchange didn't like Clinton, but none hated him enough to kill. She only met Ginny that night, but she didn't look like a person who would kill anybody. "I'm as baffled as everyone else."

"Have you talked to people at The Exchange since the party?"

"Of course."

"Who?"

"Paul, of course. Some of the others."

"Sally?"

"No."

"You say you don't know if Sally knows about you and Paul."

"She'd be very dense not to see it," Marilyn said. "I think that's why she invites me to these parties."

"To show she doesn't care?"

"Something like that. Paul and Sally have a marriage of convenience."

"Does Sally have a boyfriend—" I had a better idea. "Which one at The Exchange is Sally's partner?"

Marilyn considered the question as if thinking about it for the first time. Finally she said, "I don't think she has one."

"Who's a possibility?"

She shook her head. "She spends more time with women than with men."

"You suggesting she's a lesbian?"

"No." Another shake of the head. "I don't think she has anyone—man, woman or machine." She laughed, then quickly cut it off. "Maybe that's why she drinks so much. Maybe that's why she's so fat."

Until this moment, I'd been attracted to this woman behind the desk. Now I cooled. There's something grotesque about the mistress of a married man criticizing his wife.

"I know what you're thinking," she said. "I shouldn't go to The Exchange. But when you're in my situation, Sunday is a lonely day."

I'd heard that before.

A young receptionist, barely out of high school but more stylishly dressed than Marilyn or any of the brokers, entered the office. "Someone waiting for you in the conference room," she said.

Marilyn looked at me. "Are we finished?"

"For now," I said.

Marilyn stood. "Since you've taken up this much of my time, the least you can do is to ask Maureen to give me some stock tips."

"I'll ask," I said.

"I'm sure she'll like that." The Candy Cane started with a little smile, then let out a big laugh. "Yep, I'm sure Maureen would love to give me some really good tips."

I started to walk out the door without saying anything more, but she insisted on escorting me to the elevator. As I stepped in, she said: "Remember what I told you. All men are assholes. But everything else is negotiable."

I waved, trying to pretend I didn't understand what she was talking about.

#

Down in the lobby, I remembered I hadn't asked Marilyn what the banker, Raymond Siegel, was doing at The Exchange. Probably gay and probably childless, he didn't belong there. I took another elevator up to the brokerage offices, waved at the receptionist as I passed, and walked down the hall. Marilyn's office door stood open. I looked in to see if I'd be interrupting.

Alan Schneider, in a short sleeved shirt now but still wearing three gold chains was standing beside Marilyn's desk. He handed her a large manila envelope. She dropped it in a desk drawer. Alan looked up and saw me watching. I waved, turned around and took an elevator down. These two had just shown me more than I could get from asking a zillion more questions of Marilyn.

Mo was right. There's a lot more going on among these charming people than any of them was telling us. Much more happened at The Exchange than appeared on the surface. But, again, what?

Chapter Fifteen

I was barely in the door of our apartment in Lauderdale when Mo asked, "What did the Candy Cane have to say?"

"She said she sleeps with Paul Brophy."

"What?"

"Two or three times a week, Marilyn Brooks and the host of The Exchange take off their clothes and hop in bed."

"How in the world did you worm that out of her?" Mo asked.

"I'm very good with candy canes," I said.

"I've got to hear all about this."

"Aren't we forgetting something?" I said.

She smiled, walked over to me, and we engaged in a long, full-body hug, the type that's almost as good as sex and much easier to pull off in public.

"Hugs are good," I said.

Mo pulled back. "Is that what the Candy Cane said?"

"Don't I get a drink to loosen me up for this interrogation?"

"I'll put some coffee on," she said, walking toward the kitchen. That was when I noticed she was wearing a short sundress, one with vertical blue and white stripes, exactly like the one Candy Cane wore except for the color.

"Like your dress," I said.

"They didn't have pink," she said over her shoulder. I knew to leave the subject alone.

Mo and I still lived in the same one-bedroom apartment on the Isle of Venice that I rented when I moved to Florida.. She could, of course, afford a much fancier, larger place with the money she made on Wall Street, but she said this was sufficient for now. You can only sleep in one bed at a time, sit in one chair at a time, shower in one, make love on one rug, she went on and never got around to explaining all the financial reasons, all the money we were saving. Almost every other building on the street had been torn down to make way for multi-million-dollar condos, but then the housing boom burst and builders stopped threatening to move me out of my little apartment.

At this point I hadn't had a drink of alcohol for a year and a half, since my slip, my one and only in the last seven years. We lived modestly in other ways, too, something that sometimes goes with sobriety. Mo's said my one remaining addiction was spending too much time caring for others, but I told her not to complain since she was a beneficiary. "The kids need my help," I kept telling her.

Mo had a cup of coffee in each hand when she reappeared. I was sitting in the chair shaped like a seashell. "You look silly sitting in that chair," she said.

"It's a challenge," I said.

Mo sat on the sofa, near the poster with a Gandhi quotation, one Mo had given me years ago. "Now start at the top and tell me everything the Candy Cane said."

"You mean the financial wizard?"

"Out with it."

So I did as instructed and gave her an almost verbatim account of what transpired in Marilyn's office, leaving out only the come-ons and the fact that our knees touched, which weren't at all germane to the story but would have been blown all out of proportion in Mo's mind.

When I finished, Mo said: "How big was the envelope? The one Alan handed Marilyn in her office."

"Eight by ten." I made the shape with my hands. "Maybe nine by twelve."

"Big enough to put stock certificates in?"

"Is a stock certificate the size of a diploma?

"Yep."

"It was big enough," I said.

"But nowadays nobody under fifty takes possession of stock certificates."

"Why?"

"It's all in computers, now; certificates are too much trouble. But if someone wants to hide the purchase or sale of certificates..." Mo let it trail off, closed her eyes, and began meditating. Occasionally her lips moved, a few times I heard a sharp intake of breath, but mainly she sat still, her breathing slower and slower. When Mo got like this, she couldn't or wouldn't communicate with me in any way until she was finished. I sat there a while, wondering what was going on in her brain, then got out of my chair and headed to the kitchen for more coffee.

Almost there, I heard her say "Go, what do those people have in common?"

"What people?"

"The people at the Exchange."

"Children," I said.

"But they don't. About half of them don't."

She was right. "What then?"

"Libidos?" I said.

"Yep. But try again."

I thought about the question. They're all divorced. No, not all of them. They're all wealthy. Again, not all, not even the majority.

"You don't see it because it's not your field," Mo said. "It's mine."

Right then in one of those of-course-and-slap-yourself-on-the-fore-head moments, the answer came to me. "They all work with money."

"Exactly," Mo said. "Banker, stock broker, CPAs, real estate agent, builder, clothing store chain owner, even day school operator—they all collect, distribute, borrow, invest or account for money."

"But everybody does," I said.

"Not to the degree this group does."

An image of Cindy's frizzy blond hair came to mind. "Cindy Cathcart doesn't have money," I said, somehow delighted to find a flaw in Mo's theory.

"Look at her as the twenty-first century equivalent of the gang moll," Mo said.

I smiled. I'd never heard Mo use the word moll. "So, they all deal with money, so what?"

"I don't know. But it's a start."

"A drug ring?" I said, not really thinking this was a possibility but wanting to get things started.

"Could be."

"Right in the middle of Palm Beach?" I said, already arguing against my idea.

"What better place? Easy water access. A town where a couple of million bucks more or less won't be noticed. A community where expensive cars and flashy dress are the norm."

"The location's too obvious," I said. "The Coast Guard and DEA would have smelled it out and busted it up years ago. It was probably an episode in the old *Miami Vice.*"

"Maybe not a drug ring," Mo said. "But something to do with money."

"Even if it is, what connection would it have with Clinton Drake's death?"

"It's a start," Mo said. "That's all I said."

"So what do we do next?"

"Keep talking to the people at The Exchange."

"That isn't getting us much," I said.

Again Mo closed her eyes, moistened her lips and went into her trance-like thinking thing again. This time I made it to the coffee pot in the kitchen and filled my cup. When I returned she was she was still at, eyes still closed, her breathing barely detectable. I headed toward a chair that was more substantial than the shell-shaped one.

"We've got to turn up the heat," Mo said.

I turned around. "What?"

"Make them think we know all about it."

"How?"

"From now on, whenever we talk to one of them, we'll say we want to join them."

"That's a lousy idea."

Mo ignored my objection. "You'll tell them, 'We want in. We want a full share.' "

"Of what?"

"I don't know and you don't know," she said. "We want to find out."

"I'll tell them this?"

"Two of us can't be there when we make the demand," she said. "If it's only two of you there—you and the person you're propositioning—they're more likely to respond."

"No witnesses," I liked the idea in the abstract. "Later, it's just one person's word against the other."

"You're a quick learner." Mo stood up.

"So we split up the list, you interview half, I take the others?" I said.

"Can't," she said. "I've got a foundation to run."

"And I've got children to counsel."

Mo stood, walked over and sat in my lap. "You know what we haven't done in a long time?" Mo said.

"Nothing I can think of," I said, lying.

She placed a hand on the back of my neck, ran her tongue along my upper lip, then the lower, gave me soft kiss and pulled away. I put my arms around her, pulled her toward me and kissed the back of her neck, tiny little kisses up and down, punctuated with the warmth of my breath and a touch of my tongue.

"I've give you just five hours to stop that," Mo whispered.

I kissed her ear. I felt myself hardening. I unbuttoned the top of her sundress. She wasn't wearing a bra. I slipped one hand inside, rubbed one finger over a nipple. It responded.

"Right here, right now on the tile floor," Mo said. "Woman on top."

"Better idea." I put my arms under her, stood, and carried her toward the sofa.

"Beds are better," she said.

As usual, she was right.

Chapter Sixteen

We were at the Egg and You, a dinner on Federal Highway. Mo had suggested we take both cars and I was too sleepy to ask why.

"The banker, Raymond Siegel," Mo said, holding a piece of dry toast in her hand. "He's the one to interview next."

I tried to remember exactly what I'd agreed to the night before.

"When you call him—" Mo started.

"I'm calling him?"

"Of course," she said. "You're the one who's going to see him."

"But—" I started.

"You don't have any appointments this morning."

"What do we want to find out from him?"

"The usual. What were you doing at The Exchange? What do you know about the people there? Who do you think killed Clinton Drake? Follow wherever his answers take you."

Times like this I never know whether to argue with Mo or go along. She doesn't ask much of me and usually when she does there's a pretty good reason. But now I was thinking she wasn't being fair. I was doing all the work. I had a right to complain.

Across the table I heard her phoning St. Mary's. When she put down the cell she said, "They still won't allow anyone but law enforcement officials inside Ginny's room. I'll drive up there this evening and while you're at work and see if I can talk my way in."

I'm glad I kept my mouth shut that time.

#

After Mo left I phoned Raymond Siegel's office.

"Just a minute, I'll see," a secretary said after I gave her my name and explained I wanted to talk to her boss. She was back in a surprisingly short time. "Mr. Siegel invites you to lunch at one o'clock."

"Fine. Where?"

"Come by the bank," she said. "The dining room is on the second floor."

"I'll be there," I said, surprised at his choice. Most banks have private dining rooms to entertain clients, but I was surprised Siegel wanted to hear my questions with bank employees and others close by. It was a better choice for him, though, than the Governor's Club or the Executive Club where many bankers and attorneys lunch in West Palm and where we'd be seen by outsiders.

At exactly ten minutes to one, I entered Siegel's bank, a two-story yellow structure with a white-tiled sloped roof that made it look as if it belonged in the middle of Bermuda, which of course was the intent. Rich people like a bit of foreign atmosphere with their money changing.

A guard directed me through an ornate alcove and up a set of marble stairs. At the top of the stairs a tall white door stood half open. It seemed like an invitation so I walked in. Inside there was only one table with two chairs and a matching buffet, an elaborate French period piece. The walls were covered with rich red wallpaper, the woodwork gilded. Our talk would be private; there would be no one else around, no other customers, no employees..

An elderly black waiter in a formal white uniform asked if I wanted a drink. Ginger Ale, I said. This whole set-up looked as if it'd been in a time-warp, the last fifty years forgotten. The Old South. The waiter poured my Ginger Ale into my wine glass, then red wine into Siegel's. The man himself arrived right at one.

"Nice room," I said to get things started.

"It saves time." Siegel touched his tie, maroon with a pattern of little blue diamonds, a good match for the dark blue suit. "And as they say, 'time is money.' "

"Not everybody who says it has money," I said.

"Clichés stick because they're true." He tasted the wine. "A stitch in time— Take care of the pennies and— Everything has its price—"

"I've heard, 'Every man has his price.' "

"Why, yes." Siegel looked at me with new respect. "And often, I've been truly amazed at just how little so many men and women will sell themselves for."

The waiter asked if we wanted beef or fish. Siegel asked some questions about the fish, ordered beef for both of us. "If that's all right with you," he said as an afterthought. I didn't object, interested only in viewing this man in his element, much more relaxed in his double-breasted suit than in sports clothes around the pool Sunday night.

Over the soup, a thick French onion, Siegel talked about his work on the boards of the local opera and ballet companies and of helping raise money to pay operating expenses of the new performing arts center. "Most of what I do is behind the scenes, but that will change, Mr. Overman. Eventually this community is going to have to deal with me."

Maybe. But I knew that so far the people who run Palm Beach hadn't let him be chairman of anything important. He was an outsider who became too successful too quickly for their tastes. Or maybe it was just old-fashioned homophobia. Either way, they'd put him on hold.

After the waiter put plates of beef and vegetables before us and left, I figured it was my turn. "What can you tell me about Clinton Drake?"

"A snoop. But not all that bad. Amusing in his way."

"I've heard he was asking a lot of questions."

"I'm not surprised," Siegel said without expression.

"Questions about you. Questions about Cindy." It seemed pretty obvious why he wanted a bikini on his boat, but I wanted to see how he'd handle the question.

"Not at all surprised," Siegel repeated.

"Tell me about Cindy."

He smiled. "You'll have to do better than that, Mr. Overman. What about Cindy?"

The smug bastard. "Anything about her. How long have you known her? Did she have any reason to want Clinton dead?"

"I've known Cindy for several years," he said, vague amusement in his voice. "I consider her a close friend."

I hadn't explained why I was asking these questions, and Siegel hadn't asked. I knew he wouldn't. When he agreed to see me, I figured he'd listen to my queries even if he wouldn't answer them truthfully. It's the same technique many powerful people use: They put up with interrogations to find out what the other person knows. So I plunged ahead, asking about every adult still at The Exchange when Clinton's body was found. Siegel had something to say about each of them but nothing particularly revealing.

He considered the Brophys close friends. Marilyn's a bright person, full of promise, and who knew how far she could go? In the brokerage business or something more challenging? Stephanie, too, with all those contacts at day care centers. Lots of potential. Alan may have peaked as a builder, but you never knew. Wilbur with his little CPA business, too bad about that little man, but Siegel couldn't or wouldn't say more about him. Helena wasn't his cup of tea, just a subjective opinion, of course, and he didn't know her well, certainly nothing negative and some of her real estate business came through his bank. Duane Saunders, now there was mystery. Siegel didn't know much about him but would like to.

The waiter cleared the plates. Siegel asked if I'd like pecan pie or peaches and whipped cream floating in Irish whiskey for dessert. I picked the pie as the lesser of two evils. A piece of it was halfway to my mouth, when Siegel said, "I'm so sorry to hear about Ginny Stonridge's troubles. If you see her, please give her my regards."

We'd been together almost an hour and this was his first reference to Ginny. He didn't give a damn about her but wanted to be mentioned to her, just in case. Maybe she'll have a court case involving him or his bank someday.

"And by the way," he said. "Cindy told me to tell you she hopes to be a subject of one of your interviews soon. Stephanie and Wilbur, too."

He watched me for reaction, but I didn't give him anything. I was thinking plenty, though. If we needed any more proof that they're all in this together, that's it. Maybe not all, but most of them. But in what?

Siegel tried again. "You like boats?"

"I've never owned one."

"That's smart," he said. "Stick to O-P-B's."

I knew I didn't have to ask.

"Other people's boats." Siegel smiled at his little joke. "I take Courtesan to Bimini every other weekend. Would you like to go along sometime?"

"Maybe." I looked him in the eyes, straight and steady. "But what I really want is a piece of the action."

"What?" For the first time since Siegel walked into the dining room, his face showed genuine expression. Surprise.

"I want a share. A full share."

"Of what?"

"You know damn well. A share of what goes on at The Exchange."

"And what's that?"

"If Maureen didn't have a financial background and I didn't work with children, we couldn't have figured it out."

Siegel wiped his lips with a napkin. "Mr. Overman, I don't know what you're talking about. And you don't either." He stood.

"Consider it." I rose, too. "Adding partners might be the most profitable route The Exchange can take."

"Mr. Overman, this interview is over." With that, Siegel turned and walked from the room, almost running as he reached the French doors.

I stared at his back. That'd been almost too easy. Anyone who didn't have something to hide would have pushed me harder, demanded again and again that I explain myself. But not this banker. At the mention of Maureen's background and mine, he fled from the room. Guilty, guilty, guilty. But, again, of what? I'd been bluffing; I didn't know what I was talking about. But something I said— What words, what tone of voice, triggered his reaction?

Chapter Seventeen

The next morning I phoned Wilbur Gantz, the only male on Siegel's list of people supposedly looking forward to a visit from me, thinking Mo should confront the women. "It'll be a wasted trip, but come on," he said and gave me a Belvedere Road address in West Palm. "Anytime will do."

I'd worked late the night before, making up for appointments I'd missed during the last few days, and slept late. Mo had been sleeping when I got in and left before I woke. As a result I still hadn't had a chance to tell her about Siegel's reaction to my—our—proposal. Driving from West Palm after talking with the banker, I'd started wondering about the legality of what we were doing. Were we breaking the law? Was what we were doing blackmail? I really wanted to talk to Mo before I continued. But every time I phoned her office, she'd been in a meeting. I decided to keep following our plan, thinking, damn I really am hooked on this chase.

Wilbur's office was in the middle of a strip shopping center, a check cashing store on one end and a little bar on the other. A bell rang as I walked in. A worn sofa and cheap desk sat in the front room, no chair behind the desk, much less a receptionist. Wilbur's voice came through an opening in the plywood wall. "C'mon back."

The back office was even less distinguished than the front. The badly scarred oak desk reeked of Salvation Army heritage. Behind it, a personal computer and a Mr. Coffee brewer sat on a table consisting solely of a laminated turquoise top and chromed metal legs. A floor lamp stood between the computer and desk, close enough to cast dim light on both.

Wilbur sat on a chair covered with peeling brown vinyl and motioned me to the equally ragged green one. "Coffee?" he asked. I shook my head. He poured himself a cup. Now I saw Wilbur more clearly than at The Exchange, the brown mustache exactly as it was before, but the tiny red lines on his face were more pronounced. He didn't get those from drinking lemonade.

He said, "I've heard you're investigating Clinton's death."

"Maureen O'Neal and I are trying to help Ginny," I said.

"Why?"

"Maureen's an old friend of Ginny's."

Wilbur sipped from his cup and stared at the wall as if making a decision. "I don't think Ginny killed Clinton," he said finally. "But she's a good target for them."

"Them?"

"What you'd call the Establishment anywhere else. They run this county."

"Who?"

"The unholy alliance between the good ol' boys and the condo commandos," he said. "The condo commandos supply the votes, the others their local knowledge and contacts."

I knew about the commandos, bloc voters lead by retired old guys who knew more about political organization than the younger locals may ever learn. But I said, "So?"

"None of the people at The Exchange is part of the power structure. We're all outsiders one way or the other."

I nodded.

"Seymour Topping the state attorney, is in the Establishment, though." Wilbur sipped from his coffee. "Ginny embarrassed him. Ergo, pin it on Ginny."

I worked the idea around in my mind, trying to make it add up. Not enough there.

Wilbur turned and poured himself another cup. "I told you I wasn't going to be much help."

"Everything helps. What can you tell me about Clinton Drake?"

"He was arrogant."

"Who disliked him enough to kill him?"

"Don't know." Wilbur said, but clearly thinking about something. I didn't rush him.

Finally, Wilbur said, "One thing did happen."

I waited.

"Clinton came to see me a couple of weeks ago." Wilbur spread his hands, indicating the office. "Came here and asked a lot of questions."

"What sort of questions?"

"He asked about Paul and Sally. He asked about Stephanie and Cindy. And he wanted to know about Raymond Siegel."

"What about them?"

"He wanted to know about personalities, relationships," Wilbur went for his coffee again. "A few questions were about money, but mostly he asked who liked who, who didn't, who might be sleeping with who—or is it whom?"

Matches what the others said, I thought. The banker, Siegel, said Clinton was a snoop. Sally Brophy called him a snoop and a pest.

Wilbur turned his back to the wall. "He even wanted to know if I thought Cindy was sleeping with Raymond."

"Is she?"

"Don't know. Wouldn't have told him if I did." He turned quickly. "Clinton's not working for the *Enquirer* now, is he?" He caught himself. "I mean, wasn't."

"I've been told he wasn't working for anyone."

"I didn't think so."

Wilbur looked in his coffee cup, stood and moved toward the Mr. Coffee again. "I told you I didn't know much."

"Mind if I ask you a personal question?"

"Try me."

I waved a hand around the grubby room. "Wouldn't you be better off working for Paul Brophy or one of the large accounting firms?"

Wilbur smiled for the first time since I walked in. "This place is crappy, isn't it?"

I waited.

"After Stephanie left me— After Stephanie and I split up, I started hitting the bottle pretty hard. Mostly at night, but eventually I needed a shot or two in the morning to get started. One thing lead to another and I started missing deadlines for tax filings."

He looked up to see if I understood. I nodded.

It cost my clients money, and eventually most of them left. I hit a bottom. No clients, no money, no respect. Now I'm starting all over again."

"That wasn't my question," I said as gently as possible.

"A national firm like Brophy's wants its new hires to be young, right out of college," Wilbur's expression was one of acceptance. "When you get my age, you should be a partner already."

Like a big law firm, or a small investment business, I realized. Thank God they don't have that structure in the counseling profession.

"But Paul tosses business my way when he can," Wilbur added. "And I do some work for Sally."

"Did Clinton ask you about either of those arrangements?"

Wilbur stared into his coffee up and thought about it. "No. I don't believe he did." Then, emboldened by two cups of coffee and the prospect of a third, he squared himself, looked me in the eyes and demanded, "Mr. Overman, what do you want?"

"I want a share," I said. "A full share."

Wilbur pushed back from his desk, but to his credit his eyes remained fixed on mine. "What are you talking about?"

"You know," I said. "I want a full share, an equal share of what's happening at The Exchange."

Wilbur looked away, toward a wall, as if the Walgreen's calendar hanging there was the most important thing in the world. He turned back. "You talk to Paul Brophy about this?"

Bingo. No denial, no nothing. He just wanted to know if I'd cleared things with Brophy. I'd been guessing that Brophy was the boss of whatever was going on, but now there was no question. "I will," I told Wilbur.

"Then I've got nothing more to say." Wilbur got up and walked around the desk toward the outer office. I knew the interview was over, but I took my time following him. As I passed the crummy reception desk, Wilbur said, "Will you be talking to everybody? Everybody else who was at The Exchange."

"Probably."

"When you see Stephanie, give her my love."

Wilbur's ex. Don't these people ever quit? Let it go, I wanted to tell him, let her go. She wasn't a good match for you then, she wouldn't be good for you now. But I asked, "You and Stephanie have any children?"

"No. I wanted some, but—"

Then I understood. Wilbur went to The Exchange for a chance to see Stephanie. This is the poor guy Cindy wanted to dance with her. Dancing for an hour's as good as fifteen minutes foreplay. Not with this guy, Cindy. Wilbur's not available for either one.

#

Outside Wilbur's office, I phoned Mo again. This time I got through to her, but she said, "I have another meeting in ten minutes."

"You gotta hear this." As quickly as I could, I filled her in on my talks with Raymond Siegel and Wilbur Gantz, and their reaction to my demand for a share.

"Marvelous," Mo said.

"What's so marvelous about it?"

"You've stirred things up. Now we know for sure that something's going on, and we know Paul Brophy is the leader."

"The leader of what?" I asked.

"Something that got Clinton Drake killed."

"Circular thinking if I've ever heard it,"

Mo ignored that. "Now what are you going to do?"

"I drive back to Lauderdale and go to work. You come up here and confront Cindy Cathcart and Stephanie Royce. Then, after I finish my appointments, maybe we we'll go to a late dinner."

"Why?"

"Because Siegel says Cindy and Stephanie are looking forward to a visit from us." I was fudging a bit there.

"Yes, but why me?"

"We need a woman's point of view. I've met them."

Mo took her time answering. "This afternoon I'm up to my ears in a meeting to plan our big fund raising dinner."

"Good, send me an invitation and I'll be your escort."

"I'd like that, but—"

I knew what was coming.

"It's more important that you stay in West Palm and talk to those two women."

"I can't get to both of them."

"Try that Cosmo girl first," she said. "You should like that."

I tried to think of some excuse but couldn't. "Okay. But remember, you were my first choice."

"A girl has to take her chances," Mo said. "But somehow I don't think she's your type."

"Me either. My weakness is very smart, bossy, self-satisfied women."

"I'd love to discuss that problem with you sometime," Mo said. "But now I've got to go. Kisses."

"Kisses," I said without enthusiasm. Didn't Mo get us into this mess? Isn't she supposed to be leading this investigation?

#

Information had a phone number for Cindy's residence so I called it, not expecting her to be home so early but even more not wanting to talk to her while she was working at Paul Brophy's office. To my surprise, she answered. I gave her my name, and I started explaining that I saw her at The Exchange.

"I remember you," she said. "They call you Go."

I told her I had some questions I wanted to ask her.

"Let's do it right then" she said. "My place for drinks this evening. Then, a sport like you might buy me dinner."

She made the idea sound tempting, but for many reasons I didn't think about it twice.

"Would you settle for lunch?" I said, trying to match her tone but failing.

We agreed I'd pick her up at noon and we'd work out the details from there. I liked it that she didn't say noon-ish. People who turn times into adverbs plan to be late.

#

I had an hour to kill, nothing to do and no place to go. Call Stephanie? No, save her for Maureen. Phone Paul Brophy? Absolutely not until we find as much as we can from others. We'll get only one chance with him. "Don't talk, look." The message popped into my consciousness, and it didn't take much figuring to know what it meant. I decided to see what the Blue Heron Bridge looked like when I wasn't involved in an accident on it.

I slipped a Beatle's album into the CD, "Hey Jude" filled the car. (I know, the Fab Four are old-fashioned, out-of-date, and all that, but I happen to like them, partly because I'd been a kid when they were at the height of their popularity and drinking too much later on to really appreciate them.) I drove to Broadway and stopped at a gas station, the Miata with all its superb gas mileage still needing to be filled now and then.

A dusty white Ford Victoria pulled up to the curb on the other side of Broadway. I'd seen it before. Where? Outside Fathoms on Singer Island? One like it, certainly, but I couldn't be sure it was the same one. I tried to see if the Santa-with-a-Rolex was driving, but the car's interior was too dark.

I pulled onto Broadway and turned west on Forty-fifth. The Ford Vic followed, hanging about a block behind, still too dark and too far away to see the driver. I slowed and he slowed. I sped up, so did he. Okay fellow, let's see how good you are. I made a U-turn, drove back to Broadway and pushed the accelerator hard. The Miata jumped ahead. I passed two cars before an oncoming truck forced me into the right hand lane. The Vic followed. I leapt past, almost hitting an on-coming BMW. The driver shot me a finger. The Ford hung tight behind me.

I took a sharp left at Inlet Boulevard, punched ahead of a big truck, turned right onto Old Dixie Highway where it parallels the railroad and then jammed the accelerator to the floor. The speedometer snapped to almost to eighty, the road so rough it felt twice that. A mile down the road, maybe more, I braked, slowed enough to turn right into an alley next to a warehouse, went around building and parked on the opposite side. I could see cars passing by but unless the drivers looked backward, over their shoulders, they couldn't see me. A dozen trucks passed by in the next five minutes, but no cars and particularly no dusty Ford Victoria's.

Seagulls flew over a garbage dump to the west. Above a helicopter flew northward, a traffic chopper, I guessed, first report of the afternoon to radio stations below. Odd. Usually they flew over the interstate or turnpike. This one hovered farther east, over the railroad. Why?

When the Vic finally appeared, it came from the wrong direction, from the south, not the way he would come if he'd followed me. But, by God, the Santa with a Rolex was driving. When he passed, I pulled out of the warehouse lot and turned north to follow. The Beatles disc clicked to "We Can Work It Out." Ha! Not with this guy. Duane Saunders, that's this guy's name. I knew it from the newspaper accounts. Not much known about him. . Now I'm going to find out what he's all about.

The Vic picked up speed. The Santa must have seen me. I pushed down on the accelerator, and the Miata jumped ahead again, the little engine straining. I was almost to the Ford now, no way he could escape. Suddenly a green and white sheriff's car emerged behind me, siren screaming. I eased up a notch to let it pass. It cut back into my lane, separating me from the Ford. Damn! I tried to pass, but the green and white pulled to the left and blocked me. Ahead I saw Duane Saunders pulling away. I tried to pass on the right, but the deputy again moved in front of me. Again and again, he blocked me.

He's doing it deliberately, I finally concluded. With his greater horsepower and bigger bulk he can do it as often as he wants. To-hell-with-it. I pulled to a stop. I'll deal with Duane Saunders later. Now I'm late for lunch with the Cosmo girl.

Chapter Eighteen

The address Cindy gave me wasn't far away, a condominium between Dixie and the Intracoastal near the Florida Power & Light plant. At the entrance gate, an elderly rent-a-cop walked over with a clip board. "Are you going to spend the night?" he asked. What kind of question is that? I shook my head. He wrote my license number on his sheet, got me to sign it, said, "Park over to the right," and walked back to the little gatehouse. The barrier across the road went up.

Upstairs Cindy, her hair the same frizzy blond as at the party, greeted me with a little hug and turned her check for me to kiss. I went through the motions. "The rules are different here," said a little sign on the wall. An old advertising slogan for Miami. In fact, Cindy's apartment looked like a set from the old "Miami Vice." White leather sofa and chairs. Throw pillows of pink, turquoise, purple and black. Abstract wall decorations, their colors matching the pillows.

"Know what the guard asked me?" I said.

"I can guess." She wore tight jeans and a T-shirt but her face was made-up like a like a magazine cover. How long did it take to get her face looking like that—perfect but almost natural? Her mouth formed an impish little smile.

"What do you guess?" I asked, willing to play her little game to get things started.

"He wanted to know if you were going to spend the night," she said.

"He ask that of everybody, or just your visitors?"

"Nasty, nasty." Her smile turned to a frown. "Old people make the rules at these condos. They don't get many visitors, and they don't care how the questions sound."

"But—"

"The condo board claims it has something to do with security in the parking lot—where they'll tell you to park and whether you have to sign in as an overnight guest."

"Still—" I said.

"I think some of those old guys get turned on by the whole thing."

"I don't think I'd like to live here."

"There are ways around the rules. The easiest way is to lie."

Into the spirit of things now, I said, "Isn't that always the case?"

Cindy laughed, then motioned toward sliding glass windows at one end of the living room. "Go sit on the balcony while I fix drinks."

"A Coke or coffee for me," I said. Cindy frowned as she disappeared into the kitchen.

The view from the balcony, twenty-seven stories above the parking garage, was spectacular, Lake Worth and the town of Palm Beach on the left, downtown West Palm straight ahead, the interstate and little houses spread out for miles to the west. From this height, nothing seemed real. The world seemed like one big model, tiny people making their way around toy buildings. That is the way they look to whoever runs the government, I suppose. Little people to be manipulated, ordered about, and enticed. Toy people. But I knew the struggles of the tiniest of those people, the children. They had the same feelings, frustrations, and foibles as the bigger people but neither the strength nor experience to look out for themselves.

Cindy came back with the drinks. She handed me a Coke and held up her glass. "This is a Bay Breeze. It's like a Sea Breeze except you use pineapple juice instead of grapefruit."

And generous amounts of vodka and a little cranberry juice, as I remembered.

"So what did you tell him?" The imp look was back.

"Tell who?"

"The guard. Did you tell him you were going to spend the night?"

No, I told myself. Don't go down that road. "Cindy, Maureen O'Neal and I are trying to help Ginny Stonridge."

"I heard."

"We don't think she killed her husband. Ex-husband."

"I heard," she repeated. "What do you want to know?"

"Start by telling me why you were there. At the Exchange, I mean."

"You want my big dark secret?" She flashed a mischievous grin.

I waited.

"Cindy's not my real name," she said. "My parents named me Barbara Jane, but I changed it to Cindy to go better with Cathcart." She smiled. "Now you know." Trying to sound dramatic. "Now you know my big, dark secret."

"Cindy, cut the crap." It came out sterner and a few decibels louder than I'd intended, but Cindy was acting like a big child, and I wasn't going to be put off.

She pulled back. "Okay. I'll answer your questions, but you've got to ask them."

Fair enough. But I won't keep repeating the same questions. Eventually it'll all come out. I waved my left arm around the apartment. "Is your salary at Paul Brophy's enough for you to afford this setup?"

"I have help."

"From Raymond Siegel?"

"He helps."

"Does he spend a lot of time here?"

"It's not like that."

"How is it?"

"Just look, I've already finished my drink," Cindy stood up. "You sure you won't have one?"

Cindy came back to the balcony, a pitcher in her hand. When she poured, she spilled some of the Bay Breeze. She'd been drinking before I got here, I realized. Quite a bit, as a matter of fact. I'd better get what information I can as quickly as possible.

"I'm not going to tell you everything about Raymond," she said. "But it's not what you think."

"I didn't say what I thought."

"People think I'm a slut." She drained the glass. "Sure, I take money from Raymond. And I answer personal ads. And sometimes I go to bed with the guys who answer. But that doesn't mean—"

I wasn't interested in any of this, but she kept going, talking faster and faster.

"It's so hard." She filled the glass again, and her voice took on a pleading tone. "I mean with all the glitz and everything, I can't meet one man who—"

"Cindy, I don't want—"

"Let me tell you about this last guy," she said, her expression seeking understanding. "He was an airline pilot. Witty, charming, a lot of fun. I'd said in advance I wasn't going to bed with him on the first date, and I didn't."

"Cindy, this isn't—"

"But, of course I did on the second and the third. Then we decided to take a trip to Nassau together. He was going to phone me on a Monday night. But he didn't. I phoned him and left a message on his machine. He didn't call back. I must have left six messages, but I didn't get one damned call from him. Not one."

"Cindy, I'm here to talk about The Exchange."

"The son of a bitch! Does he think I need him to go on a trip?" Tears showed on her cheeks. She stood, walked the balcony railing, and leaned over. "What am I doing wrong? All I want is—"

I'd found the weak link in The Exchange. Would it be unethical; to exploit it? I was at Cindy's apartment to get as much information as possible, but in my profession my mission was to aid and comfort. I got up and moved to her side, considered putting my arms around her but didn't yield to the impulse. I put a hand on her shoulder.

She wiped her checks with her arm. "Oh this is so stupid. All I really want— all I really want is children. A lot of them. Four or five or six. I'd give all the girls two first names, Mary Sue and Bobby Jo and things like that. The boys would wear cowboy hats." She pointed inside to the Miami Vice set. "But all I've got is this."

The tears began again, stronger, with loud sobs. Her makeup smeared as she tried to wipe away the tears with her hand. "Just a minute." She walked back into the apartment. I waited a minute or two then followed. Water ran in the bathroom. Five, maybe ten minutes passed, as I sat in a leather chair trying to figure out what to do. I felt sorry for this woman but told myself I couldn't afford sympathy. My mission was to help Ginny. No. Not really. My mission was to help Mo. What would she want me to do?

When Cindy returned, her make-up restored but her face expressionless, she sat on the sofa, facing me. "This is not the way this day was supposed to go." She forced a smile.

"We were supposed to go to lunch," I said.

"I was supposed to take you to bed, then give you a message."

Is that what Paul Brophy told her to do? I wondered. Or was it Raymond Siegel? But I was more interested in the last part of the instructions someone gave Cindy. "What message?"

"Money." Cindy concentrated, picking the right words. "There's money waiting for you if you just cooperate."

"I've told them I want a share."

"They won't do that," she said. "They don't trust you enough."

"Who told you to tell me all this?"

"I'm not supposed to say."

I pressed on. "Is this from Raymond?"

"I'm not supposed to let you get me into a game of twenty questions," she said. "And I'm not going to."

"What else?"

"Only that Maureen has been on Wall Street and she can figure out how to take the money without leaving a trail."

"What am I supposed to do in return?"

"Nothing. Just stop," she said. "Stop investigating Clinton's death."

"Then what?"

"Then nothing."

Is she telling the truth? I wondered. Something close to it, maybe. Why would she make this up?

"You can tell me if you're interested in the deal," she said. "Or if you don't want to tell me, tell Marilyn Barr. You know Marilyn, don't you?"

I almost nodded my head automatically, but I wasn't going to give this drunken courier anything. She'd get it wrong or she'd get it right; either could be dangerous.

"Oh, Greg, it wasn't supposed to come out like this."

I put a hand on her shoulders, gently because I knew any touch could be misinterpreted. "Cindy, tell me the details. Tell me how The Exchange works."

Now it was her turn to stare. "You don't know?"

"I need the details. Who? How? When?"

Cindy stared again, this time with more intensity, her eyes unblinking. Had I blown it? Had she realized I didn't have a clue about what was going on? Or, and God let this be true, was Cindy so drunk she wouldn't remember any of this? She slid closer to me on the sofa, rested her fingers on the back of my neck, and said, "We can still do it."

"What?"

"Go to bed."

I moved away.

"I'm very good," she said.

Maybe, back in my drinking days before I got together with Mo, I might have said, "Sure, let's do it." But every pore of her smelled of danger. And now, Mo is the only woman I want in my life, all the woman I want for the rest of my life.

I stood. Cindy tried to push herself up but fell. Failing that, she put a hand on the inside of my thigh, started rubbing it higher. I pulled back. "Don't get up," I said. "I'll shut the door as I leave."

She sighed, slouching into the sofa. "Promise me one thing. Promise me you won't tell anybody what happened here tonight. Or didn't happen."

"You mean Raymond and Paul and the rest?"

"Yes."

"If you'll promise the same," I said.

"Deal," she said, holding out a hand.

I pantomimed shaking hands from where I stood, walked to the door and shut it behind me. This Cosmo girl will be passed out before the elevator reaches the ground floor, her makeup smeared again, her instructions forgotten, everything forgotten until she woke up with a hangover and half-formed memories. I didn't believe for a minute that she wouldn't tell Paul or Raymond or whoever was her handler everything that happened—or didn't happen—if she could remember. That was it. If she could remember.

Driving home, I put the CD on, again turned to random play. It started on the Lady Madonna tract. Oh Cindy, Lady Cindy, if they only knew. All you want is children at your feet.

I wondered how much of what went on at Cindy's apartment I should tell Maureen. Would she understand? She will, I told myself, driving the first mile. She won't, I said the next. She will, she won't. My mind switched back and forth as I-95 rolled by. She will, she won't. My God, I'm going seventy-five. I slowed to sixty.

Why did Duane Saunders, the man I still thought of as a Santa-with-a-Rolex, follow me? The question started small, then grew into a tall weed. Saunders had been outside Fathoms just before the truck rammed into the back of Ginny's car. So was a green and white sheriff's car, one just like the car that blocked me when I chased Saunders earlier that day. Ginny was in the hospital now, so they couldn't have thought she was riding with me. They were after me, me alone. Suddenly the thought that the guys in the pickup truck were trying to kill Mo and me didn't seem so farfetched. But why? And who are they?

Chapter Nineteen

After I finished with clients—at work I never call them kids—that evening, I stopped at a 7-Eleven and bought two pints of Ben & Jerry's to share with Mo. And walking up the stairs to our apartment, I vowed to tell Mo everything that went on in Cindy's apartment—but none of my fears.

I gave her a complete account of my three encounters—the conversations with Raymond Siegel, Wilbur Gantz and Cindy Cathcart—leaving out nothing. Mo can do this too—remember what people tell her and repeat it almost verbatim. She says it goes back to her news reporting days. Even without notes, she had almost total recall of an event or interview when she got back to the office and started writing, Mo told me. It was the same when she typed up notes for her stock market reports, everything there, stored near the surface of her mind, for about twelve to eighteen hours. Then, zap, it vanished, and she moved on to other things.

But I think her ability goes back further than that. When we were kids and I was recovering from polio, she'd come over after school and tell me what had happened at school or around the neighborhood. That's where she practiced noticing, remembering and reporting. Me? I've thought about it of course, but I'm not sure. Maybe I caught it from Mo. If she can do it, I can do it, the child in me must have decided.

As I was reporting to her this evening, Mo sat in the shell-shaped chair in loose jeans and a T-shirt, nodding, asking questions, occasionally smiling, every now and then spooning a bit of Chocolate Fudge Brownie into her mouth. I was eating Phish Food. She often predicted I'd get very fat if I didn't give up the habit. Occasionally she swore she would never again join me. When she said that, I'd tell her I liked a girl with a lot of soft spots to grab. Then, more often than not, she threw a pillow at me. Not that night, though. She listened hard, and from past experience I knew she didn't miss any of it.

"So you see," Mo said after I'd finished. "You got much more out of Lady Cindy than we could have together."

"We'll never know," I said.

"Do you think she realized you don't know what The Exchange a front is for?"

"I thought about that driving all the way back." I shrugged. "No way to tell."

Mo nodded.

"So what do we do next?"

Mo acted as if she was thinking about my question, but I knew it was all for show. She probably knew ten or fifteen minutes before. Finally she said, "Be safe. We'll act on the assumption that Cindy will tell her boss you don't know what you're talking about."

"She'll tell Paul Brophy."

"If he's really the leader. From what you've said, it could just as easily be Raymond Siegel."

"I'd put my money on Brophy."

"No bet."

"So we'll interview Brophy tomorrow," I said, wanting to get her committed.

"I can't," Mo said.

"What now?" I heard the irritation in my voice, told myself to put a lid on it.

"Ginny's getting out of the hospital tomorrow," Mo said. "I agreed to drive her home."

"What am I doing?"

"Delivering quick messages to Alan and Stephanie, then having a long face-to-face with Brophy."

She made it sound so easy.

"Meanwhile, I'm going to bed." She yawned in a way that made her T-shirt stretch tightly across her breasts.

"Want company?"

"Bet I'm better than Cindy," she said. "When I've got the right guy."

#

We slept late the next morning, so late that Mo was in her I'm-late-I'm-late-for-a-very-important-whatever mode but taking forever in the bathroom. I used the time to phone Helena Katz Schneider, who just as I figured, was already at her real estate office.

Any idea where I can find Alan this time of day? I asked after the preliminaries.

Well, how should she know where her ex was at any time of day, Helena said, she certainly didn't want to have anything to do with him as long as he kept up the payments, which he hasn't, and if she ever wanted to find the son of a bitch in the morning, which she doesn't and never will, she would go to the gym on Congress Avenue.

The conversation took about ten minutes and Maureen was out of the bathroom in time to hear the end of it. "Stephanie will have left for work this time," she said.

"You're guessing."

"Keenly honed analytical mind," She was smiling liked any fool should have been able to figure this out. "Mothers bring their children to day care centers on the way to work; Stephanie's got to be there when they arrive."

"So I'll drop by her day care center," I suggested.

"Bad idea. Too many kids around demanding attention. Leave a note in her mailbox."

"I don't know where she lives."

"You can find out," Mo said, blew me a kiss and was out of the door.

This sharing the same bathroom was a nuisance, and we could certainly afford to rent or buy a bigger place, but Mo says if two people can learn to share a bathroom they can get along under any conditions. Time will tell.

#

The Gold Coast Health Club was a gymnasium and spa, a mixture of fitness center and Meat Market, and the only such establishment the phone book listed on Congress Avenue. I told the receptionist I was thinking about joining but wanted to look around first.

"One of our counselors must be with you," she said. "They're all tied up right now, but if you'll just have a seat—"

I didn't want to get stuck with a salesman, so I said "I'm really in a hurry" with as much urgency as I could summon.

"I'm not supposed to—" The phone rang. The woman shrugged her shoulders. "I suppose you could start looking around. I'll send a counselor to find you as soon as one is available." She buzzed me through the door.

Four guys and one woman were working out with free weights, but Alan wasn't among them. At the other end of the room a half dozen women and a couple of guys were pumping away on stationery bicycles, treadmills and Nautilus-like exercise machines. Still, no Alan.

"Anybody seen Alan Schneider?"

"He was here a minute ago," said one of the women.

"Try the sauna and steam room," said a guy.

I headed in that direction. Alan, a towel around his waist, came out of the sauna. He started to walk past me, then recognized me, and stopped, not at all happy about my presence. "What are you doing here?"

"You and I need to talk," I said

"I'm not interested in talking. I don't have a fucking thing to tell you."

"Why so belligerent?"

"I saw you peeking into Marilyn's office when I was there."

"So?"

"You're as bad a snoop as Clinton Drake."

"I know what's going on," I said.

"What—"

"I want in," I said. "I want a full share."

Alan frowned. "I don't know what you're talking about."

"Just pass the word along. I want in and I want a full share."

"I don't know what you're talking about," he repeated.

"Yes you do," I said. "Tell them unpleasant things will happen if they don't let me in."

We stared at each other. Alan moved his eyes away first. "I don't know what you're talking about," he said again, sticking to those same words without variation.

"Does that make three strikes?"

He ignored my question. "But if I see anybody who wants to get a weird message like that, I'll pass the word along."

Bingo. As good as a confirmation. "Do that." I turned and walked away.

"A counselor will see you now," said the receptionist as I walked through the waiting room.

"No thanks," I said. "I've learned what I came here for."

#

The phone book listed an S. Royce in Ocean Ridge, the beachfront community off Boynton Beach. I'd never spent much time there except to pass through it on A1A, so I stopped at a gas station and bought a Palm Beach County street map. Just like a dozen other Florida communities, Ocean Ridge should have been a part of a mainland city but wasn't. The developers and early residents didn't want a poorer political body on the other side of the Intracoastal taxing them and telling them what to do.

Stephanie's place turned out to be a large town house on a side street, one that could fetch six to seven hundred thousand, maybe more. I wondered if the day care business was profitable enough for her to afford a place like this, but quickly moved on to the more pressing question of what kind of note I should write. I thought of using the classic kidnapper's trick, cutting out letters from newspaper headlines and pasting them to a blank sheet of paper, but dismissed the idea as too terribly corny. Instead, I tore a page from my pocket notebook and wrote: *I know what's going on. I want a share—or else... Phone me at...* I wrote in my cell phone number, mounted the staircase and put the note in Stephanie's mailbox.

Then I phoned Brophy's firm, and my call was routed through to him without delay, as if they were expecting it. Can I be there at eleven-thirty? Brophy asked. I said sure and clicked off.

I had time for a Ben & Jerry's break, but I resisted the temptation. Never before noon. Instead I parked the car and walked along Flagler Drive, looking across Lake Worth at the Flagler Museum, home of the old man who built the railroad that started all this. He opened the east coast of Florida to development—and developers changing it from wilderness to bumper-to-bumper congestion. I wondered if he'd be proud of his work. Probably so. Those guys were egomaniacs. That thought took me back to Brophy.

#

Brophy's accounting occupied one full floor of Phillips Point, a large, pink structure six or seven blocks south of the Darth Vader building. The Pink Princess, some people called the high-rise when it opened, but the nickname never caught on. Brophy's office, much like Marilyn's but bigger, overlooked the Intracoastal and Palm Beach. When I entered, he stood at the center of a large window, the Flagler Museum behind him, rows of computer monitors on each side. The office was his stage, the view his back drop, the electronic equipment stage props, the old and the new, a Renaissance man who could handle anything—the image he wanted to project, at least.

Except for the doubled-breasted dark blue suit and maroon tie, he looked much the same as at The Exchange, but more polished, his pot hidden better by the double breasted suit now than the sports shirt at the party, his gray hair slicked down more, a bit paler now in the fluorescent lights of the office, the almost bleached face of a man who avoids the sun. But the artificial smile was the same and so was the gold ring with a big diamond, the one that led me to think drug money when I first saw him. Maybe my initial instinct wasn't far off.

Brophy motioned me toward a pair of leather-covered wing chairs at the far end of his office. "How's Ginny?"

"She's going home today."

"If you see her, please tell her I asked about her."

"I'm here to ask you to help her," I said.

He flashed the same self-satisfied smile as before, not an ounce of warmth nor friendliness in it. "I understood you've been taking an interest in our little group."

Did he hear that from Sally, Marilyn, Cindy, Raymond, Alan, or all of them? Anybody but Helena, who I didn't ask a share from, or Stephanie, who hadn't had time to receive my note.

"The state attorney and maybe the police think Ginny killed Clinton Drake," I said.

"That's preposterous, of course," Brophy said.

"Who do you think did it?"

"I'm told the police are considering my random killer theory."

"What theory?"

"A coke head," Brophy said. "A drug addict who didn't know me or anyone else at the party wanders by looking for money or something to pawn to get his next hit. The front door was unlocked so guests could arrive or leave at will. The bum walked in, finds the gun in Ginny's purse."

"In your house? In Palm Beach?" My hands moved up and out automatically, signaling disbelief.

"Any neighborhood. Any town. Any place." Brophy talked faster. "They want crack or coke. They need money. It doesn't matter what they have to do to get it."

"Ginny's gun wasn't in sight," I said.

"Think about it," Brophy argued. "The guy found the purses on the table. He went through them, looking for money. The gun was in Ginny's purse. He took it and the money. He sees there's a party going on. He decided to look around, see whether there's cocaine or something like it nearby."

Brophy paused and looked at me, trying to figure if I bought the story. I didn't show him anything.

"He searched the living room. Nothing there, so he goes to the swimming pool. Clinton Drake comes up from the lake and surprises him. The guy had the gun in his hand. He's frightened. He pulled the trigger." Brophy was pitching hard now, his pace faster and faster. "The poor bastard was probably scared shitless when he saw the bullet hit

Clinton and Clinton's body fall into the pool. He drops the gun and runs from the house."

I took my time responding. Let him think I'm really considering this absurd story. When I was ready, I said, "The cops haven't said there was any money missing from the purses."

"Maybe they'll remember," Brophy said.

Maybe the cops can be persuaded to remember, he was saying.

"Too many coincidences," I said. "Your random killer had to go into the room when there was nobody there. Then open the purse that had a gun in it. Then find Clinton Drake by himself."

"Police tell me most crimes involve coincidences." Brophy's voice was one of reason now, talking to me as he would a rebellious client. "A guy goes into a 7-Eleven with a gun. They give him all the money in the cash register. A pregnant woman comes in. He throws her to the floor and rushes out—into the arms of her brother, an off-duty cop. The cop fires two shots. One hits the robber, the other hits the cop's sister. Both die."

"I read that story in the papers last month. It happened somewhere out west." I got up and walked to the window.

The bridges opened only every thirty minutes, so half a dozen or more yachts were caught at every span until it rises. The money, I thought. The immense wealth accumulating in this tiny part of the world. People make big money in program trading on Wall Street or Chicago real estate or Kansas wheat or Texas oil—whatever. Then they shell out at least a couple million, often more, for these playtoys. And we're talking about a crack head killing someone for pocket change.

I turned back to Brophy. "You really think that's what happened? Someone off the street killed Clinton?"

Brophy stood. "I think that's what the police will conclude."

"And you think someone, a real person off the street, will be charged with Drake's death." I wanted to see how far Brophy would go.

He put his fingers over his mouth, as if weighing the idea. In less than a minute, he said, "Yes. They could find someone to charge."

I waited.

"There could even be a trial," Brophy said, then caught himself. "Of course the charges would be thrown out. Insufficient evidence. Probably thrown out before a trial."

Brophy stood next to me, looking out the window, his unspoken question in the air. But he couldn't wait for an answer. "Either way, it gets all this out of the way. You agree?"

Now or never. "I want two things. I want Ginny cleared and I want a full share."

"A full share?" Calmly, matter-of-factly. "A full share of what?"

"Of what's going on at The Exchange."

"And that is?"

"You know."

"No, I don't. Spell it out for me."

I took a chance. "Smuggling. Drugs. People. Maybe something else."

Brophy laughed, a big belly rumble that rolled through his body and spread throughout the room. When he stopped, he faced me, a "Gotcha" smile on his face. "I've never used street drugs, don't allow them in my house, wouldn't know where to get them. And smuggling people? In the middle of Palm Beach? That's absurd."

I'd made a major mistake and tried to recover. "That's what I expected you to say."

"And it's the truth," he said.

"About as truthful as pinning Clinton's murder on some innocent street bum."

Brophy's face turned serious. "I didn't say I knew that my theory to be the truth. I said it could have happened that way. I said the police might just arrive at the same conclusion."

"With your help, and that of others at The Exchange," I said. "Raymond Siegel, for example." A cloud, somewhere between a scowl and a frown, crossed Brophy's face at the mention of Siegel's name. "And we, the world, would never know what really happened—who really killed Clinton."

"That's the way life is sometimes,"

I turned back to the window, again watching the parade outside, the sun glistening on white fiberglass and varnished teak trim, the boats so pure compared to the dirty deal being proposed in this office. Half the owners of those boats have done things just as foul, I guessed. No, I don't know that. It's what I and everybody else assume without giving owners of the boats a fair trial.

"Raymond says you're a bright fellow," Brophy said to my back. "So does Wilbur. And the ladies like you."

So my hunch was right. Brophy is the leader of whatever's going on.

He kept pushing. "This thing is hurting us all. We're in the papers every day."

"I don't see how you can avoid that."

"It'll stop soon." He paused for effect. "If you let it."

I kept my back to him.

"You're stirring things up," he said. "The more you talk to people, the more they wonder what's going on. They're beginning to ask each other questions."

Mutiny in the gang. Good.

A buzzer sounded on Brophy's desk. He picked up the phone. "Five minutes," he said into the mouthpiece.

"Time for me to leave," I said.

"Not before I mention one more thing," he said. "I have no idea what you mean by a share, but when this is over we—I—may have need of a consultant. Or some of my clients might."

"Consulting about what?"

"You're a therapist. You know about people." He looked away, then back. "Maybe we'd ask you to give us a psychological report on people—what their motives are, what it would take persuade them to do certain things."

Like a CIA psychiatrist did on Daniel Ellsberg for the Nixon administration, I thought. Did it twice as a matter of fact. It's ethical, but slimy. At least that's the way it seems to me. Psychologists and other therapists work for people other than patients all the time. But not me. I got into the field to help people, not do something that can potentially hurt them.

I said, "I don't do that sort of thing."

"I'm talking about six figures," Brophy said. "Maybe more after that."

What a cute little package. They'll find a homeless guy, a wino or someone hooked on drugs, pin the murder on him, and if I don't dispute their version of how Clinton Drake got killed, I get a big- bribe. I wasn't tempted. Wouldn't have been even when I was drinking, I hope.

"No thanks," I started walking to the door. Brophy followed me. I extended a hand and we shook. Why is it that no matter how much men may hate each other, they always shake hands in an office like this?

"Think about what I said," Brophy said.

"I'll give your proposition the consideration it merits,"

Every smidgen of Brophy's charm vanished in an instant, the muscles of his face tightened, and his voice became harsh. "You'd better,"

Precisely the wrong thing for him to say. I have never responded well to threats. When people threaten it is a sign they have run out of reasonable things to say. They are admitting defeat. I walked through the door feeling good. Ginny hadn't killed anyone. Brophy knew who did. It was just a matter of time before Mo and I put it all together.

"You'd better," he repeated to my back. "Or you'll end up like Clinton Drake."

Or you will, I thought to myself, because by this time I've finally learned to keep some things to myself.

\#

I phoned Maureen from my car and, to my surprise, her cell clicked on at the second ring.

"I just drove Ginny home," Mo said.

"Why did they let her go so early? A coma is serious business."

"It wasn't a coma. A Grade Four concussion, the doctor said. It knocked her out for a while, but she's been conscious most of the time since."

"Not when I saw her." I said.

"She was sleeping some and faked it other times. When you were in her room, she heard every word you said."

Good, I thought. She got my message. "How's she feeling?"

"So, so. The doctor said she'll have mood swings for a few days as the concussion heals."

"Mood swings?"

"Some days she'll feel despondent and fatigued. Other days she'll have bursts of energy and feel like taking on the world."

Like any woman, I thought, but I knew better than to say it. Two times now. Twice I'd been silent when I really wanted to say something. Hooray for me.

"Where are you?"

"On the Interstate passing through Deerfield Beach."

"I'll follow you. We can have lunch together "

"Can't," Mo said. "Gotta noon appointment."

"Can I make an appointment with you?"

"Yep," she said. "Six o'clock tonight at our place."

"Want to hear how the session with Brophy went?"

"Give me the headline version."

I filled her in.

"Well, we're certainly onto something," Mo said when I finished. "Six figures to stay silent while they convict an innocent man for murder."

"That's it." I was relieved she hadn't jumped on my mistake—allowing Brophy to goad me into guessing what the Exchange was all about.

"We'll talk more tonight," she said.

"Promises, promises," I said.

I figured that sooner or later we'd have to get around to talking about the mistake I made, why I made it, and how to avoid it again. But we never did. One of the wonderful things about Mo is she never piles on, doesn't criticize me for errors I know I made. That evening played out exactly like the one before. Sometimes I felt I was the luckiest guy in the world. Other times I knew I was.

Chapter Twenty

The next morning I was sitting at a window seat in Howley's diner in West Palm eating a late breakfast, a BLT and Coke (an occasional indulgence), when I saw a dusty white Ford Victoria drive past on Olive heading north. It passed too quickly for me to see the driver, but I had more than a hunch. Too late to chase him now.

I went back to the newspapers, searching the follow-up stories about Clinton's murder for something I didn't know. The *Palm Beach Post* had the longest follow-up but even its story didn't provide anything new. My assignment that day, Mo and I had agreed, was to go to West Palm and see where my instincts took me, something that works some-time. And doesn't more times. I looked up from the papers and saw the Ford Vic pass by on the other side of the road, heading south this time, the Santa with a Rolex at the wheel in clear sight. I put the papers aside.

Again, the Vic and Duane Saunders passed. I tossed a twenty on the table next to the half-eaten sandwich, rushed to my car, drove it to the parking lot exit, and waited, hidden from northbound traffic. Saunders and the Ford Vic came by yet again. I pulled into traffic two cars behind him.

At Southern Boulevard, he turned left and I figured we were headed for the Interstate. I passed the car in front of me, wanting to be close enough to Saunders to see which ramp he took. He had other plans. When we got to I-95, he kept going straight over the overpass and continued west. Less than a mile down the road, he made a sharp right, then a quick left onto a small, unmarked road paralleling Southern. Saunders increased his speed, and I—directly behind him now—did the same. Palm Beach International Airport flashed by on our right.

A white van, a Dodge, appeared in my rear view mirror, closing fast. Private plane hangars rushed by. Overhead a big jet roared upward, toward Palm Beach and Mara Lago, giving Donald Trump something more to complain about. A small plane taxied to a gasoline pump. The Ford in front slowed down, the van sped up, sandwiching me between them almost bumper to bumper. We rode that way for, say, forty-five seconds, maybe more, until the road ended at a chain link fence.

The Ford stopped abruptly in front of a big sign:
NO TRESPASSING
FEDERAL PROPERTY
U.S. DEPARTMENT OF JUSTICE
DRUG ENFORCEMENT ADMINISTRATION

\#

Duane Saunders, his beard looking silver in the sun, emerged from the Ford and walked toward me. I got out to face him.

"Surprise," he said.

"You knew I was behind you miles back," I said.

"I've been trolling for you."

"Why?"

"Come have a cup of coffee and I'll explain."

We walked into an unpainted concrete-block building, the inside walls just as barren as outside. A half dozen gray metal desks were scattered about the room, only one occupied. A metal table stood in one corner surrounded by metal chairs with green vinyl seats and backs. Tan filing cabinets beginning to rust huddled along one wall.

"I'm DEA," Saunders said. He pointed to the driver of the van, now standing ten feet behind me. "Dan here is IRS. So is Billie over there." A woman, short black hair, tanned and muscular, looked up from a computer screen. She waved without smiling. The man, short and wiry, didn't move.

"Why have you been following me?" I tried to make it sound like a demand, but the events of the last few minutes had left me thoroughly confused.

"All in good time," Saunders said. "What do you want in your coffee?"

"Nothing."

Saunders poured coffee into Styrofoam cups and we sat at the table. The IRS agent from the van sat at a desk next to the woman. I thought of demanding identification but decided to see how Saunders played out his game first.

"We checked you out," Saunders said. "You seem okay."

"That's exciting."

"More than that, you seem like a man who can be trusted."

"But I don't trust you. You were in the parking lot at Fathoms before a truck ran us down. You tried to follow me last night."

He smiled. "You did some good driving."

"Why were you chasing me?"

"All part of checking you out."

"Am I supposed to be relieved?"

"Relax and listen," he said "If you have questions when I finish, I'll answer them. Deal?"

"I'll listen."

Saunders started from the beginning, speaking slowly and method-ically, providing just enough detail to give his story credibility. Two years ago, he said, a DEA task force bumped into The Exchange. They thought it might be a front for a drug smuggling operation but watched Brophy's house long enough to determine that nothing unusual was going on—no late-night boat arrivals, no cars shuttling back and forth, none of the usual stuff. Not satisfied with that, they followed Raymond Siegel's Courtesan to Bimini and monitored his activities there. Again, they found nothing to indicate any drug related activity. Washington told them to suspend the operation and move on.

"But I knew in my gut something was happening in that house," Saunders said. "So I persuaded a friend at the IRS to loan me two people to help with some unofficial, unbudgeted surveillance for a year. The year's about up."

I looked around the room. "This doesn't look like a government operation."

"This building was confiscated after a drug bust. We took it over, borrowed some furniture about to be declared surplus, and went into business. All three of us."

I remembered Mo's question, what do these people have in common? And her answer, they all work with money, and an idea hit me. "They're laundering money—exchanging it."

"Maybe," Saunders said.

"And Clinton Drake was about to expose them," I said. "They killed him."

"Maybe."

And maybe not. I still didn't trust Saunders. "Why did you lead me here?"

"We want your help," Saunders said.

"Doing what?"

"Continue doing what you've been doing."

"I'm trying to help Ginny."

"Because your friend Maureen O'Neal is her friend."

"That's right." I wondered how much else he knew about us.

"And in trying to help Ginny, you've been asking questions of people who were at The Exchange when Clinton was killed."

I nodded.

"In the process, you've learned a lot about personal relationships within the group—information we need if we're going to turn one or more of them into informants."

"You were there at The Exchange," I said. "You can discover those things for yourself."

"Unfortunately no," he said. "They don't trust me,"

"How did you get invited there in the first place?"

"Helena brought me."

"What's your relationship with Helena?"

Maybe thirty or forty seconds passed before Saunders said, "I can't answer that."

"Clinton Drake was asking about personal relationships. You see where it got him." I remembered Brophy's threat when I was in his office but suppressed an impulse to tell Saunders about it. "What were you doing in Fathoms' parking lot?"

"Ginny Stonridge's ex-husband had just been killed," Saunders said. "We followed her to see where she'd go to after she left the state attorney's office. You and your friend happened to be along."

"And then you had somebody almost knock us off the Rivera Beach bridge," I said, my tone harsh.

"I—we—had nothing to do with that," he said. "Believe me, we want to know who did it just as much as you do."

I sat there trying to process what I'd heard. Saunders was thinking, too, or giving a pretty good imitation of it. Finally he said, "Will you help us?"

"No," I said. "This is not my fight."

"It involves a friend of your friend. Who's to say who'll be murdered next?"

Me, if Brophy has his way. Or Mo, who's been behind my every action. "Show me some proof," I said. "Something to prove you're not just blowing smoke about The Exchange."

Saunders looked at his partners from the IRS. A signal passed between them.

"Okay," Saunders said. "I'll show you how a little piece of the operation works."

#

I sat next to Saunders in the white van, a Dodge with tinted side windows. The IRS guy drove behind us in the Ford Vic, and the woman agent lead the way in a Pontiac Grand Prix. "When I was with the DEA, we used four or five vehicles to tail someone," Saunders said. "But we'll make do with these." We followed the Grand Prix into a neighborhood called Lake Clark Shores, passing groups of children walking home from school. "One of the few suburbs in the county with more children than retirees," he said.

The Grand Prix turned into a side street and stopped near a sign that said: "*Go Preciously Slow: Very Young Children Cross Here*." Tall weeds covered the name of a child care center at the bottom. The center itself was an asbestos-shingled house with a low chain link fence around the yard, a collection of plastic play sets and cartoon characters within it. No children in sight, but a silver Mercedes, an E series costing at least sixty thousand bucks new, sat in the driveway.

"The kids are inside this time of day," Saunders said. "We're waiting for Stephanie Royce to come outside."

As if on cue, Stephanie came out of the front door and got into the Mercedes. The pout was gone, but the rest was about the same, a model's slim figure and arrogant walk, short brunette hair, red blush on her cheeks and heavy eye makeup, wearing a brown suit with a yellow blouse and moderately high heels this day.

"Used to be married to Wilbur Gantz," Saunders said. "Ran the kindergarten association."

"They don't call them kindergartens anymore," I said.

Saunders scowled, as if to say he knew that and he wasn't going to change what he called things to match prevailing moods.

When Stephanie's Mercedes got a half block away, Saunders eased the van into the road and followed. After a mile or so, the Ford Vic passed us and assumed the surveillance. We dropped back. Another half mile and the Grand Prix took the lead, giving Stephanie little chance of discovering she was being followed. She pulled into a drive-in lane at a bank on Congress Avenue, put an envelope into a pneumatic tube, waited for it to come back, and drove off. A few blocks farther down Congress, she did the same thing at a savings and loan. Then she drove to another child care center and to two other banks. Throughout the afternoon she repeated the pattern over and over, picking up money and making deposits, our little caravan playing hop scotch behind her.

"This is a big day for her," Saunders said.

"What's going on?" I asked.

"Notice she goes to twice as many banks as kindergartens."

"Why?"

"They're running cash through bank accounts. A tiny bit is a legitimate deposit. The rest is dirty money."

"Start at the beginning," I said.

"Most of these child care centers are barely making it," Saunders said. "They're started by women who need to make some money but want to stay with their kids during the day."

The van pulled in front of us.

"The women who run these places work hard—ten to twelve hours a day," he said. "They can't leave the centers while children are there. Money's a constant hassle. People drop off their kids and promise to pay next week. People give them bad checks. There's a lot of cash, too, and if they employ help, they want to be paid off the books."

"So?"

"Stephanie and her so-called association go to these kindergartens and offer to take over the bookkeeping, filling out the forms and all the other stuff. She tells them it won't cost a cent." Saunders dropped back and let the Ford Vic pass. "Stephanie says she'll even pay them a little premium. One percent. Tells them it has to do with the time value of money. That's bullshit, but they don't ask a lot of questions."

Ahead of us, Stephanie picked up the pace. When no car sat in the drive-in lane in front of her, she could get in and out in a couple of minutes.

"The women who run these centers love Stephanie," Saunders said. "They sign whatever papers she puts in front of them. They go to banks with her and sign signature cards. They do what she tells them as quickly as possible. They just want to get back to their centers quickly."

"More than one bank per child care center?"

"Stephanie tells them she's moving their account from one bank to another, but they really end up with two or three and sometimes four active accounts at different banks. One is the real one, the others are Stephanie's."

"What's the point?"

"There's a big demand to wash money around here these days. Not just drugs. Money from the islands. Money from Latin America. Stephanie and company have come up with a service there's a big demand for."

"But this is peanuts," I protested.

"Not the way Stephanie does it," Saunders said. "Say she picks up ninety dollars from a kindergarten. She adds nine thousand in cash and makes a deposit for nine thousand ninety dollars."

"Always less than ten thousand," I said, more statement than question. I knew from Mo that banks were under a lot of pressure then, and still are. They must report all cash deposits of more than ten thousand dollars. Also deposits that look like pieces of a transaction that could add up to more than ten thousand.

"Yep. And never more than peanuts—your word—for the first couple of months after an account is open."

Until they're not monitored, I thought, and said, "It's still small change. Even when deposits add up to more than nine thousand dollars."

"Think about it," Saunders said. "An extra nine thousand at ten stops a day and you've washed ninety thousand dollars. That's nine hundred thousand in ten business days—two weeks."

"Why don't you subpoena bank records and establish that none of the kindergartens—day care centers—could possibly bring in that kind of money? Then you arrest Stephanie."

"The money doesn't stay in those accounts more than a day."

"It's transferred to Raymond Siegel's bank," I guessed

"Yep. And sometimes into Sally Brophy's accounts, sometimes into an account of one of her husband's customers."

"So arrest them," I said.

"Not as easy as that," Saunders said. "We don't know enough to prove anything."

"The Intracoastal Waterway runs past the Brophy's. Boats come and go. They could take money to the islands."

"We've stopped some and searched them," he said. "Nothing but parents and children aboard them."

I had a moment of illumination. "Clinton Drake was working for you."

"He preferred to be called a consultant."

"But you paid him for information."

"Yep."

"And you think someone in this money laundering ring killed him?"

"Yep."

"And now you want me to take his place?" I said, my voice louder than intended.

"Not exactly."

"How, not exactly?"

"You wouldn't be paid."

"That's wonderful. A fine consolation." I tried to sound as sarcastic as possible. "You can't imagine how good that makes me feel."

"You'd be helping Ginny," Saunders said. "And your friend, Maureen."

By then our three-car tag team had followed Stephanie throughout most of southern Palm Beach County, South County to people who live here. We'd gone to banks and child care centers in Lake Worth, Boynton Beach, Delray Beach and Boca Raton—each town different, yet all the same, not a real city among them, all mostly look-alike houses and condominiums.

"She'll head home now," Saunders said. "To Ocean Ridge."

And the note I left there. I tried remember its exact wording but couldn't. Something about it bothered me. I put the thought aside.

"Remember," Saunders said. "She's just a part of this. Think about the same thing happening in each of Sally Brophy's clothing shops. Think about accounts Wilbur Gantz brings in. And, of course, think about your friend Marilyn, the stock broker."

"Not my friend," I said automatically.

"Not for lack of trying," Saunders said.

"What?"

"On her part," he said. "I noticed her coming on to you at The Exchange. We know you went to see her."

"She's wasn't after me," I said automatically. But I realized I wasn't sure what or who she was after. An image—Alan Schneider handing Marilyn an envelope and her dropping it in a desk drawer—floated through my mind. I decided to keep the information to myself, for the time being anyway. "Is everyone at The Exchange at the time of Clinton's murder in on this scheme?"

"Most of them."

"Helena?"

Saunders stroked his beard. "Probably not."

"Ginny Stonridge?"

"Doubt it. But it's strange they invited her."

They didn't have much choice if Mo's theory were right—that Ginny had been working on assignment from the state attorney's office,

I said, "If you really suspected Ginny was involved, you wouldn't have shown me any of this."

"No."

"What exactly do you want me to do?"

"Trade information with us."

"Such as."

"You're after Clinton's killer," he said. "We know things that might help you."

"My side of the bargain? What do you want me to give you?"

"The personal stuff," Saunders said. "What the relationships are really like. Wilbur and Stephanie, for example. Divorced, but could they be working together now?"

You bet. Wilbur still loves her.

"Would one of them testify against the other," he continued. "If not, who would?"

Not Wilbur I think. But Helena would reveal everything she knows about Alan in a minute. Then I understood. She already has. She's helping Saunders.

"You're looking for a weak link," I said.

"That's right," he said, nodding so eagerly that I knew I wasn't going to tell him about Cindy Cathcart that day. He'd have to earn it.

We drove back to the airport in silence, the sun setting in the west, traffic heavy now, and my mind about to crash from processing the input of the last four hours. Saunders pulled the van in front of the DEA sign and looked at me. "Well?"

"I still don't see what this has to do with Ginny," I said.

"It may be connected, it may not," Saunders said. "We don't know, you don't know—until we find out."

I couldn't argue with that.

"Are we partners?" Saunders asked, extending a hand.

"I'll let you know tomorrow." I turned away and opened the van door, leaving his arm frozen in the air. If I was going to make a bargain with the devil I wanted to sleep on it first.

Chapter Twenty-One

I dreamed about a wedding. Mo's and mine, I finally understood, the knowledge coming to me slowly through a heavy mist. We stood with our backs to the congregation, the minister— No, he's not a minister. He's wearing a sailor's uniform, and the people behind us are passengers on a cruise ship. Okay let's do it. Suddenly the ship's bell starts ringing, making an awful racket, no, not like a ship's bell but—

"Phone." Maureen shook me. "Male voice on the phone demands to talk to you."

I put the receiver to my ear.

"Now you've done it." Paul Brophy's voice, rough, loud and angry. "You and your Goddamn full share."

The digital clock beside the phone read 1:21. AM, I guessed. "What?"

"Raymond Siegel's been murdered."

I pushed myself up.

"There's no way to stop this thing now," Brophy shouted. "I told you a way to settle it. Topping was almost ready—"

Ready to help convict some poor crack addict of a crime he didn't commit. I could almost see Brophy, wearing a silk bathrobe, pacing up and down in one of the front rooms of his house, a phone with a long extension cord in his hand—a land phone he would call it to distinguish from a cellular one—so angry he could barely speak, spitting out words and phrases that barely connected.

"Well, you'll get your share," he said. "You'll get your full share of trouble."

"When?" I said.

"When what?"

"When was Siegel murdered?"

"Between ten and eleven tonight," Brophy said. "As if you didn't know."

The phone went dead. I could see Brophy slamming it down, wondering why he phoned me, maybe realizing that his anger had trumped good judgment.

"Who was that?" Mo said.

I told her and gave her a summary.

Mo sat up. "Again," she said, so I repeated the conversation word for word, beginning to end.

Mo got out of bed, found a robe in the closet. "I'll fix some coffee."

I got my robe and met her in the kitchen. She hadn't said much the evening before when I told her all about Duane Saunders, the DEA task force, and following Stephanie Royce. Now she wanted to hear all about that again.

"Yes," she said when I finished. "They could have been using Raymond Siegel's bank to pull their money laundries together."

"So why would they kill him?"

The kitchen phone rang. Mo picked up the receiver, said hello, listened then handed it to me. "Duane Saunders," she mouthed.

"Apologize for calling you at home," he started.

"How did you get this number?"

"I told you I checked you out."

"Why are you calling now?"

"To tell you that yesterday never happened," he said. "We didn't talk, we didn't follow Stephanie Royce and the DEA isn't involved."

"I thought you wanted my help."

"The DEA sign will be gone before sunrise," he said. "There won't be any desks or files in the building."

"Because Raymond Siegel's been murdered?"

"Who told you?" he said.

"I only share information with my partners."

"Did you do it?"

"That's absurd," I said.

Neither of us said anything for maybe thirty seconds, then he said. "Save yourself a lot of trouble and remember we never met except at The Exchange."

"Maybe," I said. "Maybe not."

"No one will believe you," he said.

"Goodbye, partner." I hung up.

I told Mo about Saunders' end of the conversation. She listened, nodding her head, but I could tell she was thinking about something else.

"This isn't a safe place anymore." She motioned toward the living room but I knew she meant the whole apartment. I put my arms around her.

"We've been—" She pushed me away. "Violated, I was going to say, but that's such a cliché."

"By the phone calls?"

"This used to be our hideaway, the little space in the world we could come to get away from everybody and everything. Now—"

"We'll move out," I said.

"It would never be the same."

I tried to put my arms around her again, but she moved away.

"I don't want to talk for a while." She walked to the living room, pushed the shell-shaped chair to one side and sat in a yoga position, her robe tucked between her bare legs and the tile floor. She closed her eyes and her lips began moving against each other, her tongue moistening them every few seconds. This was deeper, more elaborate version of the concentrated thought she practiced in the hospital. More like meditation, she'd explained, communing with a power greater than hers for assistance.

Mo would be this way for at least twenty minutes, I knew from experience, and nothing I could do or say would shorten the time.

Something had changed in Mo after she got out of the securities business and moved to Florida. Before, she was super-practical and driven, ready to take on any challenge. Since then she'd become more relaxed, more introspective. In New Jersey, where she lived when she worked in Manhattan, her bookshelves had been filled with books and magazines about stock market; now the bookcase on her side of the bedroom was crowded with books and tapes on spirituality.

I headed for the bedroom, thinking there might be some clue as to what she was doing in those volumes. They were all there, the big names and the unknowns—Carl Jung, Deepak Chopra, Scott Peck, Ernest Kurtz and dozens of others. I'd barely opened Kurtz's *The Spirituality of Imperfection* when Maureen appeared in the door holding her robe tightly around her body, a serious expression on her face.

"You have to leave," she said. "Now. Right away."

"Nonsense," I said.

"No argument," she said. "Either you leave or I leave."

"But Mo—"

"No times for buts," she said. "Go to a hotel. Register under an assumed name. Pay cash."

"What's got into you?"

"Pack a small suitcase." Her voice rose. "Get out of here."

"Mo, you're not yourself."

"Don't pack then. Just get out."

I'd never seen Mo like this, either as a child or adult. But wait— One time long ago, something like this happened. I couldn't recall the details at that instant, but the feeling was familiar. Maybe I should leave. Mabe she's doing this for my own good. The thought—no, the feeling— came from nowhere.

"I got you into this, and—" She stopped.

"What do you mean?"

"Get out," she shouted. "Get out, get out."

Still stunned, I pulled on a pair of jeans, a knit shirt and boat shoes. Mo handed me my toilet kit from the bathroom. I found some extra underwear and my blue blazer to take with me.

"Don't phone here," she said.

"I don't understand."

"Don't try to call me at the office, either. Now leave."

I stumbled to the front door, bewildered and hurting, wondering what evil spirit had possessed my best friend, the only unadulterated good to ever come into my life, the only person in all the world I could depend on. Until now.

Halfway down the stairs, she called out. "Wait. Take this." I turned around. She handed me my laptop computer, kissed me softly on the lips, said, "Take care," and rushed up the stairway. What the heck was going on? Maybe I imagined it, but she seemed about to cry as she climbed up the steps. I felt like crying, too, felt as if the world had ended, knew the only way I could keep my sanity was to hold on to one simple thought: This too shall pass.

Chapter Twenty-Two

The first four hotels I phoned were filled, but I found a vacancy at Embassy Suites on Seventeenth Street. The atrium was noisy in the morning when they were serving breakfast, but the bedrooms in the back of the suites were quiet.

It didn't really matter. I knew I wouldn't sleep anyway. No matter how much I tried to figure it, I couldn't understand what had gotten into Mo. Two phone calls to our apartment and she was a changed person. A bitch. No, there must be some explanation. I walked out on the balcony, my room on the tenth floor, facing north. The air had cooled, the temperature down to the high fifties, a breeze coming from the Atlantic.

I could almost see my apartment from there. Between us, on the other side of Seventeenth, canals dug from marsh and swamp long ago formed a trellis of land and water. The Venice of America they call his city, and from the hotel I could see why. A splendid view, but without Mo no scene would seem right. I could live quite nicely anywhere if Mo were with me. Otherwise it was all dirt. All I want in life is to be with one woman, the woman who so suddenly, terribly turned on me.

Without warning, my thoughts turned vicious. It was my apartment damn it. What right did she have to kick me out? About the only things she had added was some kitchen stuff and the bedspread. She didn't like the one I'd bought, one covered with sailboats. Said they made my room look like that of a twelve year old boy's. Well, so what? It took some time to get used to the one she'd found, the one with the pink hibiscus flowers and green leaves, and put it on the bed without even asking me, but I'd made peace with it. Well she could get out and take her damn bedspread with her for all I cared. The kitchen stuff, too. I'd never use all those spices, not in a million years. And the big spoons, stirring spoons she called them, What crap. All a man needed in any kitchen was a microwave oven, a supply of frozen food packages, and something to eat it with. Oh. And an ice cream scoop, of course.

I heard how ridiculous I sounded, even saying this these things to myself, and wanted to cry. Oh Lord, I have lost my mind. I thought of a drink, but knew that wouldn't help. What good would it do to numb my feelings with a central nervous system depressant? I knew the routine. Walk through the pain. Feel it. What doesn't kill you makes you stronger. Yeah, yeah, yeah. But I hurt so fucking much. Why did she do it? Why?

Somehow I've got to get through the next few hours, until stores open. Then I'll find some shorts and gym shoes, run these feelings off. But how to make it through the night? I decided to plug in my laptop computer, maybe surf news sites around the country until I got sleepy.

I felt someone in the room. I looked up. Were those darkened figures in the corner? I got up and walked there, to the corner, but when I reached the area they were gone. Must be seeing things, I told myself. Get back to work.

What I did could not really be called work. The word work implies a purpose, a sense of direction, an aim toward a predetermined goal. What I was doing on the net was mindless, poking keys without a plan. But it was making me feel better. I was thinking about things other than Mo.

They were here again! Shadows of men with dark cloaks in the corner. I shook my head. I was seeing things. I was tired, I told myself. But no, that wasn't true. I was in shock. My spirit had collided against something hard, unyielding; the most precious person in my life had suddenly, irrationally turned on me. I closed my eyes, kept them closed for a minute, maybe more, then let them open. The men in the dark cloaks, the shadows, had vanished. Back to the web.

Again I surfed without purpose. I thought of looking up psychological terms or studies, but rejected the idea immediately. They were bunk. This was real, this feeling of despair. What's the use? What's the use, God, when you do everything right and it turns out like this? How could you do this to me? The thought startled me. I am not a believer in any sort of traditional God. And yet the words seemed so natural.

Clarion bells pealed, as if from the tower of the biggest cathedral in France. Something glistened in the corner of the room. Cyrano! Damn if it's not Cyrano de Bergerac, his sword flashing, taking on all comers, creating poetry as he dispatched fools. I shook my head. Cyrano disappeared. An hallucination, but there's a hero for you. Sometimes I imagined myself as him.

I returned to the research. Suddenly Cyrano was back in the room, his cape mussed, the sword in its sheaf, bragging of his independence to that kiss-ass Le Brett. I shivered. I knew what was coming. Le Brett took Cyrano's arm, then quietly but loud enough for all to hear: whispered:

Speak proud aloud, and bitter!
In my ear, whisper me simply this,
She loves thee not!

Tears started flowing down my cheeks and I did nothing to stop the them. Mo. Maureen. Mo. Why have you forsaken me? Why?

#

I must have fallen asleep. I woke lying on the bedspread fully clothed, staring at the ceiling. I remembered the hallucinations. And my tears. Good, for me. I tell my clients that it's OK to cry and I would say the same to adults. My watch read a few minutes after eight. Time to shower and eat breakfast. I'll run later, I told myself.

It was in the shower that the whole thing came to me. I remembered what had been tickling my mind the night before, the events of years ago when she did something else for my own good.

#

When I was ten and Mo was fourteen, she discovered boys. Or maybe boys discovered her. Whichever, it was terrible time for me. One minute I was the center of her life, as she was mine, and the next I didn't exist. Not for her, anyway.

For four years after I first contracted polio, the minute she got home from school Maureen would come to my house, climb the three stories to my bedroom and yell something like, "Okay, time to get your ass out of bed and get to work!" The work was school work, but she made it fun. She taught me how to read and write, then to add, subtract and all the rest. She was so good a teacher that when I finally went to school they put me in a class with kids two years older.

Then one day she said, "Go, I'm not going to see you anymore."

"What?" I can still remember the shock.

"You've got to get some new friends," she said.

"You're the only friend I ever want."

"No. You need male friends. And you need to meet other girls."

I argued, I protested, I begged. But nothing would change her mind.

It took a couple of hours for my anger to retreat into pain, but when it did the torment became excruciating. I couldn't read, couldn't eat, couldn't do anything. Every cell of my body yelled out, I want to die. Life is not worth living without her. Finally, a week or two later, I got angry again. She can't do this to me. It's unfair. I won't let her.

So I skipped my school one day and went over to hers, a high school. I planned to ambush her at lunch break, but a teacher saw me wandering around the halls and told me to go back to elementary school where I belonged. I left the building but hid in the parking lot where I could see the front entrance. Hours passed, but I didn't notice. I hurt too much.

Finally Mo came out, but she wasn't alone. A boy walked on either side of her, or three or four others trailed behind. Even from where I stood, maybe fifty yards away, I could see they were laughing and joking, having a fine old time, good buddies for life. Did Mo put a hand on that guy's shoulder? In my pain, that was too much. I ran toward her.

She saw me when I got about fifteen feet away. "Get lost," she yelled. "I told you to stay away!"

"Leave her alone," shouted the tall guy on her right.

"You heard her," said the plump guy on the other side.

"Get lost!" yelled the others.

"Disappear," Mo said.

I stood there, numb and speechless.

During the next few weeks, we played that scene over and over, the details different but my feelings always the same. Finally I learned my lesson. If I wanted to avoid pain, I needed to stay away from her. So I did.

Eventually, out of loneliness if nothing else, I began hanging around with kids my own age. One of the guys tried to teach me football and basketball, but with my legs like they were, I was too slow and clumsy. Try softball, he said, and I was better at that as long as I played catcher and someone ran the bases when I got a hit. A year later, a girl developed a crush on me, gimpy leg and all. Soon I became interested in other girls, too. Life went on.

Years later, when Mo returned from college she made a point of seeking me out in high school, beginning from the same spot in the parking lot where I hid before, I was with a group, another guy and a couple of girls when I saw her. I started to turn away.

"Go," Mo yelled. "Don't."

I stopped and walked over to her.

"It's time for our separation to end," she said.

I wanted to feel angry but couldn't. I was off on a wonderful high, a sense of thanksgiving and relief that I didn't get from booze or drugs. (Yes, I was an early starter.) I didn't look back, didn't say goodbye to my buddies, just walked with her to her car. She drove us to a diner (maybe that's why I like them so much) and over hamburgers and fries we had our reconciliation. No, that's not the right word. To reconcile, two people must be separated, and although we were physically apart she was never far from my thoughts, nor—she confessed in that diner—I from hers.

"I did it for your own good," she said. "Can you see that now?"

I didn't want to say it, but finally I forced a "yes" from my mouth. "But it's over, isn't it?"

Mo reached across the table and squeezed my hand. "Sure it is."

And that was that, except we were never exactly like we were before. She was in college, first Georgetown University and then Johns

Hopkins in Baltimore, so she couldn't spend much time with me. We saw each other only on weekends, and then only on the weekends she was home, and not of course, the nights she had a date, and especially times she stayed at a date's apartment overnight. This last was the worse, but eventually I could accept that, too.

Sitting in that hotel room, I began to understand what was happening now. Mo kicked me out me out for my own good. Maybe she'd figured they would make me a suspect in Siegel's murder. I still felt lousy but at last I was able to get to sleep.

Chapter Twenty-Three

Downstairs I found the gift shop and headed for the morning newspapers. A big black headline on the top of the front page of the *Sun-Sentinel* shrieked:

PALM BEACH BANKER MURDERED,
CHILDREN'S THERAPIST SUSPECTED

Immediately below the headline two large photographs jumped out. One a close-up of Raymond Siegel. The other, a big fat mug shot of me.

I bought a copy each of the Miami, Fort Lauderdale and Palm Beach newspapers and retreated to my room, pretty sure the woman behind the counter didn't recognize me from the photo in the papers she sold. She barely looked up. I read every word of every story about Siegel's murder. They told roughly the same tale.

Siegel was found dead in his Palm Beach home sometime between ten and eleven o'clock the night before. He'd been shot with a pistol, probably .22 caliber, but police said there hadn't been time for lab tests. The banker's body had been discovered by a man one paper identified as Siegel's aide, another described as a business associate and the third called a yard man. The stories did not explain what the guy was doing at Siegel's home late at night. Neither did they come close to describing Siegel as gay. The story broke too late for editors to figure out the relevance or political correctness of such disclosure, I guessed.

Considerably more important to me, every story said police sought "for questioning" Gregory Overman, a children's therapist now residing in Fort Lauderdale. Overman was known to have—and here the stories retreated to "sources said"—demanded from CPA Paul Brophy and others a mysterious "full share" in their enterprise.

"None of us knew what he was talking about," one paper quoted Brophy. "We assumed it was some sort of blackmail attempt, but we don't have anything to hide."

The bastard!

"One woman who attended The Exchange had the blackmail threat in writing." Again sources said, but I knew who they got that from. Stephanie Royce. *I know what's going on. I want a share—or else. Phone me at...* Then my cell phone number. A stupid thing for me to put in writing. Mo had said to deliver the message, not write a note. Or did she? Leave a note in her mailbox. Yes, that's what Mo told me to do. And what did she say last night? "I got you into this, and—"

So that's how Mo knew. She put everything together last night after we got the phone calls from Brophy and Saunders and news of Siegel's death. She remembered what I said in the note to Stephanie. She knew I was in danger. She knew police would soon be tapping our phones.

But she could have told me, I thought, she didn't have to force me to leave the way she did. She didn't trust me. She didn't— Then the truth crept into my consciousness, unwelcome at first, but certainly a stone cold fact: I wouldn't have left if she'd explained. I'd have insisted on staying there, facing things together. And that would have been an idiotic thing to do. Mo wasn't accused of anything. I was. My presumed guilt would rub off on her and we'd both drown. Separated, we have a chance.

#

I knew I'd have to leave the hotel soon. If I hung around, eventually somebody would recognize me. But where should I go? Not much to pack. Just my notebook computer and a few clothes. I began collecting them near the front door when I had another thought. Mo told me not to phone. She didn't say anything about e-mail. Quickly I logged on, clicked to messages. Mo, marvelous Mo, anticipated me. A message from her stood at the top of the queue. I opened it eagerly, knowing she wanted me back. But her note consisted of only one word.

DISAPPEAR!

This time I didn't argue. I sent her a one-word reply.

OK.

#

The picture of me that the three Florida papers splashed on their front pages was one taken in New York four or five years ago. It went with an interview I'd given a Maryland newspaper saying that if parents were wondering what was wrong with their children, they should look in a mirror. It was and is an extreme view, since sometimes kids take weird turns for which their parents have no responsibility. But not usually. Show me a kid neglected by his parents and I'll show you one who's acting out in all sorts of ways to get attention. Show me an abused kid and I'll show you a violent kid who tries to abuse others. When they can't they seek revenge in other ways, lighting fires, bringing guns to school—well, just look at the headlines.

The Maryland paper liked the story enough to offer it to the Associated Press, which picked it up and distributed it throughout the country with my photograph. I wore a suit and tie with my hair slicked down, but the day they took the photograph my face looked fleshy and my expression—unfortunately—was one of wild-eyed fear, a fleeting instant of excitement frozen forever by a camera's flash. In the years since the original story, the picture's been run over and over throughout the nation, whenever a newspaper uses a quote from me about adolescent issues, usually completely out of context. I've quit giving newspaper interviews and given up trying to get newspapers to use another photo.

Now I'm glad I failed. I've lost weight since coming to Florida, let my hair grow longer, become rather casual about shaving, and acquired a deep tan. Wearing my jeans and knit shirt, I doubted many people could recognize me from the photograph alone. Sooner or later, though, if the police were really interested in finding me, a police artist could meld witness descriptions with the photo and come up with a pretty good likeness.

Fortunately, this wasn't the first time I'd thought about how to vanish without leaving a trace. Leave a false trail, and then cut it off, I concluded years ago in a strictly intellectual exercise. Plastic. That's the key. The idea came to me while reading stories about a manhunt. A guy in Illinois was wanted for embezzlement. He'd withdrawn a half million dollars from his employer's accounts, deserted his wife and children and taken off for Florida. On arrival, he rented an automobile in Orlando and checked into a hotel near Kissimmee. FBI agents arrested him the next morning as he left his room for breakfast. They'd found him by tracing credit card transactions. The jerk used a MasterCard, titanium no less, to charge the car rental and the motel bill. "The cards are a habit," he told the *Orlando Sentinel*. "I never planned to be in one place more than one night." He'd forgotten how quickly plastic charges are processed. Records of a transaction fly from merchant to bank computer in seconds, often via satellite. How else could Walmart and all those gas stations know our credit's good?

At the time I thought: If credit cards can be used to trace a suspect, they can be used to create a false trail, too. Maybe a couple of trails. From that start, I came up with a scheme, one I never intended to use. But the time had come to try it.

I started my disappearing act by getting as much cash as I could without talking to anyone. I found a drive-through ATM machine and, still in my car, withdrew the maximum allowed from each of three checking accounts—one for personal expenses, one for business, and one connected to my little investment account. Then, at another ATM, I used four credit cards to extract their maximums. Including the money I started with, I had more than four grand. Not as much as I'd like, but it would do.

My Miata had become a liability, much too recognizable. I drove to Palm Beach International and parked it in the middle of the "Park and Ride" lot about a mile from the terminal. I rode the Courtesy Bus to the building, walked up a flight of steps, and paying cash, bought a ticket to

Atlanta on a Delta flight that stopped in Orlando. Then I took the escalator down two floors to the Hertz counter and, using a credit card and my driver's license, rented a Ford Taurus.

The rest was easy. I drove to Miami International, ditched the Ford in the rental return lane and, again using plastic, bought a one-way ticket on an American Airlines non-stop flight from Miami to New York—a ticket I'd never use. Then I rode the Super Shuttle back to West Palm terminal, arriving twenty minutes before the Delta flight left.

If investigators got my credit-card records, they'd see I rented a car at Palm Beach International, left it in Miami and then flew to New York. They might wonder why I returned the car so quickly and eventually they'd find my Miata at the Palm Beach International lot. Even then, though, they wouldn't find any record of my flying from there.

I got off the Delta flight in Orlando, took a taxi downtown, and boarded the next Greyhound leaving for Tampa. There, I grabbed a taxi to the Tampa International terminal. The Hyatt there tempted me, airport hotels being among the most anonymous places in the world, but I thought of the jerk arrested in Kissimmee. No, I decided. I won't take the smallest chance.

Walking around the terminal, I found an exhibit with a map of the area and little lights showing the location of about a dozen motels and hotels. Phones with direct connections to each sat below the display. I picked up four in succession, asking the same set of questions of desk clerks on the other end of the line. A motel on the causeway to Clearwater had the right answers. Yes, they had a room for a week; yes, they had room service from six in the morning until midnight and, yes, a shuttle bus could pick me up in twenty minutes.

I walked to the gift shop, bought a Tampa Bay Rays cap and matching jersey, the cap dark blue with large letters TB in white, the jersey blue also, with the word Rays silhouetted in light blue, neither even hinting of the original team name. "*Devil* Rays, *Devil* Rays, Devil Rays," I said to myself, until I saw someone looking at me strangely. I changed clothes in the men's room, found a news rack, and bought a *Tampa Tribune*. Just enough time to find out who they, no, we, were playing before the shuttle pulled up.

The Baltimore Orioles. Sting 'me, Rays!

Chapter Twenty-Four

I registered at the motel using a false name and fake address, one in Maryland. If anybody ever checked, they'd find the address was that of a shopping center I hung around as teenager. "I've got some reports to write," I told the desk clerk. "I'll be needing room service for most of my meals."

"You won't be disturbed." She was young, Cuban, bored. "Credit card or cash?"

I laid twelve hundred dollars' worth of twenty-dollar bills on the counter top, methodically counting out five in each of eight stacks. She didn't blink. Happens all the time, her expression said. "Will there be anything else?"

"Newspapers," I said. "I'll need a *Miami Herald* every morning."

"Not here," she said.

I put down two more twenties. "Do you think someone could pick up one at the airport and bring it to me every day?"

"Maybe," she said. "Maybe I have a friend who could do that."

I pointed to the twenties. "One for you, one for him. And more, every day until I check out."

She picked up the bills and buried them in a skirt pocket. "My friend can get you anything you want."

I'll bet, I thought, shaking my head.

#

Can the cops trace e-mail? If Mo and I were going to stay off phones, I'd have to find out. I knew they could determine the electronic ID of a computer that originated a message, but I didn't think they could trace its location. Right or wrong, I decided to chance it. I changed my net name to LonelyInSeattle2 and sent Mo a two-word note.

I'M TRANSPARENT.

That's all. She'd know I was hiding somewhere and didn't think anyone could find me. She didn't need to know where. She'd get back to me when she could. More tired than I realized, I lay on the bed and fell asleep. I dreamed of a Middle East slave market. Every adult at The Exchange being auctioned off. Paul Brophy the auctioneer, but he took instructions from Ginny. Or was that Mo?

When I woke, I logged onto the *Herald, Post* and *Sun-Sentinel* web sites. Each carried an abbreviated version of their second-day stories about Raymond Siegel's murder, but there was nothing new. That's why I needed a paper copy of the *Herald*. I wanted to read the longer stories, stuff they didn't put on the web.

I switched back to e-mail. There was a one-word note from Maureen.

RESEARCHING.

RESEARCHING WHAT? I sent back.

But she didn't answer.

During the next three days, I settled into a routine. I had my meals delivered to the room and soon learned to stick to plain fare, BLT sandwiches and the like. I kept the coffeepot going all day, thanks to coffee and sweetener packets I bought from a maid. I watched morning and evening news shows but avoided other daytime television. Vast wasteland was a very kind description. I bought and read paperback novels on sale in the motel lobby. Most of them junk, either novels of action with flat characters and no ideas or novels about the human condition but no action. Why can't a novel have both?

True to her word, the motel clerk arranged for the shuttle driver to pick up a *Herald* at the airport every day and deliver it to my room. I gave the guy a Jackson each time, and he showed nothing, like twenty bucks was the going rate for newspapers in Tampa. When I ran out of even halfway interesting paperbacks at the motel, I gave him a list of authors and titles to buy at the airport terminal, but he found only two or three. Airport bookstores are the vast wasteland of American literature.

"Don't you want something else?" the guy asked on the first day. "A woman? Something to make you feel better?"

"No," I said then and every other time he offered, and on the fourth day he quit asking.

I hadn't heard from Mo since her last mysterious message about research.

MISS YOU, I messaged her on the second day.

MISS YOU MORE, I sent the next.

She didn't answer, so I stopped.

By this time I was so desperate for human voices I began watching Oprah and her clones. Winfrey had some class, but the others were tacky and tasteless—almost as if they were in an undeclared competition to see how low they could go. Where do they get these people? The late Raymond Siegel, gay or not, was right. He'd been amazed, truly amazed as he put it, just how just how little so many men and women would sell themselves for. What was your price, Raymond? What did you sell your life for?

#

I thought of putting my Tampa Bay Rays outfit to use, later figured the game wouldn't be worth the cab ride. I was tired of being a spectator. I used the motel weight room every other day, but knew I needed more exercise. After a little searching, I found a stretch of beach that couldn't be seen from the highway—a little peninsular on the south side of the causeway halfway between Tampa and Clearwater. I jogged along this beach twice a day, running to the mangroves and back four times. Two or three miles each run, I figured.

The footprints I left in the sand were uneven. My left leg's shorter than the right, so my feet cut deeper on the left side, shallower on the right. The story of my life. Almost nothing has been easy for me from the time I contracted polio. A one in a million screw-up, one I can usually banish from my mind. But in my solitude, the whole sorry story insisted going round and round in my head.

My father, a Foreign Service officer, was stationed in Saudi Arabia when Mother became pregnant with me. Instead of going back to Washington D.C., she decided to stay in Riyadh for most of her term and fly to a military base in Germany to give birth. All went well except for one thing. The military nurses and doctors at Landstuhl thought the embassy physician would give me all the necessary inoculations and vaccinations. The Embassy doctor, neither an obstetrician nor pediatrician, assumed these routines had been taken care of in Germany. Mother, the supposed expert, didn't check. The oversight wasn't found until my parents were transferred back to the states, and by then the poliomyelitis virus was already in me.

One bad assumption and my whole life was skewed. I'd made peace with the events and people involved, but even after I'd grown accustomed to the limp, decided against an operation and fallen into a pretty good life, I wasn't free. A ghost named post-polio syndrome, or PPS as it is so inelegantly called, stalks me every day. Sure, the chances are only one in five I'll be stricken again. But what if I'm the one?

I'd spent enough hours with shrinks to know myself pretty well, well enough to rise above memories of the past or possible dangers of the future. Most days anyway, especially when I'm with Maureen. When Mo with her love and wisdom was nearby, I'm happy to live in the here and now. But take them away, leave me isolated for three or four days as I was in Tampa, and I begin falling into a dark and impossibly deep pit of depression and despair. Where are you when I need you, Mo?

#

Hours later, my mood was worse. I felt just like I did twenty-odd years ago when Maureen first told me to get lost. This is different, I told myself, but it feels the same. If I keep going one more step like this, I'll fall off a cliff so steep that I'll never be able to crawl back. Fuck it. I know what'll help.

I walked down Courtney Campbell Causeway, toward Tampa, for miles until I found a 7-Eleven. No wimpy Ben & Jerry's for me that day.

I wanted something that would numb those feelings, make me forget about polio, bad assumptions, Mother, Dad, Mo, the murders, everything. I bought two six-packs of Bud Light. Only a drunk would worry about calories at a time like this. I planned to drink all twelve myself.

Back at the motel, I put the Buds on the round, laminate-topped table that served as my eating area and desk, brushing my notebook computer to one side. I made a line of the twelve cans, then decided a circular arrangement would be better. The little PC was in the way again, so I pushed it back again. It fell to the floor. Damn. I picked it up, saw the thing was still hooked up to the web. One more search, although surely there's nothing new.

I checked the *Herald* site first, then the *Sun-Sentinel*, leaving the *Post* for last. I read and re-read all their stories about two murders (by then, all the papers were linking Clinton and Raymond's deaths together) and saw a tidbit I'd overlooked before. About midway down one *Post* story, State Attorney Topping was quoted as saying he'd convene a grand jury to hear testimony about the crimes "as soon as all witnesses can be found."

What did that mean? Do they know of someone who witnessed either murder? Tune in tomorrow, my only choice. By then, my curiosity aroused, I didn't want the beers. I could always drink tomorrow. I carried the cans of Bud to the motel patio. Not a soul in sight. With a deliberation only a man on the brink of doom could summon, I carefully snapped open each can, upended it and poured every fluid ounce into the swimming pool. You can't tempt me again, I said to each of them. I knew this wasn't something a good motel guest would do, but what the heck?

#

The next day the *Post* went all out. SUSPECT IN 'EXCHANGE' MURDERS DISAPPEARS read the top-of-the-front-page headline. With a start, I realized they were talking about me.

As often happens, the headline went further than the story, which carefully did not call me a suspect. I was wanted for "questioning," that's all, in connection with the two murders and would be called before a grand jury when found. "The state attorney said he would begin presenting testimony to the grand jury next week but indicated that the evidence would be incomplete without Overman's testimony."

After that, a sentence that cheered me up. "A source said there was reason to believe Overman flew to New York City from the Miami airport." Glory be to the magic of plastic! They bought my fake trail. But for how long? If the cops found my car in the West Palm airport, they might be able to check airline boarding records. But even then, could they discover I got off the Atlanta flight in Orlando? So much I didn't know.

#

Mo's phone call came about noon, reaching my cell phone while I was under an umbrella near the pool. I'd been thinking: If I weren't so fucking depressed, I could enjoy this life.

"Don't tell me where you are," she said first thing.

"Mo!" I said. "Where are you?"

"I can't tell you," she said. "And you shouldn't tell me."

"Can someone overhear us?"

"From what I've been able to learn, cell-phone calls can be intercepted only between the phone and the nearest tower," Mo said. "I drove to a point when I can be sure no one's following me."

The Florida Keys, I guessed. Nobody could tail someone down the causeway without being noticed. She could be in Marathon, say, almost under a relay tower close to the highway.

"Did you see the Post story on the web?" Mo asked.

"Yep."

"You could sue."

"Nobody ever wins a lawsuit like that."

"I knew you'd say that," she said.

"I'm ready to come home," I said.

"No! You can't."

"Why not?"

"They'll drag you before a Grand Jury and no matter what you say, they'll make you look horrible."

"So?" I said.

"Ginny says—"

"Ginny? You've been talking to Ginny?"

"Of course," Mo said.

"Do they still consider her the most likely suspect in Clinton's murder?"

"There's more to Ginny's story than we knew," Mo said. "She hasn't been a real suspect since the very beginning."

"Why not."

"Ginny told me something in confidence," Mo said.

"What?"

"I'm not supposed to tell you."

"Since when have we started keeping secrets from each other?"

"Since we're talking on a cell phone," Mo said.

"You'd tell me if we were face to face?"

The air waves were silent for longer than I liked. Finally, Mo said: "Yes."

"Well, that's certainly good to hear."

"Don't be like that."

"If we start keeping secrets from each other, that'll be the end of us."

"Not always," Mo said, and I could almost see color rising in her face. "They'll be certain times we have to keep secrets." A pause, then, "For our own good."

I didn't answer that.

"Let's start over," Mo said. "The official story— The unofficial, official story is Ginny's off the hook since Raymond Siegel's murder."

"Who says?"

"Lucy—you know, her former secretary."

But could she be trusted?

"Lucy says Seymour Topping thinks you're a better suspect," Mo said. "That note you left Stephanie, and then Paul Brophy's telling police you wanted a share of the action."

"Stupid of me," I said.

"No," Mo said. "I suggested both those actions."

"And the last night I was at your apartment, you figured they'd use those things against me?"

Silence.

"Didn't you?" I insisted.

"Yes," Mo said.

More silence, this time from me.

"Maybe I should have explained," Mo said.

Maybe she should have explained. Jesus Christ Almighty, I thought, but I said, "You might have."

"I knew you'd figure it out eventually," Mo said.

So now what do I do? Lose my temper and yell and scream. No, not at Mo. As always, she had my best interest at heart.

"Are you alone?" I asked.

"No. Ginny drove down here with me."

I was surprised.

"She has a lot of time on her hands these days," Mo added.

"I want to come home," I said.

"You said that before. It would be unwise."

I held my tongue.

"I can't tell you what to do," Mo said. "But I wish you wouldn't."

I didn't answer. Another very long silence between us.

Finally she said, "I've got to go."

"OK."

"Love and kisses."

"Back to you," I said.

Neither of us said goodbye.

Chapter Twenty-Five

The next day it rained. I lay on my back, the lime green bedspread below me, the curiously marred ceiling above, tedium and restlessness growing exponentially. If I read another paperback, my eyes would crack. If I watched another TV show, my brain would surely curdle. The cracks and spots on the ceiling no longer interested me. I'd given up trying to figure out what caused the three round purple spots in one corner, the bright orange splatter in the middle.

Who shot Clinton? Who killed Raymond? Those were the only questions that mattered anymore. Who to believe? Sally said there was bad blood between Alan and Clinton, that she saw them arguing at the Exchange before Clinton was killed. Helena said Alan owed Clinton money. Also that Alan dated Stephanie and Cindy. Anything there? Alan isn't worth a dime, Helena's phrase, but he can still borrow enough to stay in business. Where does he get the money?

Mo and I did everything we could to find the answers to these questions before my exile, I told myself. Nonsense, the tough critic inside me challenged. You've both been lazy. You haven't even made a basic public records search. That's right, I admitted. But I can't now, stuck here, more than a hundred miles from the Palm Beach County government center. Bullshit, the voice answered. What are you talking about? I started to argue, but then I realized what the voice was telling me. The net, stupid, the net. The records are probably accessible through the Internet. I was excited then, glad I listen to the inner voices. Ask the universe a question and it always answers. Maybe what other people call God is what I've always called the subconscious.

The modem in my notebook computer was already connected to a phone jack, so all I had to do was click in a few commands, then go to Google and tap in Palm Beach County Records. Another click to the site and there's a message from the Clerk of the Court, Dorothy Wilkin, welcoming me but at the same time warning she wouldn't be responsible for the accuracy of the electronic version of official records, then telling me the index and associated records went back to 1993, and saying I could print uncertified, unofficial copies of the same from my computer, all available twenty-four, seven. Thank you. Thank you, Dorothy. As they say, "Take off your clothes, I think I love you."

I started work, happily clicking away, searching for anything I could find about this weird Exchange bunch, impressed once again about the amazing amount of information that could be learned about almost anyone from public records. Real estate transactions, mortgages, recorded loans, liens, court suits, divorces, even small claims, all cross-indexed by buyer and seller, grantor and grantee, plaintiff and defendant, almost everything you'd want to learn about a person except marriages, births and deaths, which were recorded elsewhere. Mo used these records all the time, she'd told me, following the money and the people who had it wherever the trial lead. Now I tried to use the net as she did, tried to think like she did, looking for the money angle in everything.

Five hours and five cups of coffee after I began the records search, my eyes felt as if rubbed with sandpaper, every muscle in my shoulders ached and my sour stomach protested the intake of so much coffee. Nonetheless, I'd finished, and I felt a wonderful sense of accomplishment, the best I'd felt in days. I'd checked records of all adults at The Exchange at the time of the murder and made a good haul.

Paul and Sally Brophy paid only eight hundred fifty thousand dollars for their lakefront house almost twenty years ago, about one-fifth the current tax appraisal. They'd refinanced it five times in the last six years, each loan coming from Raymond Siegel's bank, at one point owing almost eight million dollars, considerable more than the place was worth even at the top of the real estate boom.

It's nice to have a friend at the bank.

Wilbur Gantz's divorce from Stephanie was routine, no grounds stated, none necessary in this no-fault state. The property settlement gave Stephanie everything. Since then, Wilbur had three autos repossessed, been a defendant in sixteen small claims cases and the subject of four landlord evictions. All court action against him stopped four years ago, though, and he didn't seem to owe anyone now.

So life was getting better for Shy Wilbur, even if his office is a dump.

Helena Katz Schneider bought residential real estate as often as some women bought shoes and sold it just as quickly. Professional martyr or not, she had a sharp eye for undervalued property and quick access to financing. Made a profit of only thirty to fifty thousand per residence, but held them only four to eight months. Since she paid no commissions, her cumulative profits were substantial.

The Schneider's divorce file was thick, possible evidence of vindictiveness on both sides, but the complaint made no specific allegations—only vague boilerplate stuff. Three times after the divorce, Helena filed motions asking that Alan be held in contempt for failing to make payments, and each time the motion was withdrawn before a hearing date was set. Alan must have paid.

Helena was not a woman who needs child support payments, I thought. Her insistence must be a point of pride. Or maybe continuing anger. Angry enough to kill?

My cell phone rang four or five times during my research. The first few times no voice responded to my "hello." The last time a woman's voice said: "Is this Gregory Overman?"

"What are you selling?" I asked, my automatic response to telemarketers. No answer. "Hello, hello." Again no reply. I hung up and turned off the phone. How could telemarketers get my number? Cell phone numbers aren't compiled and listed anywhere except by phone companies and those lists are supposed to be confidential.

I continued my research. Alan Schneider had taken out enough loans to finance construction of a small city, and the paperwork confirmed talk on the street. He'd exhausted most sources of credit, at one time or another borrowing from almost every bank and savings association in South Florida and repaying them late. In the last two years he'd done business with only Raymond Siegel's bank, and by my rough calculation still owed it between twelve and fifteen million dollars. What do federal bank auditors think about a bank loaning so much money to one small, residential builder? They can't like it, but so far they haven't done anything about it. Why?

Clinton Drake's finances were a surprise. He'd taken out dozens of small loans that, except for one to finance an auto, were all just under ten thousand. His list of lenders duplicated the banks and S&Ls on Stephanie's milk run for day care centers. Most were signature loans, with the sequence of dates on the notes suggesting he took out the new loans to make payments on the old ones.

He avoided Raymond Siegel's bank. Why?

Ginny and Clinton's divorce had been settled quickly. He agreed to pay seven hundred a month in child support payments, and a deed conveying their residence to Ginny was recorded on the same day the divorce decree was filed.

Others at The Exchange hadn't done much to get their names recorded. Ginny didn't show up in the records except for her divorce, the deed to her home in Boca Raton and a mortgage. Stephanie Royce owned a townhouse in Ocean Ridge, Marilyn Barr a condominium in Palm Beach, Raymond Siegel a mansion in Palm Beach and the apartment in which Cindy lived. Cindy said Siegel paid her rent. Would she know the difference between a rental and condo assessments?

I'm finished, I thought, then remembered a name I hadn't checked. A waste of time, I figured. Surely there won't be anything incriminating against Duane Saunders, squeaky-clean federal agent.

But Saunders, the rascal, showed up in these public records more than anyone else. He was an officer—president, secretary or treasurer—of sixteen public corporations which owned more than fifteen hundred acres of land throughout Palm Beach County. Total cost: More than five million, two hundred thousand. In addition to property ownership, the corporations were involved in leasing, rental and maintenance activities.

What's Duane Saunders, public servant, doing in these corporations? Where did he get the money? Who is he, really? I never asked him or his colleagues for identification. Maybe he's a phony, running a racket of his own. Anybody could put up a sign in front of an old building. Next time I see him I'll asked him— When the heck will that be?

#

I dreamed of another slave auction. I was on the block. Seymour Topping tightened the chains. Again Brophy is the auctioneer. A woman stood behind him, not Ginny I slowly realized, but Mo. She came forward, kissed me lightly, and took the metal links from Topping. She'll release me. No! She shrugged her shoulders, dropped the chains on the ground and walked away.

I woke up sweating. Mo, kissing me but walking away. What did that mean?

Two cups of coffee and a walk down to the mangroves and back didn't help. Every moment I became more irritated, more restless. Back at the room, I lay on the bed again, staring at the ceiling. What was I doing here, on the opposite side of the state from Maureen, hiding from Topping and his Grand Jury? Am I a fugitive from justice? Maybe so, maybe not. I don't know the law, and don't care what it says. I came here because Maureen told me to. I obeyed because once long ago she told me to stay away from her, and—with the painful and hard-won benefit of hindsight—that turned out to be the right thing to do at the time. But now?

I have nothing to hide.

The words clamored throughout the room, skirted across the round table now cleared of the dozen beers, blotted out the orange and purple stains on the ceiling, and stung me like a shot of lightning. I have nothing to hide. Dear Mo wanted to protect me, just as she tries to guard everyone she loves from harm. But I don't need protecting. I can handle things myself, by myself, did in fact for twenty years when we saw little of each other.

I'm going back—back home, back to face the music, back closer to Maureen but not to her—whether she likes it or not, I decided. When I get there, I won't tell her. She said it. They'll be certain times we have to keep secrets. For our own good. OK. Two can play that game.

#

The rented Mercury Sable leapt forward as it came off the top of the Sunshine Skyway, ready to show what it could do. I let it romp down Interstate 75 with the speed odometer sitting mostly in the low eighties, pulling back only when it edged close to ninety. Slow down, a voice told me. Figure out what you're going to do when you get there. But I didn't.

At Fort Myers I turned east on State Road 80, my speed cut in half on the two-lane roads. Little towns passed by, a part of Florida tourists rarely see. I slowed even more at La Belle, Heartland America hidden away in South Florida, country folk in their Sunday best. Then sugar cane country, the monotonous brown cane fields stretching to the horizon, just as they must in Jamaica and the Dominican Republic. Cuba, too. Small world department: the owner of the biggest collection of cane fields in Florida, a Cuban exile, lives a couple of miles north of the Brophys in a real Palm Beach mansion, his lavish parties financed at least in part by U.S. government price supports. Has Brophy ever met him? Are they somehow connected?

South Bay and Belle Glade were next, tough little towns. If the Saturday night homicide rates aren't higher there than any in Florida, it's the result of flawed statistics. Miami gets a bum rap. If Mo phones my cell number, I'll pretend I'm still far away. I don't like deceiving her, but what else can I do?

Florida's Turnpike in West Palm just ahead. This is the hard part, the reason I've been making and re-making resolutions driving across the state. I could turn south here and be back in Lauderdale in an hour, back with Mo, back home. Tempting. But bad for both of us. Mo won't like what I'm about to do, but that's the way it's got to be. .I won't tell Mo, I resolved, won't tell her I'm back in Southeast Florida.

I didn't turn. Instead I drove straight ahead and checked into the same hotel I stayed at in West Palm when Mo was in the hospital. When Mo was in the hospital, my mind repeated. Even a motel she hasn't been in holds memories of her. Damn.

#

My cell phone rang just after I dozed off. I almost didn't answer, but so few people know the number I couldn't resist.

"It took you long enough." Mo's voice.

"I'm in bed."

"By yourself?"

"Of course," I said, sitting up.

"Not of course," she said. "You're a healthy male and it's been days."

"You know I don't do that."

"Wherever you are, there are probably dozens of women who'd like to seduce you."

"That's silly."

"Women like to seduce men," she said. "I think they like it because they find it so easy to do."

I laughed. It was good to have her teasing me like this again.

"Don't know why it took me thirty years to seduce you," she said.

"Maybe because we hadn't reached puberty for a good chunk of that time."

I loved to hear Mo laugh, even at her own jokes. This was like old times.

"What's the weather like where you are?"

I realized Mo didn't know I was close to her, less than fifty miles down I-95. "I haven't told you where I am."

"I didn't ask that. I asked about the weather."

"Would you believe me if I told you it was snowing?"

"I'll always believe you," Mo said. "Especially after that little lecture you gave me about not keeping secrets."

"It wasn't a lecture."

"Know what?" she said.

"What?"

"I miss you."

"Miss you too. I told you I wanted to come home."

"Maybe soon," she said.

Then silence, the awkward pause two people reach when they've run out of small talk and are reluctant to talk about anything serious.

"Anything I should know about?" I asked.

"Not really. You still reading the net?"

"Yep."

"I miss you," she said.

"You've already said that."

"Well, I do."

"I'm ready to come home. I could be there—" I stopped before I could add, *in less than an hour.*

"It's still not safe," Mo said. "Seymour Topping wants to call you before a Grand Jury."

"I know that," I said, too fast.

"Well, if you're going to be grouchy—"

"Sorry," I said.

"We'll talk again, soon."

"Goodbye."

"Goodbye."

#

I felt guilty about that conversation. I hadn't lied to Mo, but I had misled her. A small sin, maybe, but I knew I couldn't get back to sleep. To kill some time, I decided to retrieve my Miata roadster from the airport parking lot.

First I turned in the rented Taurus, a fine car that got me where I wanted to go in good time. Why do so many people spend so much more for transportation? Prestige? Status? Ego? All three, maybe. My Miata is my only extravagance and an inexpensive one at that, I kept telling myself, but the excuses seemed lame.

Next I walked to the "Park and Ride" lot, waving to the lone toll-booth operator as I passed the gate. He waved back, probably not even wondering even in these days of supposedly rock-tight airport security why I hadn't used the shuttle.

At first, I couldn't find my baby. Up and down the aisles, back and forth, an exercise I could have avoided if I'd recorded the Miata's location. The overhead lights were bright enough, but in my wandering I didn't come across a guard, riding or pedestrian. I turned a corner.

Damn! Something's happened to it. Maybe that's not mine. But it was. My Miata squatted on the asphalt like a toad, its wheels removed, its grace and beauty reduced to that of a junkyard reject. Never mind, I told myself. I can get new wheels. Then I got closer. The wheels were the least of it. Some bastard had cut the canvas top into broad ribbons, torn out the CD and radio, slashed the leather seats, scarred the thick red paint—front to back, side to side, top to bottom—with something rough and sharp, then smashed the headlights into little bits of glass.

Just a thing, I'd said of the little car, but at that moment it seemed the most important thing in the world. This wonderful little machine desecrated in some unholy ritual. Why? The bastards. Am I being punished for my deception of Mo? Absurd, but that was my first thought. No. Human beings did this. Did they set out to steal the wheels and electronics, then decide to trash the rest for the fun of it? Or was someone involved in The Exchange trying to tell me something? Maybe whoever drove the pick-up truck on the bridge. Or someone who worked for the same boss? Who was that? The puzzle spun round and round, leading nowhere.

There were many things I did not know that night, but I was sure of a couple. I would never let myself become attached to any object the way I had the Miata. I wouldn't ever buy another roadster. The Miata was an expression of ego. There's a plain little car in my future.

The second thing: I'm going to have to meet the enemy on his own turf. And I knew how to do that, exactly what I had to do next. I walked to the terminal to catch a taxi.

Chapter Twenty-Six

I slept late the next morning, then took a long run, not caring if anyone recognized me, just as I had never cared what people thought of my silly looking gait when I run. It does the job. Then, after a leisurely breakfast, I made the call—the one I knew I had to make—using my cell phone so my location couldn't be traced, at least not quickly.

"Seymour Topping," I told the woman who answered the phone.

"Who should I say is calling?"

"Gregory Overman."

"The man who—" She stopped. "Just a minute."

It took more than a minute, but eventually Topping got on. "Where are you?"

"That doesn't matter. What should matter to you is where I'm willing to be."

"Where's that?"

"In front of your Grand Jury."

"You'll testify?"

"Nothing to hide," I said, starting to enjoy myself.

"We should talk first," he said. "We need to get an idea about what you're going to testify to."

"Nope. I'll testify, but I won't talk to you or one of your aides first."

A pause. I knew Topping was playing out the chess game in his head, what I'd say if he insisted, what he'd say back, and coming to the conclusion that I couldn't be moved. They could force me to testify to the Grand Jury, but that was that. They couldn't force me to say anything to him or his aides without giving me immunity. And I wasn't going to help his political career any more than I had to.

"Be at the courthouse at eight o'clock tomorrow morning." Topping gave me a floor and room number. "We could provide a police escort if that would help."

"I can find it," I said.

By now I'd guessed he'd motioned to others in his office to listen in on the conversation. We dueled a bit longer, but I didn't budge. Finally, I said "See you tomorrow" and clicked off without saying goodbye.

There. It was done. Now I was on the offensive, and he couldn't hurt me by continuing to leak half-truths, falsehoods and innuendoes. I thought of phoning the newspapers to tell them I'd volunteered to appear, but I didn't want to open myself up to a game of twenty questions with reporters. Someone in the State Attorney's office would take care of it, at least that's what I told myself. I felt great, energy gushing through my body for the first time since I'd left my apartment in Lauderdale. I wished Mo were there to talk with. Talk with. Heck. I wanted to hug her, squeeze her so tight she squirmed, tell her I didn't like being separated, tell her I love her, damn it and please don't ever do this to me again.

#

I worked out in the hotel gym, then settled into my room to write up some notes to myself. I needed to be prepared for whatever questions they might ask, and the way I prepare is to type out rambling, almost stream of consciousness, recollections to myself, asking myself questions and answering them, trying to pin myself down, usually finding a way to escape.

My cell phone rang.

"Mo," I said as I clicked on.

"No such luck," said a male voice.

Duane Saunders, but how did he get my number? "Who's this?"

"I think you know."

"What do you want?"

"I think we should talk," Saunders said.

"We aren't partners anymore," I said.

"I have some information that may be helpful to you."

"You want to help me? Funny." Like Topping wanting to give me an escort.

Saunders persisted: "You hear the information. You decide."

"I'm listening."

"Not over the phone."

I paused, then realized I hadn't asked him an obvious question: "How'd you get my cell number?"

"I read your note to Stephanie Royce. It had your number."

"Who gave it to you?"

"I'll answer that and other questions when I see you," he said, and I could almost see him rubbing that white beard, smiling, to himself as he planted the hook.

What have I got to lose? "Where and when?"

"Two o'clock. The Marine Bar." He gave me an address.

#

I had time to stop by the *Palm Beach Post* first. It was in a squat, block-like building on Dixie, a mausoleum out-of-place in an internet world.

"I want to place a personal ad," I told the clerk behind the counter.

She handed me a form. "Be sure to check the category. Men seeking women, women seeking men, men seeking men— You know."

"None of those," I said. "I want to place a personal ad of general interest."

"Oh. That comes just before the men seeking women." She looked me over. "I wouldn't think you'd have to buy one of these."

Using block letters, I transferred the message I'd written in my head to the form.

WILL THE PERSON WHO HAS THE MATERIAL GATHERED BY CLINTON DRAKE III PLEASE CONTACT ME. REWARD.

I debated whether to add my cell phone number, finally deciding to include it. If half the cops in the county had it, civilians might as well join in. I could get a new number after this was over.

"You want a box number on this?" the woman behind the counter said when I handed her the form. "No extra charge."

"Sure."

"You're box number two-ninety-one"

#

They named the place The Marine Bar, but the only boats for miles around were on trailers in driveways, the bar in a shopping center west of the turnpike. Outside bright sunlight warmed weekday shoppers. Inside darker than dusk. I wouldn't be recognized here. Saunders either. Not that I cared anymore.

Eight television sets, six of them on, shined down from above a U-shaped bar and every corner in the room. Anchors, fish netting and old nautical charts hung on walls between them. I sat in one of the red vinyl booths, waiting for Saunders. A guy who must have weighed two fifty sat alone on one side of the bar, two shot glasses and a half-filled beer mug in front of him, stared up at visions of surfers riding giant waves. Men on the other side of the bar talked among themselves, ignoring both the lush and television. Later, they'd watch basketball. I liked the place. Not a fern in sight.

At exactly two o'clock Saunders walked through the door, blinked a couple of times, found the booth I was sitting at, and sat opposite me. "Not much of a lunch crowd here, but it's popular at night," he said.

I wasn't in a mood for small talk. "How did you get my cell number?"

"Half the cops in the county have seen copies of your note."

"You still pretending to be in law enforcement?"

He rubbed his beard, the gold Rolex barely visible on his arm. "I am."

"If you are, you're running some racket on the side," I said.

He took his time with that, finally saying. "You're an interesting guy, Greg. No telling what you'll say or do next."

"How to you explain all the property you own?"

"What property?"

I told him what I'd turned up in the records search—ownership of big chucks of real estate in the county and an officer in dozens of corporations that managed it. As I went over some of the major items, he relaxed, smiled and nodded. I stopped my recitation. "Well?"

Well, what?"

"How do you explain the corporations and the real estate?"

"I don't have to."

"Someday you might."

"But not here, not in this place and not to you."

No use arguing. "So, why'd you call me?"

"Let's order first." He waved for a waitress. Somebody put money in the juke box. Country western mingled with chatter from television. The waitress, hair dyed red, a too-tight T-shirt and too-tight shorts, cellulite beginning to build on the back of her legs, stood by the table.

"How're the oysters today?" Saunders wanted to know.

"Medium to large," she said.

Saunders ordered a dozen oysters and a draft. I asked for a hamburger and a Coke. The waitress walked away, Saunders watching every step. Then he turned to me. "We're still not partners," he said. "I've never met you and never taken you on any tour."

"That bull again."

"Listen and you might hear something new."

"From you?"

"Example. Topping's calling you before the Grand Jury for the publicity. So far, he hasn't got a case."

"I know that." Or had figured it. "But what's he get out of it?"

"He gets to see headlines saying he's bringing in a suspect."

The waitress brought our food. "These are really more medium," she said as she put the oysters in front of Saunders. The smallest oysters I'd ever seen. The waitress tossed a half-dozen packages of salt crackers on the table. "Let me know if you want more."

I wondered if she'd conned Saunders deliberately. He ignored her.

"Do you know that your buddy Fourquet hates Topping's guts?" Saunders tore cellophane from the crackers with his teeth.

"Who cares if Fourquet doesn't like Topping?"

"You might be able to use it."

"You called me all the way out here to tell me that?"

"There's more if you'll listen."

So I sat there munching on the hamburger, barely touching the fries I hadn't asked for, and listened. According to Saunders, before I left town neither Fourquet nor other professionals working on the case seriously thought I murdered either Clinton Drake or Raymond Siegel. As far as they knew, I had no motive to kill either Drake or Siegel. Now, though, they'd like to talk with me. They were confused by the note I left Stephanie Royce and by Paul Brophy's statement about my asking for a share of whatever operation was going. I'd hurt myself by running.

"How did they know I left?"

"You haven't been sleeping at your apartment. Only Maureen O'Neal is staying there now," Saunders said. "We know that because your cell phone doesn't ring there

I remembered the mysterious calls to my cell phone when I was in the Tampa motel. "That's not proof."

"And, until last night, you weren't registered at any hotel in the county."

"How—?"

"We asked the manager to phone us," he said. "It wasn't smart to check into the same West Palm hotel you used before."

Of course. "But what does it matter?

"If our information is correct," Saunders said, "You've talked to everyone at The Exchange except Stephanie. And you left the note for her."

"You've followed me," I said. "I saw you once. On Old Dixie Highway."

"I know you did." Saunders grinned. "I had to call in a second car to get rid of you."

That's the way I remembered it, too.

"Did you see our chopper?"

I thought back. "Just one making traffic reports."

"That was ours. In fact two of the choppers you see in the air over the interstate are ours. We put radio station call letters on the sides."

"The stations know the helicopters are yours?"

Saunders shook his head. "They deal with an advertising agency and think it's some form of media swap."

I finished my burger and pushed the fries away. The oysters and crackers had disappeared from Saunders' plate. The waitress came to clear the table. "More oysters?" she asked.

"Fool me once, shame on you," Saunders said. "Fool me twice, shame on me."

She laughed, Saunders smiled, old acquaintances who had been through the routine before.

"Why are you telling me all this?"

"We want you to help us."

"Again?"

"Yes," he said. "Because someday you may need us to help you."

Entirely possible, but I'd made a deal with this devil once before, and he deserted me when things got rough. "What do you want this time?"

"Same thing," he said. "Whatever you learn about personal relationships in The Exchange. Who might be a weak link?"

"You haven't mapped that out?" I liked the way that sounded when I said it. I knew more than he did.

"Tell me."

"Nope. You won't get a thing from me until you have something to trade."

"I've given you—"

"You've given me garbage," I said.

"But—"

"I'll give you this," I said.

Saunders waited, expectation showing on his face.

"I wouldn't believe a word Paul Brophy says,"

He didn't let his disappointment show. "What else?"

"That's it."

Saunders breathed in, then exhaled slowly, the first sign of discouragement or fatigue I'd seen in the man since our initial encounter. "OK.

I'll level." Just the thought of it hurt him. His lips clamped together, he twisted his head toward the bar, rubbed a forefinger across his upper lip. "We're closing the operation down. We can't find a shred of evidence to indict Brophy or anyone else at The Exchange."

"Impossible," I said. "Surely all that money Stephanie Ross flushes through day care accounts can be traced in banks. Same for the money Salli's runs through its stores. Send some auditors in, or subpoena the accounts."

"We've done all that," Saunders said. "We know where every dime goes, but that doesn't help us. The chain of evidence always breaks."

"Impossible," I said, knowing I was repeating myself. "Money has to go somewhere."

"At some point in the chain the money evaporates. If it shows up again, it's far from where it started."

That stopped me. If what he said was true, there wasn't any point—any illegal activity, that is—in the whole Exchange. Nothing made any sense. I tried another tack. "You said you wanted me to help you, but now you've said you're shutting down. Which is it?"

"Both. IRS is taking its agents back and DEA says I have to get on to another assignment. What I'm asking you is personal."

"Unofficial."

"Yes."

"So it's you, not 'us' who wants help?"

"Yes."

I liked Saunders, and at that moment I understood why. He wasn't just some bureaucrat following orders. He wouldn't quit just because they told him to. There was still no reason to trust him, though, so I said I'd think about it.

"Take this number." Saunders handed me a card. "It's my home phone."

I took the card. One line of cursive writing, nothing else. I stood up.

"You can get the check," I said, looking down at him. "And you won't get even a morsel more from me until you stop staking out our apartment." I turned and walked out of the bar into sunlight.

Fool me once, you don't get a second chance.

#

Maureen phoned late that afternoon. "I've got a feeling. Something's about to happen."

"What?"

I could almost see Mo shake her head. "Are you all right?"

"Sure."

"You're not where you were before," she said.

That was true, but she couldn't know that. She was guessing, following a feeling. "Where did you think I was?"

"We agreed we wouldn't— Oh. Now you don't care if anyone finds you."

"Another guess."

Her tone of voice turned harsh, defensive. "Based on a very strong feeling."

"Your intuition strikes again."

She was silent, then: "Go, I don't like you when you're like this."

"You're the one who exiled me."

"But you've started enjoying it."

I didn't say anything to that, because now that I was near her, I had indeed started enjoying life again. Napoleon returns from Elba, I thought, then remembered his fate. Scratch that.

"I don't like this," she said.

"That I'm happy."

"You know that's not true."

This was the point I should have stopped kidding around. But I didn't. "What then?"

"You're just so—" A pause. "I don't see the point on talking as long as you're like this."

"I'm not 'like this,' " I said.

"Goodbye," Mo said. "I don't know what's going on, but I don't like it."

I waited to hear a click or something, but nothing came over the air waves. "Goodbye," I said.

"Nothing good will come of this." Mo hung up.

My line, I thought. She's stealing my lines.

#

There was some truth in what Mo said. I'd begun to enjoy the game, the secrecy, the hide-a-seek, cops-and-robbers aspect of the last few days. Or maybe part of my mind was striking out at her kicking me out, even though I know it was for my own good. Wait until she picks up the morning papers.

CHILD THERAPIST
VOLUNTEERS TESTIMONY
TO COUNTY GRAND JURY

That was the way I envisioned the headline. It might take some work to get the lines to come out even, but headline writers could fix that. The main thing is I'm on the offensive against Topping and the whole bunch of them. I'm not hiding any more.

When I left the hotel for dinner, I noticed two deputies sitting in the lobby. I walked over to them.

"I'm going to Howley's," I said. "Want to join me or tail me?"

"They told us you were a smart ass," one of them said.

"Know why they don't send donkeys to college," said the other.

"I've heard it," I said.

That didn't stop him. "Because nobody likes a smart ass."

"Nobody likes dumb ones, either." I said, turned and walked out.

That wasn't like me at all, I thought when I got outside. But it felt so good. The deputies followed me but sat in their car in the parking lot outside Howley's while I ate. Later I saw, or thought I saw, a black Ford pickup park near them. But when I left Howley's, it was gone. The deputies escorted me back to the hotel. They were alone. Not a Ford pick-up in sight. Best I could see, anyway.

#

A few hours later, I was getting ready to go to bed when the cell phone rang.

"Mo," I said, an automatic response.

"No. This is Ginny."

Briefly I thought of asking how she got my number, but then remembered what the Santa with a Rolex told me: Almost everyone in law enforcement had my number.

"Gemini, I've heard," I said to Ginny.

"I'm trying to live that down."

I waited, figuring she knew what she called about. I sure didn't. She asked if I was all right, told me how much she appreciated everything Maureen and I were doing for her, where I was ("Can't tell you," I said) and then she got down to it.

"Are you really going to testify?"

"Of course," I said.

"What are you going to tell them?"

"Everything."

"That might not be wise."

"Why?" I said, starting to pay attention.

"Everything you say can be used against you. One tiny mistake and they can get you on perjury charges."

Can they? I wondered. She's a lawyer, a assistant state attorney, albeit a suspended one. She should know.

"And they can use whatever you say against Maureen."

"She hasn't done anything," I said. "Neither have I."

"You wrote the note," she said. "Could be construed as blackmail."

Maybe, I conceded in my mind, but I didn't like the way this conversation was going. Why was she telling me all this? What was her motive?

"And if anyone told you to write the note the cops have, you could get them in a lot of trouble, too."

Mo suggested I write it. Would I tell the Grand Jury that? Or would I lie? And if I started lying, where would I draw the line?

"Extortion is the legal term," Ginny said, not making me feel any better.

We talked some more, Ginny asking questions and me mostly evading them for reasons I didn't fully understand at the time. Finally, she gave up and I knew she was about to sign off.

"By the way," I said. "Where did you get my cell number?"

"Maureen gave it to me," she said.

So Mo really trusted her. Did that mean I could, too?

Chapter Twenty-Seven

That night I dreamed of sitting in a big pot of boiling water, the kind you see in cartoons of cannibals preparing their victim for a feast. Seymour Topping, pot belly extending over his loin cloth, was chief cook. Duane Saunders, Lt. Detective Louis Fourquet, Gemini and Mo, yes, Mo, stood on each side, all ready to quarter and devour me.

I woke up sweating, got out of bed, turned down the air conditioning, and crawled under the covers again. Couldn't get back to sleep, though. Finally I gave up, did a few exercises in my room, showered and went to the lobby to relish the headlines I knew would be there. Now they'd be in my favor, all about my volunteering testify.

Wrong. Not one letter of the bold print matched my fantasy. The biggest type, in the *Palm Beach Post*, said:

CHILDREN'S THERAPIST THREATENED THEM,
'EXCHANGE' MEMBERS TO TELL GRAND JURY

Below ran a rehash of Brophy and Stephanie Royce's accusations with fresh quotes from Topping. Near the bottom the ever-present, omniscient "sources" said Greg Overman might appear before the jury also, but officials were privately skeptical.

Headlines and stories in the other papers were much the same. Each said I'd been unavailable for comment, and all carried the same photograph of Stephanie. The photo, a studio portrait, made her look sexy but trustworthy, young but somehow mature too, very pretty and very sophisticated, no trace of the pout I'd seen her carrying around at The Exchange. One paper's credit line said the picture came from an unnamed "business associate" of Stephanie's. Paul Brophy, for sure.

OK. Round One to you Topping. But the fight's just beginning.

#

I had to do some fast thinking riding in a taxi on the way to the courthouse, and the sight of two deputies in a green and white car behind me helped. The day before I'd resolved to tell the Grand Jury everything. A lot of good that did me. The newspapers ignored my volunteering (maybe because they didn't know about it, I admitted) and Ginny warned me I could inadvertently hurt Mo. So I had to decide: Tell the Grand Jury everything or refuse to answer any questions. I hadn't talked with an attorney, but I thought I knew the law. Once I began answering questions, I couldn't hold back. I'd started down this path, volunteering to testify, to confront Topping and clear my name. But what assurance did I have I'd get that result? Back and forth my mind argued with itself, an internal tennis match. What if I decided not to talk? What harm would that do? And what good would come from cooperating?

At the courthouse, a uniformed deputy steered me to a small, stark room that looked as if it usually held prisoners. No windows. No reading matter. Only a wood bench. I settled in for a long wait. Be there at eight o'clock, Topping had said, but from the papers I knew Stephanie Royce and possibly others would testify before me.

As the morning wore on, I missed Maureen more and more. Maybe it was a mistake to keep my return to West Palm a secret from her. Maybe I should phone her now. No, stick it out until after I testify, then call her, another message from my mind said. My psyche, so much an ally in the here and now, started projecting the future, always a dangerous exercise. Newspaper headlines formed in my head, the black letters flipping to form new accusations.

DAY SCHOOL EXECUTIVE
SAYS MURDER SUSPECT

PROPOSED MONEY SCHEME
Another:
OVERMAN SUGGESTED
LAUNDERING SCHEME
WOMAN TESTIFIES
And this one, so unprofessional I knew no newspaper would use it:
USE KIDDIE FUNDS
TO WASH DRUG DOUGH
SUSPECT TOLD HER

By then I'd already imagined a story to go with the headlines. Stephanie Royce, president of the Greater Palm Beach Area Day Care Association, has given a sworn statement to State Attorney Seymour Topping alleging children's therapist Gregory Overman suggested she use collections from day care centers to help launder drug money, it would say.

I saw Brophy's hand in this. He was the only person in the world who would have allowed, even encouraged, Stephanie to fabricate such a story and swear to it. She must have known there were big risks. Perjury is a serious offense; she could go to jail. But Brophy could make a prison term sound like an absurd possibility. Or maybe he made Stephanie think jail was a greater possibility if she didn't go along. He could be persuasive.

"Are you all right?" A male voice, above me.

I looked up and saw the bailiff standing over me, his hand shaking my shoulder. "I'm OK."

"You looked like you were in another world," he said. "Don't bug out on me now."

"Not likely," I said.

He stayed in the room, so we got to talking. He told me news photographers and television cameramen had taken pictures of Stephanie Royce as she came through the lobby, the lady slowing down and standing for several moments at the elevator door to oblige them.

"Paul Brophy with her?"

He shook his head. "She's the only witness before you, as far as I know.."

When the bailiff left. I began thinking of Maureen. I could drive to Lauderdale tonight and surprise her. Our first night together in almost two weeks. I felt a sense of peace then, the fantasies curbed. I'll follow my instincts on this one, and everything will work out as it is supposed to.

It was then that I decided against testifying. I'd volunteered to appear before the Grand Jury to confront Topping and set the record straight. But Ginny's phone call and the imagined headlines changed things. If I told the truth, I might put Mo in the way Taylor's wrath. If I didn't, I might get in trouble. There was only one course I could take.

#

An hour later, maybe more, the bailiff was back. "You're up."

I followed him down the hallway and into the Grand Jury room. From that point on, many details of what happened did not stay in my consciousness long enough to recall later. I don't remember the appearance of the room, what members of the jury looked like whether the court reporter was male or female, or even what color suit Topping wore. All I recall, and I remember every detail of this, was the duel, Topping and me twenty feet apart at first, then him edging closer and closer.

A bailiff swore me to tell the truth and nothing but the truth so help me God and told me to sit down. Then:

"State your name," Topping said.

"Gregory Overman."

"What is your address?"

"I am a resident of Palm Beach County."

"What is your occupation?"

"I'm a therapist, specializing in children and adolescents."

"Who do you work for?"

"I am in private practice.

"Do you know a resident of Palm Beach County named Stephanie Royce?"

Under the law, I could give my name, address and occupation without opening doors that would allow Topping to question me about other matters. But I could not go any further. If I answered any other questions, I could be required to answer any reasonable follow ups. That was my understanding.

"I decline to answer under protection of rights guaranteed me by the First, Fourth, Fifth and Fourteenth amendments to the U.S. Constitution," I said.

"Did you know a resident of Palm Beach County named Clinton Drake III?"

"I decline to answer under protection of rights guaranteed to me by the First, Fourth, Fifth and Fourteenth amendments to the U.S. Constitution." This isn't so bad, I thought.

"Did you know a resident of Palm Beach County named Raymond Siegel?"

"I decline to answer under protection of rights guaranteed me by the First, Fourth, Fifth and Fourteenth amendments to the U.S. Constitution." Easy in fact.

"Is it your intention to answer all questions put to you in this same manner?"

"I decline to answer under protection of rights guaranteed me by the First, Fourth, Fifth and Fourteenth amendments to the U.S. Constitution." Fuck 'em.

Topping had a problem. He would delight in badgering me, requiring me to invoke Fifth Amendment and other protections over and over to dozens, even hundreds of questions. But a court reporter was taking all this down, and the transcript might someday be reviewed by a judge or a panel of judges. Harassing a Grand Jury witness is prohibited conduct, and Topping did not want to be criticized for this at some future date. He would be Candidate Seymour Topping then, or even Congressman Topping seeking reelection.

Topping turned to the jurors. "Does any member of the Grand Jury have any question to ask this witness?"

"Yeah," said one. "I know what the Fifth amendment is, but what are those others?"

"Does the witness want to explain?" Topping looked at me.

No way. No way I would fall into that trap. "I decline to answer under protection of rights guaranteed me by the First, Fourth, Fifth and Fourteenth amendments to the U.S. Constitution."

So Topping had to explain the First, Fourth, Fifth, and Fourteenth amendments to the jurors, just as I intended.

"The First Amendment protects freedom of religion, speech, the press, and the rights of assembly and petition," Topping told the juror. "The Fourth Amendment protects people against unreasonable searches or arrests. The Fifth Amendment provides that no one can be forced to stand trial for a crime punishable by death without being indicted by a Grand Jury—a jury such as the one on which you are sitting."

Topping paused, letting the jurors understand their importance.

"The Fifth Amendment also provides that no one can be tried twice for the same crime, unless there are special circumstances. It also provides that no one can be deprived of life, liberty or property without due process of law." Topping stopped again, seeming to think. "That's a very important but complex requirement. The Fourteenth Amendment extends due process protection to actions by individual states."

"What's it mean to 'take the Fifth?'" asked another juror.

Topping let the ends of his mouth turn upward, almost like a yellow happy face, then looked my way. He'd been fishing for the question, so he could answer it his way. "The Fifth Amendment also provides that no person may be required to testify against himself. And under the law, a witness who invokes a Fifth Amendment right against self-incrimination is not required to explain the nature of that potential incrimination or the possible connection of it to any other rights protected by the Constitution."

Topping looked at the jurors, turning his head slowly to form eye contact with each one individually, trying to see what impact he'd made. None. He made it stronger. "So the Fifth Amendment protects a person against self-incrimination. We have the right to compel testimony from a witness in exchange for immunity from prosecution." He stopped, stretching out the pause to make what he said next seem very important. "At this time, we have no plans to grant immunity to Mr. Overman."

Much as I disliked Topping, I had to admire the performance. He'd done everything but wink. This fellow's guilty, he was telling the jurors and all of us here know it, but we have this problem with the constitution and we'll get to the truth about this guy without his help. A person reading the transcript without being present would see nothing amiss.

Topping asked the jurors if they had any more questions. They looked at one another but said nothing. "You can leave now, Mr. Overman, but do not leave the area again," Topping said.

I started to stand.

"Remember," he said. "You are still under subpoena and can be recalled at any time."

Wrong. Nobody subpoenaed me. I volunteered. I wanted to tell this to the jury but didn't know whether that would open me up to more questions. Topping's statement was gratuitous and mean-spirited. I could travel anywhere; the state had the responsibility to give me adequate notice of any reappearance before the Grand Jury. But I let it go. Nothing Topping said could shake me from my one sentence answers.

I left the Grand Jury room feeling relieved, although looking back I don't know why. I walked down the hall, turned a corner and saw a stairway. I'll walk down and avoid reporters, I decided. Things are bad enough without those hyenas.

#

At the bottom of the stairway, I pushed through a door and stepped into the lobby. One second, two seconds, three went by, suspended in time as I took in the scene. Three or four guys with television cameras, more still photographers than I could count, a mess of microphones, and about a dozen reporters crowded around the door, waiting for their prey—me—to emerge. I'd put myself squarely in the middle of a lion's den.

A woman reporter, her perfect make-up unable to hide a gleeful "gotcha" expression as she in closed for the kill, stuck a microphone in my face. "What did you tell the Grand Jury?" I turned away, to the right.

A man, a kid really, pimples still on his face, thrust his mike from that direction. "Is it true you took the Fifth?" Two minutes out of the Grand Jury room, that sacred place where all concerned were sworn to secrecy about what transpired, and already Topping or one of his aides has leaked the news.

I plunged ahead, colliding with a reporter who pushed a business card into my hand. "Call me at the office so we can talk." Her loose red blouse and black slacks signaled danger as clearly in this courthouse lobby as in a bullring.

I turned to the left and bumped into another television reporter. "Just give us one comment," he said. Reflexes now fully engaged, I lunged the other way and into the side of a bearded guy carrying a mike on a long aluminum pole, a black box on his back. "Watch it. This is expensive stuff."

He turned one way, and I spun the other. The short end of the pole hit my eye. "God damn it," I shouted, the pain so sharp I couldn't think. I grabbed the air, looking for something to catch my fall. My hand caught the business reporter's blouse. She pulled back, and the blouse tore down the front. She shrieked. A male reporter pushed me away. Still cameras flashed and television lenses zoomed in for close-ups. My right hand held the piece of red cloth tighter. My left flailed the air, reaching for support. It hit a television camera, sending it twirling. I fell to the floor.

Desperately I got up, put my head down and began running. Behind me, the pack took up the chase. I pushed through the courthouse doors and ran toward the street. There, at the curb, a light blue Toyota Camry, illegally parked on Dixie. No it couldn't be, can't be. But it was. I knew the car. I leaned down and looked in the window.

A red-headed angel wearing jeans and a pink T-shirt sat behind the steering wheel. The closing stanza's of Beethoven's Ninth thundered all around. From on high? The car? Somewhere inside me? Doesn't matter.

"Well," Mo said. "Don't just stand there. Get in."

Riding down Okeechobee Boulevard, Maureen still driving, me in the passenger seat, I imagined myself being transported by a magic carpet surrounded by a supernatural world—CityPlace, in reality something that might be found at Disney World, transformed into the set for this fairy tale, the two larger than life black elephants on the left seeming real, the Performing Arts Center straight ahead something the Wizard of Oz might build, Mo the Good Witch arriving in a huge bubble disguised as a Toyota Camry.

I didn't and don't believe in miracles, though, so I figured my first job was to beam down to reality. When Mo pulled onto I-95, I asked, "How did you know I'd be there? In front of the courthouse."

"I read the papers and put two and two together," she said.

"Must have been more than that."

"I know you," she said. "I knew what could happen. That's all I needed."

We drove a few more miles before I said, "You're claiming feminine intuition?"

"If I want," she said.

"But it was really—?"

She didn't answer.

We were at the Lake Worth power plant when I said. "OK. Give it to me. I know you have a lot to say."

"Not necessarily," Mo said in a way that let me know she was holding back truckloads of garbage, just waiting for the right time.

A foolish thought crossed my mind, its distracting appeal so strong I didn't hold it. "Thanks for rescuing me."

"This is the Twenty-first Century, Greg. Now damsels have to rescue their fair-haired knights." She looked over in a way that I knew she was fighting an impulse to break out laughing. "It gets tiring at times, but sometimes it's worth it."

So I shut up, not saying a single word all the way though Boynton Beach, Boca Raton, Pompano and the rest, all the way down Broward Boulevard, over to Las Olas, left on the Isle of Venice until we stopped in front of our apartment.

"Come upstairs," she said.

Now. I knew I was in for it.

#

Maureen carried two bottles of water from the fridge, handed me one, sat on the sofa and patted the cushion beside her. She downed half her bottle, then turned. "Do I have to tell you to kiss me again?"

I put my arms around her and gave her a gentle kiss. We stayed that way for a while, our bodies together, her head on my shoulder.

"I missed you," Mo said.

"You banished me."

"You're such an idiot."

"I missed you, too," I said.

"I knew they were going to come after you. There was no time to explain. You'd just argue," She looked at me intensely. "So I kicked you out. For your own good."

As if I hadn't figure that out, I started to say, but that was not strictly true. It was only when she started the sentence, "I knew they were going to come after you," that the whole thing—her insight, her thinking, her quick action—came to me. I wasn't going to lie to her but I certainly wasn't going to tell her the truth.

"You want me to thank you, or something?" I said.

She reached up, placed her hands behind my head, pulled me to her, and said,. "Do I have to tell you to kiss me?"

Chapter Twenty-Eight

On one wall of the living room, not far from the sofa, hung a framed poster, a duplicate of one Mo had given me years ago, one that's haunted me ever since. Printed on stark parchment paper, it's a quotation from Mohandas Gandhi in bold black type superimposed over a burnt-orange line drawing of Gandhi's face. The withered old man, squinting from behind his owl-like glasses, stares directly at you no matter where you sit in the room.

It's the action,
not the fruit of the action,
that is important.
You have to do the right thing.

And what the heck is the "right thing," great teacher, in this day-to-day world, so full of grays, no simple black and whites, where you have to slosh through whatever the world tosses at you, barely knowing minute to minute what to do next?

It may not be in your power,
may not be in your time,
that there will be any fruit.
But that doesn't mean you stop doing the right thing.

You make it sound so easy, Gandhi. It's not so simple, fellow, not at all.

You may never know what results come from your action.
But if you do nothing, there will be no result.

Maureen and I have made love under the poster before, and usually
I could ignore it. But that day it bothered me. I didn't know why at the
time. My mind kept paraphrasing the last line as, "If you do nothing,
you know damn well there will be no result."

#

Maureen showed how much our reunion meant to her by insisting
we celebrate with a very late lunch at the Café de Paris, one of the best
restaurants on Las Olas. Or in Lauderdale for that matter. I couldn't
remember ever being there together on a weekday afternoon. Usually
Mo reserves mid-day meals for business.

It was a special treat for me. I ate at so many diners I'd almost
forgotten that you could dine before dusk at a place with white table-
cloths, good china, modestly expensive silver, and napkins folded into
pyramids. The red, white and blue awning out front was another nice
touch, a reminder that there was a time that France helped this country,
that we weren't mad at them about anything, and that time would come
again.

Mo ordered a Cobb salad, I picked broiled flounder, and I thought
we wouldn't talk about anything serious.

When the waiter left Mo reached over, took my hands in hers and
looked steadily into my eyes. "I don't like secrecy," she said.

"Me neither," I said, but a warning flag went off inside my head.

"I'll stop if you stop."

"OK," I said, no idea what she was talking about.

"Even if it means breaking a confidence?"

I was even more confused now. I knew to shut up and listen.

"I shouldn't have kicked you out without explaining."

"We've put that behind us."

"Ginny phoned me yesterday and told me something." Mo reached
for the bread basket but withdrew her hand without taking a roll. "In
confidence."

"Out with it," I said.

"I've already told Ginny our deal was off. My agreement to help her in every way I could."

I took a piece of the bread. Soft, light centers and hard crusts are a seductive combination. "What did she say?"

"She didn't seem to mind." Mo reached over and took my hands in hers again. I knew she wouldn't tell me whatever she wanted to say until she was ready. That was what the hand holding was about.

We sat in silence. "Well?" Mo said.

"What?"

"Do you want to hear about Ginny or not?"

"Of course."

"Ginny has never been a real suspect in Clinton Drake's murder. She was at The Exchange in an official, investigative capacity. As an assistant state attorney."

"So?"

"She went there with Seymour Topping's explicit approval," Mo said. "He also authorized her to carry a gun."

"But he suspended her."

"All for show. We and everyone else were taken in by an elaborate charade."

"Why?"

Mo released my hand and picked up a roll. "Your buddy Duane Saunders wasn't getting anywhere with his investigation," Mo said, breaking off half a slice of bread. "They needed someone who wouldn't be suspected by the people running the Exchange. Ginny, a single parent with a child, fit right in."

"So when I thought she was networking, she was really investigating?"

"Right."

The waiter brought our food and asked if we wanted anything else. Mo asked for more water, I ordered a second cup of coffee. Meanwhile I let my mind play with the idea of Ginny as an undercover sleuth. I couldn't find anything wrong with it. She'd been quiet, absorbed in her thoughts, when we drove to Palm Beach to attend that crazy event. I thought she was nervous about seeing her ex again. Instead she was thinking of the investigation.

We kicked the idea back and forth for almost an hour, and of course I asked why she hadn't told me about it earlier. Couldn't, she said. I didn't know where you were. Not my fault. So, by implication, it had become my fault.

"Dessert?" the waiter asked.

"No," Mo said automatically.

"We'll split a piece of cheese cake," I said. "Two forks."

Mo nodded approval, then to me: "Aren't you forgetting something."

"What?"

"I've pledged not to keep secrets from you." Mo said. "All you've done is order dessert."

"You want me to—"

"Of course."

"No more secrets," I said. "Never again."

"No more riding around the state without telling me?"

"No."

"No more volunteering to testify to a Grand Jury without telling me?"

I didn't like this interrogation, so I tried to turn things around. "How did you know to park outside the Courthouse?"

"I read in the newspapers you might testify. I figured that meant you'd volunteered." Mo smiled, barely showing her teeth like she always did when she felt proud of herself. "I knew they'd keep you there for a while. And I knew they'd sic the media on you."

"How did you know I couldn't handle it by myself?"

"I know you, Go." That smile again. "Handling excitable people isn't your strong suit."

Check. "Still, you had to make a lot of assumptions."

"I was upset," she said. "It was very clear what was going to happen."

"That doesn't make sense."

"I like to work when I'm upset. It inhibits rational thought."

"Figuring I'd be coming out of the courthouse, at that entrance, at that time of day was a million in one shot." I said.

"If I worried about odds, I'd never get anything done."

Checkmate. I wondered what Freud knew about feminine intuition and what he thought about it if. He probably didn't have a clue. If he understood it, he might have figured out what women want.

#

Mo had to get back to her office, so I didn't see her again until later that night. I phoned clients rescheduling as many of my missed appointments as I could. Then I spent the evening on the net, reading and re-reading all the stories I could find about the murders of Clinton Drake and Raymond Siegel. In the morning the stories in the papers would be all about my Grand Jury appearance.

The gun that killed Raymond Siegel was a .22 caliber similar to but not identical to the one that killed Clinton Drake, police said. They hadn't found it. A sweep of roadsides near the Brophy's home produced zip. Divers searched the bottom of Lake Worth near the house with the same result. Police hadn't said the same person killed Drake and Siegel, but acknowledged they were pursuing the possibility. The newspaper accounts read as if there was no doubt about this. What other explanation could there be?

I wasn't so sure. Clinton was an outsider. The Exchange group considered him "a snoop"—Sally Brophy's words. Siegel was an insider, maybe the one who masterminded whatever was going on. Who would want to kill one insider, one outsider,?

Police were questioning the man who found Siegel's body. Also other "acquaintances." Who could they be? I'd like to talk with Lt. Detective Louis Fourquet, but we got off onto such a bad start I know he wouldn't give me five minutes. Maybe Mo would have some ideas.

#

When Mo got home we watched the 10 and 11 o'clock local news shows together, flipping from channel to channel to see every second of my splendid adventure in the courthouse lobby. In all of them, I looked like a wild beast, a fearsome creature who attacked women and cameras without provocation.

The commentary was worse. "After repeatedly taking the Fifth Amendment before a Grand Jury investigating the deaths of a prominent banker and former news reporter, children's therapist Gregory Overman went berserk when reporters approached him in the courthouse lobby this morning. Watch." A video tape of the encounter followed, the sound of the reporters' questions muted at the beginning, then turning into shouts as I bumped into one of them, then another, hit the mike boom, tore the reporter's blouse and fell to the floor clutching the piece of red cloth like a trophy.

"Nice blouse," Mo said.

Silk? I wondered. Soft smooth cloth all feels the same to me.

"Good pictures," Mo added, her sarcasm forcing me back to the subject at hand.

None of the cameras had an unobstructed view of the entire episode, the fuzzy, blocked pictures between clear shots fueling the feeling of frenzied chaos. But when I fell down, the camera men and women circled around me, zooming in for close-ups of the lunatic on the floor clutching an innocent woman's blouse. Yeah, good pictures, good enough to make national news shows in the morning.

Finally Mo clicked off. She sat silently, saying nothing.

"What do you think?" I asked, too impatient to wait her out.

"I suppose it could be have been worse," Mo said. "Although offhand I can't see how."

I decided to take the offensive. "Little did I know when I agreed to take your friend to a party, that I'd be a television star."

"Touché," she said. "Now that we've got that out of the way, let's figure out what to do next."

"How?"

"First tell me everything you've done since we parted."

I told her about the bogus trail I'd left, the trip across the state, my routine in Tampa, even buying the beers and throwing them away, talking to Saunders at the Marine Bar when I got back, placing the personal ad in the newspaper and my Grand Jury appearance.

"Now," Mo said, "We've got to reexamine everything from the beginning. Go back to Sunday afternoon when you picked up Ginny."

So I went through the events in chronological order, putting in every detail, even the unimportant ones, the drive to Palm Beach with Ginny, our disagreement about whether divorces could be friendly, meeting Sally and Paul Brophy, watching the people and hearing the sexual by-play, the fireworks beginning, Sally rushing from the house yelling for Paul, our running to the pool and discovering—

"Stop," Mo said. "Go back."

"Where?"

"The fireworks."

I began that part of the story again, even sticking in my thought that all fireworks look alike, then becoming as fascinated as the rest, all of us looking upward—

Mo interrupted. "So anybody could have left the dock area without being noticed?"

"Yep. That's why no one is eliminated as a suspect."

"But we know for sure that one person left."

"Who?"

"Sally," Mo said. "She says she found the body and then came running for help. What if Sally killed Clinton first, then made a big to-do about yelling for Paul and everyone else to come look."

"Why would Sally want to kill either Clinton Drake or Raymond Siegel?"

"I don't know, and I don't have to know now," Mo said. "The fact is she had an opportunity to kill Clinton Drake."

No argument from me.

"And for all we know," she said, "Raymond Siegel, too."

"Maybe. But ha no more a suspect than the others."

"What are the police saying?" Mo said. "The same person killed Clinton and the banker?"

"They think it's a good possibility but aren't sure. They say the gun that killed Siegel is similar to but not identical to the one that killed Clinton."

"What's that mean?"

"Probably the same manufacturer, the same gun model but not the same gun."

Mo raised her voice. "Of course not. Police have the gun that killed Clinton."

"I could try to find out more from Saunders about other evidence."

"Forget it," Mo said. "This isn't some cheap detective novel. This is real life, Greg."

I laughed. It's one of Mo's favorite lines, right out of E.T. The Extra-Terrestrial. Remember? Elliott and a friend are helping E.T. escape. He explains to a friend on a bicycle, "He's a man from outer space and we're taking him to his space ship.: The other kid says, "Well, can't he just beam up?" Then Elliott corrects him, "This is reality, Greg!" A great inside, inside joke.

"These people aren't suspects," Mo said. "These are real people. Understand them and we not only know who killed Clinton and Raymond, we understand why."

"You're telling me?" I said. "A bigger question: Why do we care, now that your friend's off the hook?"

"Because of you, you idiot," Mo says. "You're not off the hook."

"I know I'm innocent. You know I'm innocent. What more do we need?"

Mo didn't say anything to that. Instead she eased from her end of the sofa to mine and gave me a little kiss. "For a smart man, you're pretty dense at times."

I could see where this was going, so I said: "Before we forget, we should visit Sally again."

"Not me," she said. "You. In the future we do everything differently. We'll split up when we visit people we've already talked to together. We go together when we see people you interviewed individually."

"Why?"

"Because what we've been doing hasn't worked," she said.

"Except one thing," I said, putting my arms around her.

#

The next morning we were both dressed and headed for the door when I remembered. "I don't have a car."

Mo said, "Think you can learn to drive a Toyota?"

I almost never answer smart-ass questions like that, but this time I said, "When I have the keys."

She dug in her pocket book and held them out. "Drop me at work. I won't need it until late this afternoon."

So that's what I did. When I pulled up to the place she worked, once a mansion owned by a man named Pettigrew, she leaned over, kissed me and said, "Don't park it at an airport."

"Not unless I have to," I said.

On the way to West Palm I phoned Salli's Inc. and told the receptionist I had something very important I needed to talk about with Sally Brophy. "She's booked solid all day," she said.

"Tell her it's a matter of life and death—and the police."

"I'll tell her, but I don't think—"

"Just tell her," I said.

Chapter Twenty-Nine

F ort Lauderdale and West Palm Beach are less than an hour apart on the interstate but an eon distant in attitude, style and purpose, the differences stemming partly from their origins. Lauderdale started as a small military encampment and Indian trading village on what was then no more than a creek, and by late in the last century had risen no further than a place where the boys and girls were, its wide, sandy beaches defining its national image. West Palm began as the place where maids, butlers and others lived to serve the wants of the grossly rich who lived in the Town of Palm Beach, and for decades no one would live in West Palm if they could afford Palm Beach.

When Henry Flagler built his railroad down Florida's East Coast (with considerable financial assistance from the U.S. Government), he pushed it south from Jacksonville to St. Augustine, built a hotel there, did the same in Daytona Beach and Palm Beach, then straight through to Miami, not bothering to build a hotel in Lauderdale on the sensible view that it lacked the broad expanse of water found at Biscayne Bay or the high waterfront elevations offered in parts of Palm Beach. As a result, West Palm was stunted for years by the allure of Palm Beach, and Lauderdale was thought of as a suburb of Miami. By the Millennium, though, each city had outgrown its origins. Miami became the Capital of Latin America, West Palm had become an urban city on its own, and Lauderdale had become place where corporate executives, professionals and others could live on canals halfway between downtown and the beach with a five-minute commute to work or play. Retirement communities still linked all three areas, but they were becoming less and less important, the traffic and urban sprawl making the area a less desirable place to spend supposedly Golden Years. Unless, of course, these same oldsters liked professional football, basketball, baseball, and hockey, or symphony orchestras, operas, ballet, and equity theater.

I thought about these things as I drove north on I-95 through Boca Raton, not wanting to think about the program Mo had in store for us later in the day. She said we were going to do some things together. Interview the people she still considered suspects? If so, who? I'd tackled Marilyn and Cindy by myself, so now it's her turn to visit them. Who else? She could have Brophy and Saunders, too. She can have them all.

Alarmed at my bitterness, I let my mind rattle about again. Why is Boca considered the gem of the Gold Coast? Because its development started so late? After all, until World War II, it was merely a crossroads with gas stations on the corners. If someone asked me where to live in South Florida worry-free, I'd pick one of two little towns not on anybody's favorites list—Briny Breezes, the quaint collection of mobile homes just across A1A from the Atlantic, or Lauderdale-by-the-Sea, a little community on the same ocean that bans buildings over three stories tall.

I can't imagine anyone taking themselves too seriously in either one.

#

When I arrived at Sally's office, the receptionist waved me by, a mixture of annoyance, anger and awe on her face. "Ten minutes. She has only ten minutes."

Sally met me at the doorway. "What's this about?"

"Let's sit down," I said and took one of the Queen Anne chairs.

"What's this about?" she said again when she sat behind her desk.

"We don't think you've told us the whole story," I said.

"Who's we?"

"Maureen O'Neal and I."

"Ginny's friend. And your friend."

I nodded.

"Why?" Sally said. "Don't you accept what I've told you."

"Not entirely, because one of two things is true. Either you didn't tell us everything you saw at the swimming pool the night Clinton Drake was murdered, or—" I let the half-through hang there for a for a few beats. "Or you killed Clinton Drake."

"Absurd," Sally said.

"The way things stand now, you were the last to see Clinton Drake. You could have been the last person to see him alive."

"I didn't—."

"You left the dock and the fireworks and went back to the house," I said. Why?"

"A call of nature."

"If you didn't kill Clinton Drake, you had to have seen the murderer coming or going."

Sally turned and studied the county map with its magenta stars. Then she looked the other way, at paintings of the racing sailboats. Finally, back at me. "The police asked me that too. I told them I hadn't seen anyone."

"But you did," I insisted.

Again she looked at the magenta stars that meant so much to her, the symbols of her success. A very personal, individual achievement, I figured. Paul hadn't been much help.

"I've remembered something—" She wrinkled her forehead and pursed her lips.

I kept my mouth shut.

"I've decided to tell the police about it, so you might as well know, too."

"What?"

"When I went up the house, I saw Raymond Siegel in the side yard talking with someone."

"Who?"

"It was dark over there and they were almost surrounded by shrubbery. Paul and I have never thought we needed security lights anywhere but the dock."

"Man or woman?"

"Man," Sally said. "I'm sure of that."

"If you had to guess, what man at the party did he look the most alike?"

She stood. "I don't want to guess."

I got up, knowing our interview was almost over. "For Ginny's sake. For justice sake. For your sake. Who?"

"All right," she said. "Of all the men at the party he looked the most like Duane Saunders."

Duane again, her favorite suspect.

"Now I really have to ask you to leave," she said. "The police will be here soon."

"Police?"

"My secretary phoned them after you arrived. I might as well make a clean breast of this."

I started to walk to the door. Then a thought hit me, and so I turned around. "You tell Paul this?"

She shook her head. "A girl has to look out for herself first."

#

I phoned Maureen from her car and reported what Sally said.

"You believe her?" Mo asked.

"Maybe about Raymond Siegel," I said. "Not about Saunders."

"You probably got more out of her than we would together. You scared her."

"I doubt that," I said. "She's not a woman who frightens easily."

"If you could see yourself when you get on someone's case—" Mo started. "Forget it. I need my car back."

"I'll head your way now. Then what?"

"We drive back and do some things together."

"What?"

"Tell you later," Mo said, then as an afterthought, "When you get here, put on a tie and your blue blazer."

Mo knows I've worn a necktie only two or three times since moving to Florida. I hate the things. This had better be important.

#

Mo insisted I drive to West Palm, the idea being she'd drive her Toyota on the way back and I'd follow in the rented Taurus.

"You know where the Sailfish Club is?"

"I've driven by, never been in."

"Well, today we go inside," Mo said. "Paul Brophy is taking us to lunch."

"What?"

"He phoned me and invited me to break bread with him. I asked if he'd mind if I brought you. What could he say?"

Chapter Thirty

The Sailfish Club sits at the southern-most tip of Palm Beach, on the west side where the power and sailboats docked at the club's marina are protected from the waves and wind from the Atlantic but close to the Lake Worth Inlet so there is quick access to the ocean. For wealthy people into boating, it is the preeminent location in the area to store half-million-dollar vessels that will be used, at the most, a couple of weekends a month, five or six times a year.

It is also a luncheon and dining club, its membership rolls exclusive, but to its credit not nearly as discriminatory as the Everglades Club or the Bath and Tennis. A few Jews have become members, and African-Americans have passed through its doors. You can't say that about the other two.

Paul Brophy waited in the lobby, a light tan suit, matching shirt and orange tie that day. "I've already signed you in," he said, his way of reminding us we were there by sufferance. The demonstration continued in the dining room, a sweep of lime green table clothes with pink flowers in vases at the center of each. We couldn't order in a normal way; Brophy had to write what we wanted on an order slip and hand it to the waiter. Another reminder as to who was in charge.

That exercise out of the way, Brophy turned to Maureen. "Miss O'Neal, I invited you here in the hopes that you might have a flexible approach to our mutual problems."

"More flexible than me?" I said.

"Perhaps," he said.

"Last time I saw you, you predicted I'd end up like Clinton Drake."

"An unfortunate outburst," he said. "I've been under a lot of strain."

No retraction, no apology, but Brophy's attempt at charm had returned, the hysteria of his late-night phone call gone. Does he fool anybody? Some people I guessed. How suave does a CPA executive need to be?

Maureen said, "You won't find me any more flexible than Mr. Overman if you mean to set someone up."

"No," Brophy said. "I'm here to ask your help."

Neither Mo nor I responded.

"Our group, the people at The Exchange, are extremely upset about what's happened. The cops are all over us, follow-up interviews and phone calls every day."

"I supposed that's inevitable," Mo said.

"But there's got to be an end to it."

"It will end when it ends," Mo said.

"I invited you here to solicit your help," he said. "You have a reputation of being a problem solver–before when you were an analyst and now as an administrator."

"If you think I have any influence over Gregory, you're wrong," Maureen said.

That was one of the few times I'd ever heard Mo tell an untruth. She was, of course, the Significant and Only Influence in my life. And I could tell from the way Brophy looked at her, then me, that her influence on me was exactly what he'd wanted to, in his word, solicit.

A waiter put gigantic bowls before us. We'd each ordered various salads, and between us we had enough lettuce and vegetables to feed a small rabbit farm. The arrival of food stopped the conversation. I wondered what Mo had in mind when she accepted this invitation. What good could come of it? She wouldn't answer any of my questions on the way here, frustrating in itself, and my mood worsened when I'd walked in and saw, contrary to what she'd told me, that not all the men in the dining room wore neckties. I tried to enjoy the view. Bright sun shown down on the rich men's toys as they bounced gently among the docks. Beyond them, toward the inlet, the water took on a lighter tone, a hint of the azure green sea offshore. What was I doing here? I'd rather be sailing a small racer, a J-22 or something, in the ocean.

"Did you have an Exchange at your home last Sunday?" Mo asked, bringing me back into the room.

"No," Brophy said. "Of course not."

Mo let him stew a minute, then asked, "Why not?"

"Because of the— The accident. No one would bring a child there again."

"If you really want to get the authorities off your back, the most natural thing in the world be to resume your Sunday evening exchanges," Mo said. "If you have nothing to hide."

Brophy stopped chewing, stared at Mo, then me, then out the window at the yachts. Neither Mo nor I spoke.

Finally, Brophy said, "Why do you suggest that?"

"Because you asked my advice."

Again Brophy went through his three-point stare, but this one ended more quickly. "We have nothing to hide."

"I think Gregory knows something that might be helpful to you," Mo said, her look toward me about as subtle as if she'd kicked me under the table. I knew what she wanted me to say, that Saunders told me his operation had been shut down. But should I?

"Greg has friends in law enforcement," Mo said.

Now I had Brophy's complete attention. What the hell? Mo knows what she's doing. I said, "I understand an investigation into what might have been happening at The Exchange has been terminated."

Brophy's mouth stayed open for a long three-count. Then, "Who told you?"

I shook my head. Brophy looked toward Maureen. She searched for green peppers in her salad, pushing each one to the side. Brophy resumed eating.

"A wonderful view, isn't it?" Maureen said, looking toward the yachts.

"Better than the one at the polo club," I said. That got a little smile from Mo, happy to hear I knew she'd imitated Helena Katz.

Mo turned to Brophy, and said, "If you stage another Exchange, I'd appreciate being invited."

So that's what she's been after all along.

"Of course," Brophy said, not thinking twice about it, so I knew the promise wasn't worth a penny. People who quickly agree to suggestions don't mean it.

"We have common interests," Mo said. "You want to get the police to stop bothering you and your friends. I want to get Gregory off the front pages."

Brophy nodded slowly.

"So if you hold another Exchange and nothing happens, police may figure it was a stranger who killed Clinton Drake."

"That's what I told—" Brophy looked at me, then stopped. "We wouldn't bring the children, of course."

"With the children, of course," Mo said. "That would show you have nothing to fear."

Really, Mo? I wondered. Is that safe?

Brophy said, "I need some time to think about it."

Maureen stood. I followed her lead. "We'll skip dessert," she said. "Thanks for lunch." With that we walked out of the cold dining room and into warm sunshine.

#

We didn't talk for a while, each of us processing what we'd heard from Paul Brophy. Strong winds from the west flattened Lake Worth, the precursor of a cold front to come. Great sailing weather now but rough and raw in a few days. Halfway across North Bridge, officially Flagler Memorial Bridge but nobody calls it that, I asked, "Why didn't you tell me you wanted them to hold another Exchange? And that you wanted to be there?"

Mo, who'd been looking out the window, turned toward me. "I wasn't sure until we started talking with Brophy. He seemed vulnerable, so I tried it."

"What do you expect to accomplish?"

"I don't know," Mo said. "At the least, I'll get to meet these people."

"You don't trust my observations?"

"Of course, I do Greg." Mo said. "I just want to see them first hand."

I thought about arguing the point but desisted. I would have felt the same way in her place.

"Let's see if anyone answered your personal ad," Mo said.

"It ran for the first time this morning," I said. "A million to one shot anyone's answered so far."

"You know how I feel about those odds," Mo said.

#

The woman behind the counter at the *Post* recognized me. Maybe the limp.

"You're in luck," she said. "A very good looking woman brought in an envelope this morning."

I had a hunch. "Let me guess. Frizzy blond hair, young, attractive, well dressed."

"You know her?" Part question, part statement.

"I know a woman who reads the personals every day."

"Well, good luck." She winked as she handed me the baby blue envelope.

The note inside, also on baby blue stationery, said: If you're who we think you are, we might want to make a deal. A phone number followed. That was all.

I pulled out my cell phone and checked the numbers I'd stored. Sure enough, Cindy Cathcart had answered my ad.

"Million to one payoffs always look so easy after the fact," I said, handing the envelope to Mo.

Mo laughed, took the note out of the envelope and read it. Then, "You want to phone or should I?"

"Depends. You want to talk to Cindy Cathcart by phone or at her apartment?"

That stopped her. "How'd you know?"

"A million to one shot," I said.

"You're learning," Mo said.

We decided a surprise visit would be the best approach, which left some time to kill before Cindy might be home. I proposed a Ben & Jerry's break, but Mo said it was much too early in the day for ice cream, that she wasn't hungry, and she had to watch her weight. We compromised by getting a pint of Chocolate Chip Cookie Dough with the understanding that I'd eat most of it. I tried to keep my part of the deal, but I'd swear Mo's plastic spoon scooped up almost as much as mine.

Then I phoned Cindy's apartment. She said sure, come on up. I said, I'm bringing a friend, and hung up before she could object.

Chapter Thirty-One

The odor of pot, unmistakable and undeniable no matter how long you've been away from it, hit us even before we crossed the threshold of Cindy's apartment. The supposed Cosmo girl stood at the door, but I was more interested in the man standing in the middle of the room behind her. Shy Wilbur. What was he doing here?

"Hi," Cindy said in a little girl voice. I introduced Maureen, and the two women shook hands. Cindy's faced betrayed her disappointment that Mo was with me. A woman like Cindy wants to be the only woman present. And Mo, I could see, wasn't impressed with Cindy. On the way to the apartment she'd told me, "Don't you know *Cosmopolitan*'s become nothing more than a glamorous purveyor of superficial sex advice for women willing to put themselves second to their boyfriends?"

Mo shook Wilbur's hand, making no effort to hide her inspection of the man. Surely she saw the thin-red lines on his face. Her question had to be whether he was still using, maybe stopped drinking but continued on what some drunks call a marijuana maintenance program. "Hi," Wilbur said, trying to appear casual but unintentionally echoing Cindy.

Cindy's living room, so neat when I saw it before, showed signs of either argument or play. The pillows—pink, turquoise, purple and black—were scattered throughout the room, mostly on the floor, as if thrown there. One of the prints on the wall hung unevenly, a white leather chair shoved aside. Was all this the result of a mad, sexual romp between Wilbur and Cindy? No. Can't be. Couldn't be. Not with this spent man, standing there, guarding his coffee.

No ashtrays in the room, I noticed, so I walked to the glass doors that opened onto the balcony and looked out. A half-smoked roach and the remains of others sat in an ashtray on a glass-topped table. I made an exaggerated nod toward it for Maureen's benefit. I think she understood.

Cindy offered to fix drinks but everyone declined. She shrugged and sat on one end of the sofa. Mo took the leather chair and I sat in a straight chair under the sign that said "The Rules are Different Here," leaving Wilbur no place but the other end of the sofa. He picked up a pink pillow and put it on the middle cushion, a barrier between him and Cindy.

I looked at Cindy, "Your note said you wanted to make a deal."

"Did it?" Cindy said, still not sure how to play things with Mo present. "I thought we'd be by ourselves."

"I don't have any secrets from Maureen," I said. "Is Wilbur the other half of the 'we.' "

Wilbur said, "We're still discussing what we want to do." Cindy frowned. I glanced toward Maureen, who bowed her head almost imperceptibly, her signal for me to continue.

"I don't know who to trust," Cindy said, still looking at me. "I want somebody to help me."

"Start at the beginning," Mo said. "Take your time."

"Well, you know Raymond Siegel is, was, gay?"

"No big deal," Mo said. "Some people have blue eyes, some people have brown ones."

"That's not the way Raymond looked at it," Cindy said. "He was convinced he couldn't go any higher in the corporation if the big bosses in North Carolina knew about him. Knew he was a fag."

"He was right," Wilbur put in.

Probably, I guessed. Two of the biggest bank chains in Florida—in the nation, in fact—were located in North Carolina and the rules aren't different there. Not at all.

"So I was his cover," Cindy said. "An escort. The bikini on his boat. You know what he told me? He said, 'You can't tell much about a book from its cover, and a cover is exactly what I want.' That's the way he talked."

"I know," I said.

"He bought me clothes I couldn't possibly afford. He paid my apartment rent and gave me jewelry." Cindy paused. "And now he's dead."

None of us had anything to say to that.

"And I'm alone," she said, looking to Maureen for help. "Stuck with that awful bunch of people at The Exchange."

"You have Wilbur," Mo said.

"Wilbur and I are pals," Cindy said. "But he can't—"

Wilbur reddened.

Mo straightened in her chair. "Cindy, we might be able to help you."

"Are you an attorney?" Cindy asked.

"No," Mo said. "Just a woman who's been around the track a few times."

Cindy smiled at that.

I said, "Do you think you need an attorney?"

"I might," she said, turning back to me. "I'm thinking of going to the police."

Again Mo signaled me to lead. I said, "Cindy, if you want us to help you, we'll need to know some things."

"What do you want to know?"

"Did you kill Clinton Drake?"

"Heavens, no."

"Do you know who did?"

"No."

"No suspicions?"

"No."

"Did you kill Raymond Siegel?"

"Absolutely not."

"Do you know who did?"

Cindy rubbed a hand through her hair. "The man who found Raymond dead was his boyfriend."

"Had they quarreled?"

"Not that I know of."

"What's the purpose of The Exchange?"

"Well—," Cindy started to say.

"Don't!" Wilbur said. "Don't tell them that, or we'll both be killed."

"Wilbur," I said. "If you want to make a deal with the police, you'll have to tell them all you know."

"They'd kill me," he said. "The people who run the Exchange."

"They could put you in the witness protection program."

"They don't work," he said.

"You don't know that."

"I'd need immunity from prosecution."

"Most deals are made in exchange of reduced time."

"I couldn't go to jail." Wilbur's voice had become shrill. "They'd kill me there."

"Wilbur, stop it!" Cindy screamed. "You're such a coward."

Mo stood up and said, "Maybe we should take a break."

Cindy went to the kitchen. Ice cubes clinked in a glass, the gurgle of a bottle, then something else being poured. It was Bay Breeze time.

Wilbur got up and went to the balcony. Maureen walked to me, leaned down and said, "We need to talk with them separately." I nodded. She headed toward the kitchen, but Cindy walked out and past her, holding a glass of yellow liquid. "I want everybody to get out," she said, then looked at me. "Except you, Go."

"I can't— I won't," I said. "I'm with Maureen."

"Actually," Mo said. "I think Cindy has a very good idea."

Surprised me. Wilbur, too, we could all see. "But Cindy—," he said.

"We've talked enough, Wilbur," she said. "Now it's time for action."

They went back and forth like that for a while, giving Mo a chance to whisper in my ear, "I'll wait for you downstairs." Eventually Wilbur left with Mo, Wilbur casting one last woeful look backward before the door shut.

"Sit down on the sofa," Cindy told me.

I sat on the straight chair.

"You're such wuss," she said. "If you'd just try me, you'd find I'm a lot better in bed than her."

"Mo and I are together for life," I said.

She put her drink down on a table, kneeled on the floor beside the chair, and put a hand inside my thigh. I stood. "Cindy, I may be able to help you, but not for that."

"Damn." Cindy picked up a pillow and threw it across the room. It bounced on the glass door and fell to the floor.

"You and Wilbur fight before we got here?" I asked.

"I threw things," She retrieved her glass. "He just sat there."

"Why do you need him? Make a deal by yourself."

"I don't really know anything," she said, sitting on the sofa. "Wilbur has records. Photo copies of everything he's done."

"You must know some things."

"All I know is the little Raymond told me." She moved her shoulders forward. "And he never took me seriously."

"What did he tell you?"

"Not to tell anything to Duane Saunders or Helena Katz," she said. "And not to trust your friend, Ginny Stonridge."

"What else?"

"To stay pretty and smile a lot." Her eyes were wet. "Damn."

"What's the purpose of The Exchange?"

"I don't know." Cindy looked up. "Really."

Could she be telling the truth? While I wondered that, Cindy stood and walked to the balcony. She held the joint in her hand when she came back. She lit it, closed her eyes, inhaled slowly, held it in her lungs longer than I could have, and released. Then she handed it to me. I held it between my fingers, remembering college days. Good days, those, but I don't want to go back to them. No, not today, maybe never. I shook my head and gave it back. Again Cindy shrugged, her face serene or zonked, depending on your point of view. I knew I didn't have long before she couldn't or wouldn't answer questions.

I said, "Cindy, do you know anything that might help us learn who murdered Clinton Drake and Raymond Siegel?"

"Guns," she said, her voice low and dreamlike.

"What about guns?"

"Wilbur has a big gun collection," she said.

Could be. He's the type. Isolated, with few friends. And Cindy, here, turning in her buddy. No honor among thieves, no honor among any of these people.

"And I've heard Paul Brophy has some guns, too," she said. "Alan Schneider, too."

And half of Palm Beach County, I thought. "Do you see any of the three of them—Wilbur, Paul Brophy or Alan Schneider—do anything unusual the night Clinton was killed?"

"You were there." Cindy giggled. "And your friend who I happen to know is named Gemini."

I waited.

"Maybe if you and Gemini hadn't of come to the party, none of this would have happened," she said.

"What have you told the police?"

She leaned forward. "Those pigs. They were horrible."

"How?"

"They kept saying Raymond was gay so I must be gay, too."

"So what?"

"They said they would pass the word around," she said.

I could see it, a couple of bored cops deciding to have fun with a dumb blonde after they realized she didn't know anything.

"They kept asking me when was the last time I slept with a man? Who was he? How many men I'd taken to bed in the past year."

"What did you tell them?" I asked.

"I wasn't going to tell them the truth," she said. "So I told them the last man I slept with was you."

Adrenaline flushed through my body, preparing every cell to fight or run. I wanted to hit something, but I'd never hit a woman and I wasn't about to start that night.

"I hope you don't mind," Cindy said. "I had to tell them someone."

Until then, I'd thought bimbos were harmless. Now I understood how dangerous they could be. "Damn you, Cindy. You know what you told them wasn't true." She recoiled, the fright making her smaller. "I'm not going to harm you, Cindy. But I'm going to get out of here." I stood, walked toward the door, then turned. "Don't ever again ask me for help."

As I walked out, I heard her say, "Everybody's so mean to me,"

#

Mo was in the condo's lobby when I got downstairs, but we waited until we were in her car driving down Dixie Highway before we talked.

"Wilbur is a very lonely man," Mo said.

"And frightened," I said.

Mo nodded. "He wants to talk in the worse possible way, but he doesn't trust anybody."

"Same as Cindy." Then, seemingly out of nowhere, came a thought. She might trust me if I slept with her. Involuntarily I gasped for breath. The id is so strong it can banish all reason. I tried to banish the thought. In its place I wondered, should I tell Mo what Cindy told the police about sleeping with me? Not now. Not until I've had a chance to think about it.

"Cindy trusts you," Mo said. "I'll bet she came onto you as soon as Wilbur and I left."

"With nothing to show for it," I said.

"I know that."

"How in the world did Wilbur and Cindy get together?" I asked, not really expecting an answer.

"You remember how Duane Saunders was looking for a weak link?" Mo said.

"Yeah."

"Cindy and Wilbur are both weak links," she said. "They must sense that, so they sought each other out."

"Get anything new from Wilbur?"

"He might talk to you. He said, he just needs more time."

"You think he will?"

"Yes," she said. "Men like that find surprising strength when they get their new life together."

Women, too," I said.

Mo reached over and took my hand, acknowledging what I'd said and more. We both had new lives, hers working for charity, mine working clean and sober, and she was glad to spend her new life with me. Me too. There was no one in all the world I'd rather be with.

Chapter Thirty-Two

The next day I got a call from Wilbur. "Know where the park off the Southern Boulevard Bridge is?"

"I can find it," I said.

"Meet me there."

We agreed on noon.

As far as I know, the causeway connecting the southern end of West Palm Beach with the Town of Palm Beach has no nickname. The northernmost bridge between the two communities is always called North Bridge, and the span six blocks south of it is often called Middle Bridge. But I'd never heard the Southern Boulevard bridge called South Bridge, perhaps because it is more causeway than bridge.

A smallish bird sanctuary borders the causeway on the south, and the green areas on either side of the road are usually deserted. A couple of picnic tables and garbage cans sit within one small clearing on the south bank, although it, too, is usually devoid of patrons. On that day, though, an old burgundy Nissan badly in need of a wash and wax had come to rest about twenty feet away from the nearest table.

I parked and walked toward the car. Wilbur got out, and not saying a word, lead me closer to the water and behind a clump of cabbage palms where we couldn't be seen from the road. He stood straighter than when I'd seen him before, his eyes looking directly into mine.

"No way anybody can see or hear us here," he said. "Unless you're wired."

"Why would I be?"

"Doesn't matter anyway." He looked up to the top of a palm, then back to me. "Cindy was a disappointment."

I nodded.

"I thought we could help each other. But now—"

"Now she'll try to cut her own deal," I said.

"I know." Again, he stretched his neck toward the palm leaves, then looked toward me. "She doesn't know anything."

"And you do?" I prompted.

"I hear things," he said. "Two days after Raymond Siegel's murder a half dozen bank examiners flew in from Atlanta. They're digging into that bank in ways it's never been examined before."

"Interesting."

"I know things that no bank examiner will ever be able to find," he said.

"I'm sure you do."

"I kept photocopies of everything," he said. "I've even got copies of some computer tapes."

"So now you can call the shots."

"I don't want to go to the police," Wilbur said. "Some of them may be tied into this."

I thought about the idea. Improbable, I figured, but if Wilbur believed it, the notion was true for Wilbur. The DEA agent, Saunders, had said Deputy Fourquet hated the state attorney's guts, but Fourquet was in Seymour Topping's office when Ginny took us there. Sooner or later, one way or the other, Topping learned everything the cops knew and vice versa. And since Wilbur was convinced Topping and Paul Brophy were both part of the Palm Beach County Establishment, he couldn't trust anybody.

"I know something you might do," I said.

He waited, more interested than I'd ever seen him.

"Go to Duane Saunders." The Santa Claus with the Rolex, I thought, but to Wilbur I said, "The bearded guy who came to The Exchange with Helena Katz."

"Him? Why?"

"Of all the bunch, he's the one most likely to help you. He's the good guy in all this. And he's got the authority."

Wilbur thought about it, slowly reaching a conclusion. "You mean he's the law?"

I handed Wilbur the hand-written card Saunders had given me, the one with his phone number. "I haven't said that."

"But you're not saying he's not."

"Been nice talking with you, Wilbur," I said and walked away.

#

The next call came, came from Lt. Detective Louis Fourquet of the Palm Beach County Sheriff's Department, one of the hordes who, by then, knew my cell phone number.

"Know where the Banana Boat is? The one in Boynton Beach?"

"Yes." Just across the Intracoastal from Ocean Ridge, I knew.

"If you want to talk, meet me there at two."

"Okay."

He hung up.

Things are looking better, I thought. Unless this is a set-up, with me the victim.

#

The Banana Boat is a restaurant and drinking establishment on a very narrow stretch of the Intracoastal just off Federal Highway. Fourquet chose it, I guessed, because it is one of the last places in the world you'd expect to find an undercover cop. You can eat on the veranda and watch boats go by so close you feel you're riding along with them. Or you can imagine yourself on one of the dive boats and drift fishing rigs that depart from the canal between it and the Two Georges Waterfront Restaurant across the way. The music, sometimes rock, sometimes calypso, helps stimulate such delusions.

Less adventurous souls can eat at tables or booths inside the restaurant that was where I found Lt. Detective Louis Fourquet. He skipped the preliminaries "I need to ask you a few questions."

"Go ahead."

"Where were you the night Raymond Siegel was killed?"

"At Maureen's apartment. I was asleep when I got the news."

"At home asleep," Fourquet said. "You all say that."

"If you're talking about suspects, it's probably true for all except one of us. The one who did it. "

A young waitress, clad like the others in a chaste white leotard and short flowered skirt, brought menus and left.

"The waitresses here used to wear flesh-toned leotards and little bibs." Fourquet said. "They looked almost nude."

"Progress?" I said, my tone was non-committal as possible.

"More of that God-damned political correctness stuff." Fourquet picked up a menu and began reading it. Minutes passed, enough minutes in fact for him to have memorized the thing. I recognized the tactic. Make the other person talk first. Not me. I could keep silent as long as necessary. The waitress, who couldn't have been out of high school more than a year or two, broke the impasse by suggesting the most expensive item on the menu. No sale. I ordered the fresh seafood Cobb salad, while Fourquet asked for a hamburger with mushrooms, fresh peppers and sautéed onions. Coffee for both of us.

When the waitress left, Fourquet said, "Your dime. What did you want to talk about?"

That was not true. He had asked to talk. But I said, "I'm involved in this whether I want to be or not. I know I didn't murder anybody, so I'm interested in hearing what you guys have found out."

"Sure," he said, smiling like this was the biggest pipe dream he'd ever heard. But to my surprise he began a ten-minute monologue on what the police had discovered to date, the whole bit, gun calibers, how far away the murderer stood, the fact that no one at the Exchange had been eliminated as a suspect in either murder, that "some people" would like to pin it on me but the only development that pointed to me was the stupid thing I'd done in leaving town, etc. The more he talked, the more disappointed I became. I'd read every bit of this in the newspapers, or heard it from Saunders. Time to challenge him.

"You left out the part about your hating Topping's guts," I said.

Fourquet stopped, coffee cup in mid-air. "Who told you that?"

"A source close to the investigation;" Corny, but I couldn't think of anything else.

"Duane Saunders, the agent," he said, bringing the cup to his lips.

"I didn't say that."

"You're an asshole. But a clever one."

I let it pass.

"I don't like grandstanding," Fourquet said. "It interferes with investigations."

"I can appreciate that more than anyone in the world," I said. "State attorney Topping hurt me for political gain."

The food came then, and we took our time demolishing it, talking about little but the view outside and the waitresses in the room. Fourquet had a daughter their age, he said, and she faced a different world than he ever imagined. Later, over a second cup of coffee, he said, "Duane Saunders tell you he was closing down his operation?"

"Yes."

"You believe him?"

"Yes." At least I had until that moment.

"You believe everything people tell you?"

"No," I said. "In fact rarely."

"How do you know someone's lying to you?"

Good question, that. "Sometimes when what I'm being told is too good to be true."

Fourquet smiled.

"Saunders lied to me?" I asked.

"I didn't say that." Fourquet was on his feet. "Thanks for lunch."

#

That night when I told Mo about the conversation while sharing a pint of Cherry Garcia, she said, "That was Fourquet's way at getting back at Saunders for telling you he hated Seymour Topping."

"So Saunders used us," I said. "He wanted us to tell Brophy his operation was shut down." "Doesn't matter," Mo said. "In this instance, our interests are the same as his."

"Which are?"

"Break up The Exchange, solve the murders and let us get back to living our lives."

"Is that all?"

She laughed, the sound of angels happy to be out playing in good weather.

"Are we making any progress?"

"I've been thinking," she said.

"Spill it."

"I'm not ready. So far I've got nothing but conjecture, speculation and wild guesses."

"But no secrets?"

"Of course not." She laughed again, rendering me powerless. "But we're making progress."

"How?"

"People are coming to us. Cindy and Wilbur wanted to talk with you. Duane Saunders, too. Even Fourquet was willing to lunch with you."

"At a place he wasn't likely to be recognized."

"Even so, why?"

"You guess," I said.

"They all think you can help them somehow, and they don't trust each other."

"Us," I said. "They think we can help them."

"But we can't trust any of them."

I nodded.

"Saunders said he was forced to close down his surveillance team, but he's still up to something." She said. "He has all that property he won't talk about, not to mention the big Rolex he couldn't possibly afford on a government salary."

My nod was shallower this time.

"Fourquet may or may not be in league with Saunders. Or Paul Brophy."

"Everybody lies, suspects and cops alike," I said.

Mo reached over and took my hand. "So far, you're the only one taking any heat. Nobody else has been hurt."

"I can take it."

"Idiot," she said. "The board of trustees won't let me keep you as a consultant if this keeps up."

"I can do without the dollar a year," I said. "I could take off for Fiji like that banker."

"I want you around me, and around the people I've got to work with."

"We could both go to Fiji."

"I like what I'm doing and I'm doing a bunch of good for a bunch of kids," she said. "I wouldn't be happy anywhere else."

"OK," I said. "We're in this together."

We hugged, a long, close embrace that on other occasions might have led to more intimacy but not that time. Mo broke away. "Forgot to tell you. Stephanie Royce left a message on our answering machine."

"Everybody has our numbers," I said. "We'd have more privacy if we changed our phone number to 9-1-1."

"And Duane Saunders phoned again."

"Good. Time for you to meet him."

"Can't," Mo said. "Today's conference left me with a couple of fires to put out and three or four preemptive strikes to plan."

"So I'll sleep in."

"Nope," Mo said. "Tomorrow you talk to Saunders and possibly Stephanie Royce. I'll meet them if and when there's another Exchange."

#

The next morning I drove by the former DEA office near Palm Beach International to see if it was open or closed. The sign on the chain link fence was gone, and the gate wasn't locked. The door on the building wouldn't yield, though. I banged on it. Nobody answered.

Saunders had left a cell phone number, so I started to phone it. Before I pushed all the digits, Billie, the IRS agent I'd met before, drove up in the same Pontiac Grand Prix she'd used in the surveillance of Stephanie Royce. She saw me, her brow rippled, and she turned the steering wheel. I ran to the car and threw myself on the hood. The hot metal stung the side of my face. I turned my palms flat against the hood, pushed myself up inch by stinging inch to the windshield. Finally I blocked Billie's field of vision. We stared at each other through the glass, our eyes making such close contact I could almost read her mind. She could push down on the accelerator, turn sharply and let centrifugal force throw me to one side. Or she could stop and talk. Which would be easier to explain to Saunders and the others?

She braked. The action pushed me back on the hood with nothing to hold onto. I slid off the front of the car, onto sand and weeds. Now she could drive forward and run me over. Fortunately, that wasn't her day to demolish taxpayers. She got out of the Grand Prix and walked over.

"I'll have to phone this in," she said.

"Funny thing," I said, getting up. "I was just phoning your boss."

She studied me, her hands on the hips of beige slacks, her arms still tanned and muscular. A decision made, she pulled a cell phone from the holder on her belt and began pushing buttons. Just for the hell of it, I dialed the number Duane Saunders gave me. Her call got through first. My phone rang busy.

I brushed sand off my trousers and listen to Billie's side of the conversation. She told Saunders she'd found me outside the building "snooping around." After that, she said only a series of "Yes," "OK," and "All right," all the while looking at me as if I were a prisoner about to skip.

When she clicked off, looked me in the eyes, and she said, "Saunders says to phone him." She began walking toward the Grand Prix.

"Just a minute," I said. "If your operation is closed down, why are you here?"

She turned. "You won't get anything out of me."

"I asked a simple question."

She pivoted, marched to her car and opened the door. She stood there, looking me over. "For the record," she said. "If you'd have tried anything, I could have taken you."

I was not willing to concede that, but I knew it would have been a good fight. "Go in peace," I said.

Chapter Thirty-Three

I waited until the Grand Prix was out of sight before phoning Saunders again, but when I did he picked up on the first ring. "You want to meet at the Marine Bar again?" he said, not saying hello, not even waiting to find out who was calling.

"No," I said. "I've been there."

"I have information you might be interested in."

"You can tell me over the phone."

Saunders paused, weighing whether to press the point. Doesn't matter, he must have decided. "You remember Stephanie Royce?"

"Head of what you called the kindergarten association."

"We checked her criminal record after she volunteered to testify," Saunders said. "Turns out—" The roar of a jet taking off drowned out his words.

"Say again," I said. "No. Before you say another word, tell me if you believe Stephanie's story."

"About you asking her to launder money?" Saunders asked.

"That and everything else she told the Grand Jury."

"You're forgetting. I know better," he said.

"From one of those conversations we never had? Or the surveillance ride we never took?"

``You're sounding bitter," he said. "It doesn't become you."

"So you don't believe her story, and you know better," I said. "Why don't you tell that to Seymour Topping?"

"Who says I haven't?"

"Have you?"

"This isn't getting us anywhere."

He was right, but I wasn't in a mood to concede the point. "You phoned me, us, Maureen and I. What do you want?"

"I have a tidbit for you," he said. "One that if you hear it, you'll owe me one."

"Not unless I think so."

"So meet me at the Marine Bar," he said. "There's just so much I'll tell you on the phone."

"Not interested," I said.

A silence. Then he said, "When is the last time you went to the zoo?"

"Long time. Childhood, I guess."

"What's your favorite animal?"

"Quit kidding around."

"That's the last question," Saunders said. "Your favorite animal?"

"Giraffes," I said without really thinking about the answer.

"OK," he said. "Meet me in an hour at the West Palm zoo near the giraffes."

Ridiculous. I clicked off.

#

Not long afterward, I drove by the *Palm Beach Post* and claimed a stack of replies to my personal ad, then parked on the Southern Boulevard causeway and opened the envelopes, still in my rented car. Wish I'd had time to buy a car of my own, but first things first.

One correspondent, one who signed his name Larry at the bottom of a typewritten letter, said he knew all about material gathered by Clinton Drake III and for ten thousand dollars he would share it with me. Write him at his Post box number, one he already had for another classified ad. There was no indication he knew anything except what had been in my advertisement.

The others, twenty-six in all, were not much better. One woman, Rose according to her scented letter, said she knew "Clint" very well and before he died he'd given her a diary. Why don't we get together over a drink? She listed a phone number. A man, said he had had an intimate relationship with Clinton and might be able to help. Another box number. A poorly printed note on lined school notebook paper said he or she had what I wanted. No way to contact him or her.

I went through the envelopes quickly the first time around, then started through them again slowly. Almost an hour had passed. When I'd started through the notes and letters I had no intention of meeting Duane Saunders at the zoo or anyone else. Now I wondered, should I? Then a more important thought came.

The police had surely seen my personal ad, maybe gotten a subpoena or whatever they needed to get the newspapers to show them the letters first. Could they have unsealed the envelopes and made photocopies? Yes. So if there was any real lead among them, they knew it already. Maybe they'd taken it out of the stack.

Maybe Saunders knew what they'd found. Damn. Do the right thing, all over again. I thought of calling Mo, but decided to wait until after I'd visited the zoo.

#

To this day, I do not know why I told Saunders that giraffes were my favorite animals. What did I know about them? Vegetarians, maybe, their necks high enough to eat leaves from tall trees. Fast, I guessed, with their long legs. Fast enough to evade a lion? Maybe, but I doubted it. Spots for camouflage, but do they really provide cover? Maybe in rocky areas.

I sat on a bench watching these strange animals. Their strengths are their vulnerabilities. What if a lion approaches when one has his head up in the trees? Don't they draw attention to themselves in grassy areas? You think too much, the still, quiet voice said.

"Why giraffes?" a voice behind me said.

Damn if I was going to repeat my thoughts to Duane Saunders. "Why don't you level with me about who you really are?"

He sat down beside me, keeping enough distance between us so his hands were free. "I've told you."

"That Rolex," I said. "How can you afford it?"

"Look closely," he said and stuck out his arm for inspection.

Something about it looked wrong, but I couldn't be sure. "Can't see it well enough," I said.

Saunders took the watch from his wrist and handed it to me. "Look at the dials."

Sure enough, from close up I could see that the three little dials that were supposed to be slowly advancing were fake. They'd been painted on.

"Twenty dollars from a sidewalk vendor in New York," Saunders said.

I handed the watch back. "You paid ten dollars too much."

"You'd know better than I would," he said.

I let it pass. "Where'd you get all that property?"

"Can't tell you." Saunders rubbed his beard. I'd always thought most men with beards have something to hide. Certainly Saunders does.

"Then maybe we don't have anything to talk about." I shifted my weight forward, about to rise.

"I have some more information about Stephanie Royce."

That was all it took. Among my many defects of character is an irrational curiosity, a wanting to know more about anything and everything, pertinent to my interests or not. I sat back.

"When this thing first broke we ran a criminal record check on every adult who was at the Exchange at the time of the murder." Saunders lowered his voice. "When Stephanie came up with her story, we ran another background check, one that was more detailed than the first."

In front of us, the giraffes stretched their necks higher, as if to hear him.

"We didn't find anything new, but we started putting new interpretations on what we'd turned up before. We were particularly interested in this lady's activities before she married Wilbur Gantz."

I'd almost forgotten that Stephanie and Wilbur had been married.

"There were a couple of arrests on Stephanie's record, but nothing that looked significant. A mess of traffic violations she paid fines on, one DUI charge that was reduced to reckless driving. A possession of marijuana charge she got probation on and one disorderly conduct. Nothing important on the surface."

I nodded. One of the giraffes nodded back.

"But when we looked at the record again the possession charge stood out like a sore thumb," Saunders said. "Nobody gets cited for possession any more unless there's something more important involved. So we got the original arrest reports out of the sheriff's office, and we found cross references to a lot of other reports."

Saunders paused, and I sensed he was striving for effect. "It seems our gal Stephanie spent a lot of time around modeling studios, private dance instruction joints, and places that used to be called massage parlors. Not to put too fine a point on it, the president of the Palm Beach County Day Care Association was a not-so-highly-priced hooker."

If Saunders expected me to be surprised, I disappointed him. Mo had told me of brokerage clients who moved in and out of the business as their economic situations rose and fell. It paid so much better than waitressing. In fact, the new information about Stephanie explained a lot. Wilbur had been Stephanie Royce's ticket out of The Life. Maybe Wilbur was a customer, maybe just somebody she met in a bar. She could see the financial potential in him, and he probably found her gloriously uninhibited. The strains came after the marriage, and the property settlement that went with the divorce had left Wilbur poor and broken.

"Stephanie owns a day school in Green Acres City, but she doesn't manage it," Saunders said. "It's an investment she made with some of Wilbur's money. That may be how she met Paul Brophy. Or maybe Brophy arranged the purchase for her."

Yes, but so what?

"Of course, at this point, we don't know when Brophy began using day care centers as part of the money laundering ring," Saunders continued. But we figure he knew about Stephanie's past, and he used it to get her cooperation."

"She probably didn't need much urging," I said. "With the money he could offer her."

"Not much at all." Saunders stood up. "So we'll take care of Stephanie. We'll learn things about her she's forgotten. When the time is right, we'll confront her with them. She'll turn, and be our witness."

"She won't have much credibility," I said. "She perjured herself before the Grand Jury."

"Depending on the circumstances, a trial jury may never learn that. And if jurors do learn it, they won't care. They may figure she was lying then but telling the truth at the trial."

I knew that could happen, based on my experience serving as a juror once. Jurors believe whatever they want to believe, for whatever reasons they bring with them to the jury box. I stood and took a step away from Saunders. "So why did you tell me all this?"

"To even the score," he said. "You sent Wilbur Gantz to me."

Yes.

"Maybe this makes you a little indebted to me," he said.

"No. To me, the information is useless."

"Maybe," he said. "But my hunch is you'll pass it on to Maureen O'Neal first chance you get."

I couldn't think anything to say to that, so I turned and walked past the lions, the elephants and, finally, the monkeys. They laughed at me, saying I had wasted my time. Or had I?

#

Just as Saunders predicted, I phoned Mo from the car and luckily caught her between calls. It didn't take long to fill her in on what Saunders had to say.

"I'll talk with Stephanie," Mo said.

"You don't trust me."

"I'm probably more sympathetic than you or Saunders to someone who sells sex to make ends meet," she said. "Men use women like that but condemn them. Most women sympathize."

"If they aren't threatened," I offered.

"I guess," she said.

"I've learned from my clients that there's a bit of prostitution in many marriages."

"If that's true," Mo said, "we shouldn't ever get married."

What can you say to a statement like that? It was like a scene in a war movie, bombs raining down from overhead, explosives going off on all sides, gunfire all around—no matter which way you turned you could get severely injured if you were lucky, maimed or killed if you weren't. I didn't say anything. There was nothing but clear air between our phones for a moment, maybe, two.

Mo finally broke the silence, saying only, "See you tonight," and hung up.

Maybe it would have been better to take a risk.

#

Later Mo changed plans. She phoned and said she was going to have a late dinner with Stephanie and I shouldn't wait up for her. I waited up, of course, killing time by reading while doing the laundry, my chore in the division of labor we agreed on when Mo moved in. I'd finished and was watching the ten o'clock news when she got home. I offered her a Ben & Jerry's, Karamel Sutra this time, but she said she couldn't possibly eat another bite. I believed her, until half way through the pint she went to the kitchen and got a spoon.

"So what did Stephanie have to say?" I asked when Mo took a second spoonful.

"She's a very frightened, insecure woman," Mo said.

"She's afraid they'll find out she's lying?"

"Not what I mean. She's frightened and insecure every day of her life."

I scooped another spoonful from the pint, thinking if I didn't watch out, Mo would devour the whole thing. "Tell me."

"Her looks give her away," Mo said. "She starves herself until she's thin as a teenage model. Her make-up, her hair, her clothes, every bit of her outside appearance is perfect. When you see a woman like that, you know she's extremely concerned about what others think of her."

"You're good-looking, but you're not afraid," I told her, knowing she was right but wanting to see how she could make the distinction.

"I don't overdo it," Mo said. "I run for twenty or thirty minutes, not two hours. I don't eat a lot, but—" She held up her spoon half-filled with Karamel Sutra. "And when I make a choice, I'm more concerned about what I think of myself than what others think."

True. "So why did Stephanie want to talk now? Instead of earlier?"

"Wilbur told her he was going to make a deal with the authorities."

Of course. I thought, Wilbur's still so much in love with his ex that he wouldn't do anything without telling her. And he knew from his experience with Cindy, he had to do something quickly. Otherwise he'd be the last person to grab for a chair. Once the music stops, the quick movers win. "How'd you get all this from Stephanie?"

"Two glasses of wine, a lot of listening, and Cognac for dessert."

"You too?"

"I stopped after the first glass of wine."

That sounded like Mo.

"You know what?" she said.

"What?"

"Stephanie isn't afraid of being charged with perjury. She's afraid that people will find out about her past."

"How did she know they'd found out?"

"Saunders must have told Wilbur. Wilbur told Stephanie."

"Wilbur stills loves her," I said.

"Of course," Mo stood and walked to the kitchen.

"That all you got from a three-hour dinner?"

Mo came out of the kitchen without the spoon she'd walked in with. "Two more things. She kept saying, 'I'm more important to this operation than anybody realizes. Without me, they couldn't pull it off'."

"What does that mean?"

"She wouldn't say, no matter how hard I worked to find out," Mo said.

"What's the other thing?"

"Stephanie said they're going to hold another Exchange next Sunday."

"How? Why?"

"Don't know," Mo said. "I'm going to bed. You coming?"

Chapter Thirty-Four

The drive to The Exchange this Sunday evening was so much better than the first. Mo sat in the car beside me, not Ginny. We'd spent the day together, a wonderful lazy day with nothing to do but enjoy each other's company. Late in the afternoon Ginny phoned and said she'd get to The Exchange by herself.

We were running early, so after we crossed South Bridge and entered the Town of Palm Beach I took the long way to the Brophy's, turning left onto North County Road, then over to North Ocean Boulevard, driving north as far as we could until we reached Palm Beach Inlet. The route brought us near the former Kennedy compound and other oceanfront mansions hidden out of sight, past the mostly Jewish Palm Beach Country Club where old man Kennedy played golf because the other clubs wouldn't let him in, and where more recently Bernie Madoff solicited money for his Ponzi scheme, and then past scores of lesser houses with sculptured shrubbery and lawns smooth as putting greens.

"Ever wonder what these people do all day?" Mo asked.

"Same as we do, I guess."

"Can't be," she said. "Instead of going to the grocery store, their cook goes. The chauffeur goes out to buy gas or get the car serviced. If anything around the house needs to be fixed, someone else makes the phone call and deals with the repair man."

"Don't forget they have to arrange tennis and golf dates and plan charity balls."

Mo shook her head. "You're being sarcastic. I'm serious."

Then I understood what was going on. Mo had escaped from the brokerage business with a tidy seven-figure sum. She could have opted for a life of ease, gotten into the society circuit or something. Instead, she accepted a full-time job that paid almost nothing—a dollar a year—and chose to work fifty or sixty hours a week. She was wondering what it would be like to trade places with a Palm Beach society matron. Or simply stay home, like her friends with children.

"I guess what I'm asking," she said, "living in places like these with, servants and tennis courts and swimming pools and all, you think they're happy?"

We had circled around East Inlet Boulevard and were going south on North Lake Drive now.

"Ah," I said, dragging it out. "Are they happy? And I suppose you want a simple answer?"

"Of course."

I saw this as a great opportunity to show off. "There have been a lot of studies on the subject and they show that in general rich people are happier than poor people. All those Depression-era movies were wrong."

"But people flocked to them in droves," Mo said. "They made a pile of money."

"When people are miserable they seek fantasy," I said. "But here's my point: while it's clearly better to have money than not, it's possible to have too much money. Really, really, rich people can buy almost anything they want. They can change almost any physical thing around them in any way they want. Eventually, though, they find it doesn't work. In fact it backfires. The rest of us can say, 'If only I had more money. If only I had a better job...If I could only lose more weight...If only I had my own personal trainer.... If only I had a better car.'"

Mo nodded.

I kept going. "Really rich people don't have those excuses. If they want something, they buy it. If they want a personal trainer they get one. They don't need a job. They can't use more money. They find money doesn't get them what they really want, which is something else entirely. Usually something is missing inside them. Something that money can't buy."

"Like a rich girl who gets everything she asked for at Christmas but is still unhappy because the neighborhood kids don't like her," Mo said

"Exactly."

"People like the Brophy's," Mo said, "Are they happy?"

"Are you kidding? He invites his mistress to parties she's hostess at? What do you think? Why do you think she works so long and hard to make Salli's a success?"

"Now she's going to the cops." Mo smiled. "So you're saying —Look!"

I saw it, too, a black Ford pickup F series sitting in a driveway three or four houses from the Brophy's.

"That's the truck that hit us," she said.

"Probably isn't," I said, "There are tens of thousands of trucks just like that in this country, and hundreds in Palm Beach County. The Ford F-series is the most popular truck in America."

"But what is this one doing in a Palm Beach driveway?"

I didn't have time to answer before we pulled into the Brophy's driveway. "This is the scene of the murder," I told Mo. "The murder scene, as they say on TV."

#

Paul Brophy opened the door. He shook Mo's hand, ignored mine. "Same rules as before." He nodded toward me. "He knows what they are." Before I could reply he turned away, took a few steps, then did a one eighty. "Remember, you're guests. I'll be watching you." He started walking away again, but once again rotated and looked at me. "We can kick you out anytime we want." Then we were looking at his back as he hurried toward the swimming pool.

"He's really glad to see us," Mo said.

"We wouldn't have been invited if our pal Saunders hadn't insisted."

"It's good to know a Santa Claus." .

"I'm glad Brophy left us alone," I said. "This way I can give you a private tour." I took her to the television room where Ginny had left her purse and gun, then to the living room where the cops herded us into after Clinton's Drake's body was discovered.

"How do we know Ginny left the gun in her purse?"

"She said she did. You think she didn't?"

"It was just a question." Mo looked around the room. "Ever notice that interior designers hide the personality of their clients."

We walked out to the screened enclosure around the pool to join the party. Everything was the same, but everything was different. Music, softer than before, flowed from overhead speakers, but nobody danced. The adults stood in groups of three or four, talking quietly. No sexual innuendo, no joking, no threats or arguments, not much of anything going on that Mo or I could hear as we walked across the patio.

The children were different, too. They still arrived in autos driven by the parent with weekend custody, still rushed to the other parent's arms full of stuffed toys and bags of clothes from their overnight stays, even a small suitcase or two. The hugs and kisses lasted longer than at the last Exchange, but some still ran to the lakefront afterward.

About half the parents, though, refused to let their children leave them. The children begged, pleaded and cried, but these mothers and fathers were resolute. Their children could not go down to the lakefront, not after what happened before when they watched the fireworks. The fact that other children could be seen playing and yelling down by the water made no difference.

I didn't see Eric in either group.

"Where's Eric," I asked Mo. "For that matter, where's Ginny."

"Ginny phoned and told me she's coming deliberately late. By now almost everybody here knows she's an assistant state attorney, and she wants to avoid questions."

Did that explanation make sense? Somehow it didn't, but there was no time to think about it then. Trying to see where everyone was and what their children were doing at once, my sensory perceptions were on overload.

Some of the pairings at this party, which I viewed in my mind as Exchange II, were the same were the same as Exchange I. A few were different. Duane Saunders, dressed in the same bright red and white sport shirt as before with his fake Rolex on his arm, stood to one side with Helena. Our eyes caught, but neither of us acknowledged the other.

"Helena's helping Saunders," I said. "Probably thinks it will benefit her politically."

"No," Mo said.

"What do you mean, no?"

"Don't you see it?" she said. "Helena's doing everything but grabbing his privates."

Sure enough, when I watched them longer I could see from Helena's body language that Mo was right. As she talked, Helena touched Saunders' shoulder, then his arm, then put her palm behind her neck, then the same palm on his shoulder, the pattern repeating.

"That lady's in love," Mo said. "Or in lust. Is Saunders married?"

"Not that I know of."

Cindy Cathcart, in low-cut skintight jeans, stood seven or eight feet away from Helena and Saunders, waiting her turn to talk to him. Too late, Cindy, I thought. You missed the train.

Wilbur, looking the happiest I'd ever seen him, sat on the other side of the pool alternately looking from Cindy to Stephanie Royce. Stephanie ignored him.

Sally Brophy, in a subdued, pale blue version of the wrap she'd worn before, walked around the pool with a little tray, offering nuts and chips to anyone who would take them. When she got to us, she said, "I'm not sure this was such a good idea."

"Why?" Mo asked.

"Don't know," she said. "But if something bad happens, it's your fault."

"Something bad like what?" Mo said.

"Don't know," Sally said again. "But you've got me drinking ice water."

Mo put a hand on her arm, but Sally pushed it off, turned, and walked away. Mo shrugged. "Let's split," she said. "Let's see what we can find out individually."

I nodded, then watched Mo make her way through the crowd. For my money, she was the best-looking woman at the party. Not the youngest or the slimmest, perhaps not innately the prettiest, but taken as a package and allowing some extra for her warmth, there wasn't another woman at the party who came close. She was wearing her short sundress, the one with vertical blue and white stripes she'd bought after she learned I thought Marilyn look like a candy cane in a pink and white one. No purse but wearing a fanny pack.

The woman I now knew as Paul's mistress, Marilyn, wearing slacks that evening, walked over to me as soon as she saw Mo leave.

I said, "I'm surprised to see you here."

"I never miss an opportunity to participate in something interesting," she said.

"You didn't have to be here for a child, and Paul doesn't need you. The only thing you can get here is trouble."

"I'm just a bystander," she said. "An innocent bystander."

"Unlikely. You've got something at stake."

"All I am is a stock broker," she said. "People give me stock certificates and if there're legitimate, I sell them. The money goes in an account, and that's the end of it."

No it isn't, I thought. You wouldn't be making a point of this if you weren't more involved. "You'd make things easier on yourself if you tell everything you know."

She stared, giving a good imitation of thinking. Finally, "Not tonight. But next time you want to talk, I could be more cooperative. We all want to help you."

"I'm not interested in stocks and bonds," I said

"I've seen the way you looked at me. I thought maybe you and—"

"Have you met Maureen?"

"I saw the woman you were with."

"She's my soul mate for life," I said. "Also my stock and bond expert."

"Too bad," she said. "Your loss."

No, my gain, I thought, but said: "Paul Brophy send you over?"

Marilyn—sexy stock broker during the week, lonely heart on weekends—took another moment to think. Then she said, "I'm my own person," turned, and ambled away.

Stephanie Royce, the slim (much too thin, I thought now that she was close) model, replaced her. There was a time I'd have been flattered by all this feminine attention but now I disliked the game. They all want something from me or they wouldn't be giving me the time of day. Thank God Maureen O'Neal wants me for who I am. I decided to take the offensive.

"You lied about me," I told Stephanie, right off. "Under oath."

"Nobody's perfect," she said. "Tomorrow I might remember things differently."

The gall, the cheek. "You can go to jail for perjury."

"I've been through some rough times in my life, Mr. Overman," she said. "I've learned you do what you have to do. I was wrong about you before. Now I'm saying, 'Welcome to the club.'"

Yep. This woman's had experience as some kind of call girl, just as Saunders said. She had the come-on smile down perfectly but her words didn't really say anything. Her proposition was completely deniable.

"Isn't there a joke about that?" I said. "'I don't want to join any club that would have me for a member.'"

"Laugh if you will, Mr. Overman, but you would find it very profitable," she said. "And we could arrange some very interesting fringe benefits, depending on your tastes. If you get tired of Maureen, that is."

"That include you?"

"Everything's negotiable." No pout now, but a hint of a smile. I remembered Marilyn had used the same line.

I saw Maureen across the pool, watching us, a broad smile on her face, one that said, Okay, partner, you can handle yourself. I wasn't so sure.

I told Stephanie, "You told Maureen that you were the most important part of this operation. Things would be easier on you if you explained yourself."

"Who says I haven't?" she said.

"Have you talked with Duane Saunders?"

"Of course. I've got to look out for myself."

"Then tell him everything you know and leave me alone." I walked away.

#

Soon Cindy got on Wilbur to dance with her and to my surprise, he agreed. Not long afterward others joined them and it was almost like old times again. Three of us—Duane Saunders, Maureen and I—stood at the back of the screened area, across the pool from the dancing couples.

"I suppose I can talk in front of her," Saunders said, nodding toward Mo.

"Of course," I said. "I tell her everything."

"Things are about to pop. We've got almost everything we need."

Neither Mo nor I responded.

"Wilbur has furnished us with heaps of records, photocopies and computer tapes. Stephanie realizes she made a mistake by lying to the Grand Jury and offered to give sworn testimony in trade for a light sentence."

"So why don't you act?" I said.

"We really need something tangible, any little thing, to tie it all to The Exchange—to what's going on here."

"The tapes, the photo copies," I said.

"A good lawyer could come up with a plausible explanation for the money transfers," Saunders said. "And Wilbur is a shaky witness. He could recant."

Mo said, "What are you looking for?"

"Something real, something concrete found on these premises that will tie it all together."

A loud splash at the far end of the pool interrupted us. Alan Schneider, fully clothed, surfaced sputtering. "Good going, Cindy," Helena shouted. Schneider half swam, half dog-paddled to a ladder at the side of a pool. Sally Brophy bent over to help him. Alan grabbed her hand. Sally lost her balance and appeared ready to tumble in the water beside him. Alan let go, Sally pulled back, a disaster averted.

"You men don't see it, do you?" Maureen said.

Saunders and I turned back to her.

"You're so busy looking at low-cut blouses and low-rider slacks, listening to talk about dancing and foreplay, paying attention to who's fussing with an ex and who still loves one, so busy concentrating on all that, that you don't see the big picture. You don't see what's really going on going on," she said, each word pounding out distinctly, accusingly.

I looked at Saunders, he looked back, obviously not understanding any more than I what she was talking about. But it was something Mo was sure of. She never spoke that emphatically unless she had thought long and hard about the subject.

"Forget the adults," Mo said.

Saunders and I stood quietly, obedient pupils ready to learn whatever was coming.

"What is it that binds all these people together?" Mo said.

It seemed too obvious. "The children," I said. "They—most of them, anyway, brought children to this gathering."

"Yes," Mo said. "Exactly."

"So?" Saunders said.

"You've been ignoring them," she said.

I had a glimmer then, but Saunders was still clueless.

"Think about it," Mo said. "Say you wanted to exchange something from one person to another. Say it was money. Say it was drugs. Whatever. Say you wanted to do it in a way that wouldn't draw attention from others."

I began to understand.

"What better cover could you ask than children who carried small parcels—toys and suitcases—back and forth every weekend? And the children wouldn't know a thing."

The boy who carried the clown, the one with its head sewn on backwards, came into view.

Saunders said, "Is that the boy?"

"Yes," I said, both of us thinking the same thing after Mo painted the picture for us. We started running toward the lake, me four steps behind Saunders, almost bumping into him.

Saunders grabbed the clown with the head sown on backward from the arms of a boy wearing a Spiderman T-shirt. He twisted the head one way, then the other. It wouldn't budge. "Don't," screamed the boy. Next Saunders jerked first one of the clown's leg's, then the other. They remained solidly attached.

The boy's scream got the attention of children around us. They started yelling. "Stop! Stop!"

Saunders banged the clown's head against the top of one of the dock's pilings. By now everyone in the garden, children and adults alike were looking our way. "Look at them." "You crazies." "Somebody stop them!" Children cried all around us. Silhouetted figures ran from the house.

The clown's head cracked in two. Saunders pulled the two sides of the head apart with his fingers. He lifted it to his face and looked closely at the inside of each half. "Damn," he yelled. He held it out for me to see. The clown's head was empty Nothing there but the hollowed out inside of the plastic head

Saunders looked at me, disappointment showing in his face. "I thought we'd find a bag of white powder."

"Try this." Mo having reached the dock by now handed Saunders a nail file. He cut gashes in the clown's legs and then its belly. Cotton stuffing fell out. Nothing more.

"I'd thought we'd find packs of hundred-dollar bills," Saunders said. All around us children screamed and cried.

I pulled a Raggedy Ann doll from the arms of a little girl, five maybe six years old, wearing shorts and pink shirt. "Excuse me," I said, knowing it was as stupid thing to say but not caring. I pulled the doll's head. It wouldn't bulge. "Stop!" the girl yelled. I turned the doll around, tried to tear its stomach. The girl screamed, "Don't, don't." I grabbed one leg of the doll in each hand, pulled and twisted at the same time. It tore apart, but nothing fell except bits of cotton.

The three of us stared at each other, looking for explanations. Finally Saunders turned to Mo. "You had a good idea. But it was wrong."

Mo wasn't ready to concede defeat. "You're giving up too easily," she said.

"I don't have a warrant to go any farther," Saunders said. As it is, I'm going to get in big trouble with headquarters. Saunders shoulders drooped, his face whitened. I felted as let down as Saunders looked.

"I've had troops standing by ready to raid this place," he said. "If we'd found something—dope or cash, they could have invaded this place by land, sea, and air. Now I'll have to call it off." He reached for the little radio strapped to his belt.

So this was it. The wimpy climax of a chase that started with an innocuous phone call to Mo on a Sunday morning, lead to a bizarre party and a murder, took me around to offices and apartments all around

Palm Beach County interviewing every one of these strange people, leapfrogging from one bank to another watching deposits of money from day care centers being made, learning more about the life of single adults after divorce than I had ever wanted....

All for naught, I thought. Maybe I should stick with treating children.

Chapter Thirty-Five

Psychology is my field, but there are some things neither I nor anyone else can explain. Where do new thoughts come from? Are they hidden away just waiting to be triggered by some something outside of us? Or do two or three squiggles of an idea somehow come together in our brains for no external reason because they are ready to emerge into our consciousness?

I'll probably never know the answers to those questions. But in that instant, as Saunders reached for his radio to call off his planned raid, everything I'd seen or heard since Ginny phoned Mo that Sunday morning came together.

I put a hand on Saunders arm, the one reaching for the radio. "No. Mo is on to something here. It *is* all about the children. But it's not about dope or money. It's them." I pointed toward the children.

Many of the children were still in tears, others wiped their eyes, all glared at us, two mad men and their female companion. Maureen stared at them, trying to figure out what I saw. They were a varied group, just as I said before, brown and white, Latin and Anglo, even Asian. Now the differences seemed even sharper. But there was something else, something wrong about the scene. *The children don't match their parents.*

"It's right here before our eyes," I said. "They exchanging something all right. But it's not what we thought."

"It's children!" Mo shrieked, coming to the same conclusion.

"Children?" Saunders asked, not hiding his skepticism.

"It's children!" I was almost yelling. "The purpose of The Exchange is to show off children to prospective buyers. They're marketing and selling children."

"Can't be," Saunders said.

I walked to the nearest group of children and started talking with them, keeping my questions short and unthreatening.

"Where are you from," I asked a little girl who looked for all the world as if she had come from Pennsylvania or Illinois or some other place in heartland America. "Where were you born? *Donde esta su casa?*"

The children looked at each other, puzzled. Finally one answered and the rest caught on, answering with proud smiles.

"Russia," said the girl.

"Mexico."

"Vietnam."

"America." that answer came from Eric, Ginny's son.

"Brazil."

I knew I was on the right track now but I wanted to pin it down.

"Your parents," I said. "*Su padre y su madre. Aqui?* Are they here? Now?*"

Again puzzled, the children whispered to each other, then understood and began shaking their heads.

"No." a girl said.

"Not here," said a boy.

"Back home."

I didn't wait for Eric to answer.

I yelled to Mo. "That's it. We're right."

"Damn," Saunders said.

"Do you have jurisdiction?" I asked.

"Damn right, I do." he said. "We're here looking for drugs or money laundering. But if there's evidence of any other crime, we have to act. And I wouldn't be surprised if we don't find at least a roach or so or some powder on some of these fine people."

He stopped almost in mid-sentence. "But it's just so preposterous."

"See that guy over there," I pointed a young, blonde-haired, man who could have been a surfer in Hawaii Five-O. "Ask him what his name is and make him point to his child." Saunders rubbed his beard, then walked to the dude. His words were so soft that from this distance I couldn't hear what he said.

Slowly the guy reached for his wallet, pulled it out of a pant pocket but left it closed. Then he spoke louder and we could hear him.

"What's this about?"

"Remember the cops asked everybody for ID at the first Exchange, then let most people go home. Surely you remember the cops. I'm one of them." Saunders showed the guy his badge.

Reluctantly the man pulled a driver's license from his wallet.

"Now show me your kid," Saunders said."

The guy pointed to the little black-haired girl I'd questioned, the one who'd told me she was from Russia.

"Let's go talk with her," Saunders said.

"Why? I don't want—"

Saunders took the man's arm and gently pushed him toward the girl who was supposed to be his kid.

"You can't do this to me," the man said, his voice louder than before. "I've done nothing wrong."

"Greg, Maureen. Do me a favor and talk to the kid. Ask her if this is her father."

The guy, excited now, said, "I didn't say she was my kid. She's a neighbor's kid."

"And you just happened to bring her to this party of divorcees – one where parents are supposed to be returning children they've had weekend custody of?" said Saunders, his voice a mix of skepticism and sarcasm.

"Make a list," I said, by now close to Saunders. "Ask the children their first and last names. Try to match up names of parents with the children. If they're really offspring of divorcees, then the children will have the same last name of at least one of the parents."

Duane hesitated, then rounded his fingers around his mouth to amplify his voice. "Everybody stay where you are. Nobody leave."

"You can't tell us what to do," said the guy who belatedly decided he'd brought a neighbor' kid. "I'm leaving." Other adults heard him and took up the cry. "You can't keep us." "I'll get my kid and leave."

"Hell with that," Saunders said and unsnapped the tiny radio from the belt under his shirt. He spoke into it briefly, words we couldn't hear because of the screaming children and cursing adults.

"Go, look!" Mo pointed out to the lake.

Four boats twenty-five to forty feet long, amber lights flashing on their bows and sirens screaming, sped toward shore, their hulls planing across the water, a marine version of cavalry charge, a magnificent sight. The two green and white sheriff's patrol boats landed on either side of the dock, a dark blue and white police boat on the left of them, a yellow and black state vessel to the right.

Next came the sound of choppers overhead, blades flapping, spotlights glaring down at us, three landing into the back yard and another over the street in front. Children and adults scampered to sides of the yard. Suddenly blue, green and brown uniforms were everywhere, more uniforms than Exchange guests, cops spilling through the Brophy's house from cars parked outside to join the officers who landed from the boats and choppers. The DEA guys wore dark blue jackets with big yellow letters proclaiming, DRUG ENFORCEMENT, the sheriff's deputies were in green and white, the cops in blue, the state patrolmen in brown, a handful of others in civilian clothes, a kaleidoscope of energy .

There was no "up-against-the-wall" stuff, or anything close. The raiders counted on surprise and organization to handle the situation, and they achieved total control in minutes. They ran to every room of the Brophy's house, every corner of the screened pool enclosure and every section of the yard. The few parents who attempted to run were soon stopped. Soon at least two cops, deputies or agents stood close to every child and adult at The Exchange, so well-briefed they called Exchange guests by name.

Through the garden we heard parents talking quickly to their captors, trying to explain. Each was handcuffed and told to stand still by the child they had brought to the party. The children, who might have been expected to cry or yell, became still, clinging to an adult or holding hands, They'd never seen a group of men and women like this—men and women who could tell people like their parents what to do.

Lt. Detective Fourquet of the Palm Beach Sheriff's Department stood in the center of the yard, beside Saunders, coordinating the effort, a picture of cool competence, the unlit cigar in one hand, a two-way radio in the other, grace under pressure. No wonder he didn't like a grandstander like Seymour Topping.

All around, cops, deputies, and drug agents read adults their Miranda rights from three-by-five cards, stuff they knew by heart but preferred to read. There was only one scuffle. It happened when a deputy tried to move Alan Schneider toward others who'd been arrested. "Take your hand off my arm,'" Schneider said, still wet from his dunking in the pool.

"No problem." The deputy moved his hand and Schneider swung with his right. The deputy's partner grabbed Schneider from behind, pinning his arms against his body in a bear hug. Schneider pushed backward and to one side, breaking the hold but stumbling. The first deputy pushed Schneider to the ground, spun him around, and pressed his knee into his back. His partner handcuffed Schneider's hands. After a minute or two, they let him stand up. So much for weight-lifting prowess.

Sally confronted Saunders. "You can't do this," she said. "This my property."

"Sure it is," Saunders said. "And so are your little clothing shops. Suppose we look at the books and bank accounts of your stores. Maybe we'll find that some parents in want of children have paid extraordinarily large amounts for dresses?"

"My books are audited."

"Not by us," Saunders said. "And maybe a night in jail will help you remember who you really saw near the pool when the murderer and banker Raymond Siegel were close by. It wasn't me."

"Of course not. I didn't say—"

Maureen shook her head. "You did," she said. "You tried to blame him."

"Maybe it was Allen. Maybe it was–."

"Maybe it was your husband," Saunders said.

Sally looked away, thinking only briefly about whether she wanted to testify against her husband. "Maybe it was."

"You can think about it in jail," Saunders said. He motioned to an officer to take her away.

Saunders walked over to Stephanie, the haughty woman I now thought of by her full name, Stephanie Royce Gantz, because of her triple roles as Wilbur's former wife, owner of a day school in Greenacres, and president of the Greater Palm Beach Day Care Association. "And you, Miss Barr, when we audit the banks of your little kindergartens we'll probably find some parents paid you extraordinarily high sums for day care."

"I'm not telling you anything."

"And when we talk to the children here, we might find many of them came from those day care centers," he said, beginning to relish his role now, master detective explaining everything at the end of the play. "Maybe you kept the children until they were ready to market. Maybe you were the one who found parents who wanted to sell their children."

"Never!" Stephanie screamed. "All I ever did was— No, you'll never get anything from me."

"We'll see." Saunders waved for cops to take her to a van.

Soon, the agents, cops and deputies divided people into two groups. Those who were arrested were herded inside the screened pool enclosure. The others, innocent bystanders, were taken to a spot near the lakefront. "You can leave soon," I heard one deputy tell them. "We just want to check your ID." There was more grumbling from this group than from the people arrested. To be expected, I guess. Always more outrage from the innocent than from the guilty.

Mo and I were left out of either group. A drug agent stood near us but didn't talk much. "Just stay here until things calm down." Helena Katz, standing maybe twenty feet from us, got the same treatment. I looked around for Ginny. Not in either group, nowhere in sight.

Saunders walked over. "We're got them all except Brophy. He disappeared when the raid started. "

Mo said, "With all these cops he couldn't have gone far."

"We've started a search of the grounds.

"He must be the ring leader," I said.

Duane nodded. "We've thought that all along. He was the one who told one of these bozos—probably Alan—to slam into you and Ginny and Maureen on the Blue Heron Bridge. We'll catch him and find out."

"But where is he?" It was Mo's question, but we were both thinking the same question. All three of us—Mo, Saunders, and turned in a circle, looking at each side of the garden.

Saunders pointed: "There." He began running toward a barely perceptible rustle in a firebush hedge near the water. Brophy saw him coming, broke through the hedge, and darted for the water. I joined in the chase. But Brophy was too far away to catch before he ran out onto the dock.

Voices of agents rang out. "Halt. Stop."

The boat's motor started, emitting a loud guttural sound.

Saunders voice rose above the rest. "Get him. Halt or we'll shoot."

The speed boat pulled from shore. Within seconds two Coast Guard boats pushed from shore and followed in pursuit. On the shore Duane raised a portable radio to his ear and mouth. "Stop him at any cost."

Corny, I thought, surely he doesn't mean *any* cost. But from the distance we saw rockets shooting from the Coast Guard boats. toward the fleeing speed boat followed by a loud explosion. Flames shot up into the air.

People in the garden looked up in awe.

Mo asked, "Was that necessary?"

Sanders nodded. "Remember, he was trading children for money, maybe for dope."

"You overreacted," Mo said.

"Maybe," Saunders said. "There'll be an investigation. The higher ups usually side with the arresting officer."

We left him to walk to the dock. Toward the street, DEA agents herded parents toward vans; female agents gathered children together and took them to cars.

Saunders stood in the middle of the garden, alone. We could hear him say, "Things never turn out the way we expect."

#

Later, Saunders walked over to the dock. "You can leave. too."

"We'll stay a while," Mo said.

"Sure."

"Who do you think killed Clinton Drake?" Mo asked.

Saunders rubbed his chin as if it were the first time he'd thought of the question. "Maybe that's one reason for this operation. A night in jail might refresh some memories."

That's the way cops handle penny ante stuff, I knew. An overnight stay in jail has helped many a petty thief separate his self-interest from that of his companions. But none of this bunch is going to be in jail that long. Their attorney, probably one who works for Brophy, can get them out on bond in two or three hours, tops.

"I don't think it's going to work," I said.

"I don't either," Saunders said. "But that's not my problem. Not your problem either." He looked at me. "You won't have to worry about the Grand Jury any more, and eventually Seymour Topping will make some sort of public statement. We're trying to get him to say that you were cooperating and never were a suspect. He's stalling now, but he'll come around. To help in his election campaign."

"I'll believe that when it happens," I said.

Saunders looked toward Helena. "She wants a political appointment out of this," he said. "I can't manage that."

"That's not what she wants," Mo said. "Take her to dinner."

Saunders frowned, looked as if he had a question but thought better of it, then turned and walked away.

"Will she?" I said.

"Sure," Mo said. "No telling what will come from it."

We watched Saunders as he walked to the center of the yard and joined Fouquet. The two men walked toward the house, a slow, proud victory march from the scene of battle. Wait, I wanted to say, you haven't finished your job. You haven't identified and arrested whoever killed Clinton Drake and Raymond Siegel.

Instead, I turned to Mo. "Do you?" I said, mostly talking to myself.

"Do I what?"

"Know who killed Ginny's former husband and the banker."

"I have some ideas," she said.

Chapter Thirty-Six

M aureen and I stood to one side of garden, watching the gaggle of cops, suspects, and children from afar. Maureen reached for my hand. "I still don't get it. The very idea. Selling unwanted children."

"I've heard of cases," I said.

"Explain it."

"Well first you start with the truth, that most qualified people who want to adopt a child can do so in this country if they are sound in body, mind, and finances. It can take a long time and a lot of patience but eventually things work out."

Maureen nodded.

"But some people are impatient. They hear you can save time by adopting a foreign kid. And they can. The standards in less developed countries are more lax. And the whole process goes faster if the prospective parents gives money to a few people."

Mo gasped. "Money for children?"

"They don't say that, of course," I told her. "The money is for processing costs, investigating the prospective parents, counseling children—you get the idea. Some of the money goes to people in this country, some to officials overseas."

"Bribes?"

"No one comes close to calling them that."

"Are the parents of the children paid?" Mo asked.

"Everybody swears on a pack of Bibles that they aren't."

I could see Mo was getting upset. I put a hand on her arm to calm her down. "Let me finish. Many of the people who adopt foreign children are good people and the kids grow up fine. But sometimes people adopt children for the wrong reasons. Their lives are a mess and they think the adoptions will fill a big hole in their lives."

Maureen stared, wide-eyed, beginning to get it.

"The children don't, of course, and in fact they complicate lives of these unhappy people. The new parents realize they're just as miserable as before. Maybe more so. Their unhappiness comes from inside them. And the amazing thing is some of the adults don't learn. Some of them even adopt a second kid."

"And become even more miserable," Maureen said, filling in the thought.

"Exactly. Then they want to give the kids back. But they discover that's easier to decide than do. If they even mention it to anyone, adoption officials here and in foreign countries start investigating."

"As well they should," Maureen put in.

"That's when the unhappy adoptive parents hear about The Exchange or something like it and see if they can sell their kids."

"Horrible.!"

We sat silently, letting the dreadfulness of the act sink in. What other animal would sell their offspring? Sure, there are many animals who routinely push their offspring out when they can make it on their own. But not before they can survive by themselves. Maternal instincts are among the strongest animals and people are born with. What other animal would attempt to trade or barter their children?

Only people like these. These ugly human animals.

Chapter Thirty-Seven

Nightfall on the waterfront, the sunset gone but lights from across Lake Worth shimmering on the surface, the quiet especially deep in contrast to the chaos before. Mo and I sat at the end of the Brophy's T-shaped dock, our feet swinging just above the water, the floodlights off, the lights around the pool dimmed now that the cops and everyone else had left. We watched the boats passing in silence, serene in each other's company until I spoiled things with the unanswered question.

"So, who did it? Who killed Clinton? Who killed Raymond Siegel?"

"Your turn first," Mo said.

"Brophy. He masterminded the Exchange, and they were onto Clinton," I said. "Remember I told you Alan Schneider was arguing with Clinton at the first Exchange."

"Brophy doesn't seem like someone who would have the guts to kill another human being."

"He could have had someone else do it. Alan, for example."

"You think Schneider was the driver of the truck that hit us?"

"Probably, but I can't be sure," I said. "Everything happened so fast, I only saw the truck's grill."

"You're assuming the same person who killed Clinton killed Raymond Siegel, too?" Mo said.

"Yes."

"Why?"

"Things were going well for Siegel and everybody else until Clinton died. Then things started unraveling."

"Cindy said the man who found Siegel's body was his boyfriend," Mo said. "It could have been a lover's quarrel."

"Any other time, maybe. But given the events at The Exchange, too coincidental."

"There are coincidences," she said.

"You're playing with me," I said. "Avoiding the subject of who committed two murders."

"I thought we were working this out together."

There was nothing I could reply to that. Mo did that sort of thing, turning my arguments around against me, so often I'd quit complaining about it.

"Something's bothered me from the very beginning," Mo said. "On the night of the murder, Ginny said she left her gun in the purse on a table in the television room."

"Yep. And somebody found the gun."

"No mother I know would do that," she said. "Not with kids running around."

I saw where she was going. "We don't know that Ginny left the gun there. Only her word."

"Remind me what she was wearing that night."

"A loose, pink blouse, cut a little low in front, and white slacks." I could see her in my mind.

"Were the slacks tight or loose? Did they have pockets?"

"Not tight," I said. "Could have had pockets. I was paying more attention to the purse that didn't match the outfit."

"She could have had the gun in the slacks pockets all along," Mo said. "Until she used it to kill Clinton."

Could have happened. But why? "What was her motive?"

Mo said, "Remember what you told me Ginny said in your car on the way to your first Exchange? About divorce."

"She said hers was friendly."

"And you said you'd never seen one that was completely friendly."

"Yep. I said most times there's a winner and a loser. "One person wants out more than the other."

"But Ginny insisted hers was different," Mo said.

"You saying she doth protest too much?"

"Maybe she was stuffing her anger," Mo said. "It was all inside, ready to burst out at the first opportunity."

"But why would she kill Raymond Siegel?"

"You remember what Sally said about seeing Raymond Siegel in the side yard with Duane Saunders?"

"Yes."

"That could have been half-right," Mo said. "A lie about Saunders. Right about Raymond Siegel."

"So Siegel saw Ginny kill Clinton," I said. "When Ginny figured this out later, she killed him."

"That's my guess too."

"But could we prove it?"

"Not our job. When the time comes we tell the police, and they'll find witnesses and whatnot to build a case."

"I told you Gemini meant two-faced," I said.

"No," said the voice behind us. "Two of everything." We turned. Ginny Stonridge stood on the dock ten feet behind and above us, her body silhouetted against the dimmed pool lights, the angle making her look tall and powerful, arms extended, each hand holding something pointed toward us. "Two two murders, two guns left over," she said.

Yes guns, two guns aimed at us, probably .22 caliber, the same as the one found at the bottom of the pool when Clinton Drake was murdered. Same size that killed Raymond Siegel. Small, but deadly enough to do the job.

"A gun for each of you," Ginny said. "One to kill each of you. Then one in each of your right hands."

"Why?" Mo asked, pulling her legs up and twisting her body to face Ginny. I did the same.

"They'll find you two here at the dock," Ginny said. "They'll draw the obvious conclusion. You'll have killed each other."

"Not what I meant," Mo said. "Why did you kill your ex?"

"Roughly what you said," Ginny said. "You don't know how hard it is, getting up and going to work every day, logically presenting a case in court, rationally explaining to a jury why people who break the law should go to jail, when all the time I was hurting so badly inside—" Her hands and the guns dropped a few inches.

"I understand," Mo said. We sat side by side now, three or four feet away from each other, facing Ginny with our hands on the dock behind us.

"There was no legal way to get back at that shit," Ginny said. "That cold son of a bitch." The guns came back up.

"Did you try therapy?" Mo asked.

"I couldn't," Ginny said. "Not in my position."

Wrong. Just an excuse.

"You told me you were at the Exchange investigating for the state attorney's office,"

Mo said.

"Just a ruse to throw you off track." Ginny tossed off the explanation as if it wasn't at all important, then went back to her story. "Then came the final straw. I wanted to move, to go to another state and start over. I hate this fucking state. The heat and humidity in the summer time. The threat of hurricanes five or six months every year. The traffic. The rudeness. Everybody on the make all the time. Nobody you can trust."

There was some truth in what she said. But not about the people. The people here are the same as anywhere else, there're just jammed together closer. No more tightly than in places like New York, Chicago, or San Francisco, of course. The difference is in the expectation people have that South Florida will be paradise. It isn't. No place is. So when people come here from somewhere else, whether it's another state or another country, they're often disappointed. Jam five million people into a hundred mile stretch of coastline and you find hundreds of thousands of people with a major complaint.

"So I decided to leave the state," Ginny told us.

Ginny looked out over Lake Worth, as if seeing a scene with her ex somewhere on the mainland. "But with a joint custody order, to take your child from the state you have to get agreement of the other parent, and Clinton said he'd never agree. Not in a million years, he said. Unless I'd come up with enough money to make it worthwhile."

This was the friendly divorce Ginny had told me about driving to The Exchange.

"I could petition the court to allow me to take Eric out of state, but to have even a half a chance over Clinton's opposition I'd have to prove the move would be overwhelmingly better for Eric than staying in Florida. And the odds against proving that are about ten thousand to one."

Again she looked across the water, in the general direction of the courthouse. "These God-damned women judges bend over so far to be fair to the fathers that—" A tiny convulsion ran through her body and disappeared. It would take hours of therapy to figure out why this sentence—one about women judges—would evoke this strong response when none of the other topics—children, murder, former spouse—had not. My bet, if I allowed myself to bet on such things—would be something to do with Ginny's mother.

"And I didn't have anyone to talk to," Ginny said. She must have realized how lame this sounded. "I couldn't talk with other lawyers, and of course I couldn't complain to judges. And I don't know anyone else."

"You could have talked to me," Maureen said.

"Don't tell me what I could have done," Ginny said. "Now is now."

"You killed Raymond Siegel, too," I said.

"He saw me at the pool after I'd—"

"Then you hired someone to bump into us on the Blue Heron Bridge."

"No," Ginny said. "That wasn't me. They were trying to kill me."

"Why?"

"Brophy and the others knew I was a threat," she said. "They knew I was an assistant state attorney."

"Who was driving the truck?" Mo asked.

"How should I know?" Ginny raised her voice. "I didn't see him. Or her."

Of course. Why did Mo ask the question?

"I thought you might have heard. When you were exploring the case."

The word explore, Mo used it out of context. Why?

Mo pushed her arms against the planks behind her, enough to lift her body barely off the dock and shift it four or five inches away from me. "What will you do with our bodies?" she asked Ginny. "Drag us up to the house and drop us in the swimming pool?"

Absurd. But Mo must be saying these things for a reason. Sending me a message.

"Or take us out to the polo field?"

Explore. Swimming pool. *Polo* field?

"Or mark an X on the dock where our bodies will be found."

Explore. Swimming pool. Polo. Mark. Marco Polo! The game I so much wanted to play when Mo took me to that swimming pool so long ago. Ginny's "it." We'll confuse her by constantly moving, keeping her unbalanced. I eased my body a few inches farther away from Mo.

"You're talking gibberish," Ginny said. "I won't let you stall me." She pointed the gun in her right hand toward Mo.

"Marco!" Mo yelled, turning her body so it lay flat against the deck, then rolling toward the end of the "T" on her side of the dock.

"Polo!" I yelled and rolled in the opposite direction.

"Stop it!" Ginny screamed.

"Marco!"

"Polo!" I was almost at the end of the "T" now and knew Mo must be also.

"Shut up!" Ginny screamed.

"Fruit basket—" Mo shouted.

"Turn over," I finished, scrambling to my feet. Mo, already up, ran toward Ginny from another from her side of the dock. Ginny couldn't fire at both of us at once.

An explosion, the sound closer and louder than any of the fireworks at the first Exchange, broke around me. Ginny had fired a gun. Not at me. She aimed at Mo. Adrenalin flooded through my body. I charged toward Ginny.

Another explosion. Mo grabbed her arm but kept going. I ran faster, closing the distance between us. Ginny turned the guns toward me. Another explosion. Something stung my leg. Mo was almost to Ginny. Ginny turned the guns back toward her. "Here," I yelled. Ginny turned to look. A gunshot. Something jabbed into my gut.

Mo slammed into Ginny. Again, a gun fired. Inertia plunged my body into the two women. We tumbled to the wood deck, arms, legs, and bodies massing together into a confused tangle. Mo, below me, yelled, "Damn." I rolled off, screaming with pain.

"Hold her down," Mo yelled. I managed to get my arms around Ginny's waist. Mo grabbed one of Ginny's arms and slammed her hand into the deck. The gun she was holding slipped away. Ginny fought back, twisting away from my grasp. Mo lost her hold.

Ginny, up on her feet now, stood over Mo. She transferred the other gun from her left hand to her right. Mo kicked up at her, hitting Ginny's leg. The first gun lay on the dock, two feet from my hand. Straining, I pushed myself toward it. My gut howled.

Ginny regained her balance and aimed her gun toward Mo. I reached the gun on the dock, pressed one hand around it. Mo rolled away from Ginny. I pointed the gun at Ginny, not knowing a damn thing about guns, how to fire this one, whether there was a safety on, not caring about anything except the bitch who was firing at us.

"Go, don't!" Mo yelled.

Ginny turned her gun toward me.

"This way, Ginny," Mo yelled. "Turn toward me."

Ginny fired her gun in the air above Mo.

I held my gun in both hands, just as I'd seen them do on television so many times.

"Run, Ginny, run," I yelled.

Just as I hoped she would, Ginny turned and ran toward the house. I had a clear shot at her back.

"Don't," Mo yelled again at me. "Don't shoot her."

So simple, just squeeze the trigger. Do the right thing. Those damned words came back to me. Lower the gun, don't shoot her.

Mo was on her feet, running after Ginny, who had a tremendous head start, fifteen to twenty feet. I can stop Ginny with one shot, I thought. Mo's faster, stronger and taller, and ordinarily Ginny would be no match for her. Lights turned on in houses on both sides of the Brophy's house. They'll call the police. Mo pulled closer to Ginny.

That was the last I remembered.

Chapter Thirty-Eight

I woke slowly, fog everywhere, the gray mass retreating occasionally, then closing back in again. Gun shots rang from far away again and again, the muffled sounds part of the fog. Had I pulled the trigger? The thought slithered into my mind from nowhere, absurdly disconnected from everything else. Was Mo hurt? The possibility jolted me into consciousness. Where am I? Look, I told myself. Open at least one eye.

A TV set, the picture on, the sound muted, a game show of some sort. Wires, tubes and a chromed pole beside the bed. I was in a hospital room. My God, Mo's been hurt. Both eyes open now, I strained to lift my head. Pain forced me to drop back. The wires and tubes are attached to me. Damn. Where's Mo? I've got to find her and help her.

"Had enough sleep?" Mo's voice above me, then her lips kissing my forehead.

"Where am I?"

"Good Sam hospital. They had to bring you here because it's so close to where you were shot."

"Your room?"

"One just like it, a few stories down," she said.

"What happened?"

"Sure you're strong enough?"

"Yes," I said, but then the fog returned and I couldn't see or hear a thing.

#

The fog turned into fluffy white clouds, sailboats tacking among them, jibs full. I had no idea how much time had passed.

"Ready to wake up for a while?" Mo's voice a hundred miles away, then closer.

One eye open, then the other. The platinum angel around Mo's neck came into focus first, then her reddish brown hair, the overhead light giving her a halo, then her lips, orange-red and luscious.

I said, "Hi," stupid maybe but that's what came out first. Then "Did I kill Ginny?"

"No," Mo said. "You put the gun down."

"Good."

"She ran when you told her to," Mo said. "Why'd she do that?"

"Under extreme stress and excitement, people will follow whatever orders they hear if those orders are given with enough passion," I said. "That's why mobs are so susceptible to suggestion."

"She knew you were the enemy. Why in the world—"

But I didn't hear another word.

During the night I woke and asked a nurse how long I'd been in the hospital. She looked at papers in the alcove at the room's entrance. "Four days, it says here. Three days since the operation."

#

"I'm ready to go home," I told Mo when she appeared the next day.

"They're ready to get rid of you," she said. The overhead light formed a hallo around her hair again.

"Did I ever tell you that you look like an angel?"

"All horny guys in a hospital say that."

For the first time I saw the bandage rolled around her arm. "You're hurt."

"Bullet went in and came out the other side. Same thing happened to my leg."

"Climb in bed with me and I'll make them well," I said.

"Time for that later. Don't you want to know what's happened?"

I guessed I did.

"Ginny's been charged with two counts of first degree murder," she said.

"They have enough evidence to convict?"

"Probably." Mo reached down and took my hand. "I'm glad you didn't shoot her."

I wished I could be as certain I'd made the right decision. "When did you first suspect her?"

"When you told me she phoned you before your Grand Jury appearance and said I gave her your cell phone number," Mo said. "I didn't. She had to get it from someone in law enforcement."

"Where'd she get the money to buy the expensive furniture I saw in her house?"

"A small inheritance," Mo said.

"Was she a member of The Exchange?"

"No." Mo let go of my hand. "And she didn't have anything to do with the truck that tried to kill us. That was Brophy's idea. He knew what Ginny's job was, and when she showed up he smelled trouble. He paid Schneider to crash into us on the bridge, hoping to scare her off."

"Did Brophy run The Exchange?"

"A joint venture, you might say," Mo said. "The controlling partners were Brophy, Raymond Siegel and Stephanie Royce."

"Why Stephanie?"

"She had access to the children," Mo said. "People who ran child care centers center trusted her."

"Enough to borrow children for a Sunday night party?"

"When it was necessary," Mo said. "More often, she merely passed on news of The Exchange to other center operators, who passed it on to parents of children they didn't want."

She looked away and stared at a wall. "I still can't believe they could get away with this. I thought there were state agencies that kept track of adopted kids and parents were supposed to report in regularly."

"You think the system is airtight?" I said. "Remember how one of Florida's state agencies—one that was supposed to monitor and protect children placed in the custody of foster parents—literally lost a child who was in their care. Lost a little girl. Think about it. Its records showed the child safe somewhere, but the child wasn't there and foster parents said they never received her. And the agency couldn't prove differently."

"Did they ever find her?"

"If they did, they never said so." I reached out and held Mo's hand. Mo said. "As long as you have bureaucrats and agencies, there're going to be screw-ups. If kids can fall through the cracks in the states, think of the opportunities when you involve other countries. Say someone adopts a child, even two, from Russia. She or he moves to Illinois. Two months later they move to Arizona. Then to Florida. What agency is responsible for keeping track?"

"But in Palm Beach?" Mo protested. "How could they possibly pull off something like that in one of the richest, ritziest, towns in the country."

"Why not. Remember Palm Beach is where for years cocaine was served openly at parties, often in Waterford cut-glass bowls to give the sniffing a touch of class. If it was going to work anywhere, it would work there.

"Indeed, our whole culture would aid and abet such a crime. Think about it: Divorced parents routinely trade kids every weekend or for vacations. Parents who are still together send their kids off to camps they know little about. And they leave kids with neighbors they know even less about. What other animals regularly, routinely—habitually—give up the upbringing of their offspring to someone else and expect no harm will come to them?"

I realized I was breathing fast now, and knew I should change the subject. Mo had had days to find out the answers to all the questions unresolved before Ginny shot me, so I tried a safe path. "How did the Exchange get started? How did this group of weirdoes first get together?"

Mo laughed. I didn't think I'd said anything funny. "You're going to love this," she said.

"Tell me."

"Paul Brophy and Wilbur met in a nationally known rehab center in West Palm. They became friends. When they got out they introduced each other to their wives. Paul saw the potential in Stephanie's day-care route, and soon afterward she divorced Wilbur."

I laughed then. "Sobriety doesn't necessarily lead to saintliness."

Mo smiled. "Just remember, you said it, not me."

"What was Saunders' role in all this?"

"He was what he said he was—a DEA agent."

"His real estate? All those corporations in his name?" I asked.

"Held in his name as trustee only. It was real estate confiscated by the DEA."

I should have thought of that.

"What about the rest of them?"

"Wilbur and Cindy will testify in exchange for light sentences and probation. Sally's attorney is negotiating."

"She turned on her husband?"

"She knew about Paul's affair with Marilyn all along. Sweet revenge time for her."

"Marilyn?"

"Suspended by her company and probably barred for life from working in the securities business. No criminal charges."

"And Stephanie?"

"Seymour Topping won't cut a deal with her," Mo said. "She made him look stupid."

"He is," I said.

"The polls show he's trailing in the congressional race."

Justice after all. "So what will happen to the guys who drove the truck?"

"Schneider and his friend from the gym will be charged with attempted murder. Probably bargain it down to manslaughter."

"The deputy in front of Fathoms?"

"He followed us from the courthouse to guard me. Saunders heard him call in and decided to see what was going on."

"Who trashed my Miata?"

"Alan Schneider and friends."

"The chair or a life sentence—either one too good for them."

"One thing never fit together." I said. "Clinton had been going to The Exchange for weeks before Ginny went for the first time."

"He went there to spy for Saunders. He dated Stephanie to get invited."

I couldn't think of anything else. "I guess that wraps it up."

"You're forgetting about Eric."

"What about him?"

"He's practically an orphan now. Or will be, when Ginny goes to prison."

For the tiniest, briefest, instant I thought Mo was going to suggest we adopt him.

"Helena is taking care of Eric," Mo said. "I've heard talk that Saunders may move in with her."

"Nice for all three of them," I said. I wondered if Mo would consider having a child at her age. We've never talked about it. I guess we'd want to get married first.

Maureen stood over me, smiling that little cat smile that shows she knows so much more than I, the halo still behind her, the playful platinum angel sparkling. All was right with the world again.

"So what now," I said.

The angel bent down and kissed me for so long, I had a good hunch about how the other angels spent their days up there.

THE END

About the Author

After working as a reporter, editor, and columnist at four major Florida newspapers, Jack Nease earned a Master of Fine Arts degree at Florida International University and has since taught creative writing and journalism at Florida Atlantic University. He divides his time between South Florida and the Pacific Northwest.